From *Murder is a Collector's Item*

The shop on Charles Street presented its customary appearance when Emma went in. A row of chests, bureaus and sideboards stretched away to the right and left, piled high with chairs, tables and lesser bric-a-brac; chandeliers, lanterns, kettles and fire buckets swung from the ceiling; pictures and mirrors lined the walls; bedposts stood in the corners; andirons and trivets were tucked under sofas; and Emma knew, although it did not show in the picture, that every cupboard and drawer was filled with needlepoint, hinges, brasses, odd prisms, paperweights, handwrought nails, picture frames, excelsior, old dolls or miniature tea sets. The wall of the office, a tiny cubbyhole marked off from the rest of the store with a five-foot partition, was ornamented with a row of ship models. The office itself managed to contain two desks, two chairs, two ash trays, a filing cabinet, the telephone, the clock, the typewriter, some choice miniatures, an ornate Italian mirror and on the shelf over the desk to the left, which was Jeff's, Kerfoot's book on pewter, a dictionary, back numbers of *Antiques*, and whatever else neither of them knew what to do with. The opening into the office faced the front door and was plainly visible from the street. To the left of the office, and hidden from the street by the row of high-piled furniture, was the door to a small coat- and washroom which had, besides the customary fittings, a shelf, holding ordinarily a can of cleaning powder, a bottle of scotch, a siphon, two cracked Stiegel flip glasses and a blackjack. Jeff had bought the blackjack after several local hold-ups but Emma claimed the only use she had for it was to keep the cops out of the whisky.

Bending over with a groan, Emma picked up the mail from where it had fallen through the slot in the door and started for the office. At first she thought it was Jeff, passed out there, between the office and the door to the washroom. Then she realized it wasn't Jeff. It was Richard Norwitch lying there on his back in a black pool. He looked very dead.

The Emma Marsh mysteries

Murder is a Collector's Item (1939)
Murder is a Serious Business (1940)
Murder a Mile High (1944)

Murder is
a Collector's Item

By Elizabeth Dean

With an introduction
by Tom & Enid Schantz

The Rue Morgue Press
Boulder, Colorado
1998

The Rue Morgue Press
P. O. Box 4119
Boulder, CO 80306

PRINTED IN THE UNITED STATES OF AMERICA

Introduction
Meet Elizabeth Dean and Emma Marsh

IN THE 1930s, most women in mystery novels were either menopausal spinsters, deadly sirens, admiring wives or airheaded girlfriends brought along for the ride. Not so Emma Marsh, the thoroughly modern 26-year-old Boston antiques clerk in Elizabeth Dean's three detective novels. Although her publisher, the venerable Doubleday, Doran Crime Club, insisted on the dust jacket copy that the detecting chores were shared by the trio of Emma, her boss Jeff Graham, and her wealthy criminologist boyfriend Hank Fairbanks, Dean said she deliberately set out to make Emma the major player. The books all revolve around her. Maybe she isn't much at spelling or geography and perhaps she butchers the odd literary quotation or two, but Emma is a keen judge of character with awesome powers of observation, more than able to hold her own when it comes to selling antiques or solving murders.

Much of the fun in this short-lived series lies in Dean's description of what it was like to be a young woman on her own in Boston toward the end of the Great Depression. Lesser women might rankle at the barbs directed her way by Hank; Emma, instead, either ignores them (knowing they aren't really true or meant to hurt) or gives back as good as she gets—or maybe a little better. After being pursued by one dark beauty, the newly rich Hank smiles and complacently asks, " 'What do women see in me?' 'It must be your looks,' said Emma, dripping irony. 'It couldn't be your money.' " And though Hank may look at other women, Emma is more amused than upset by this—and does a little dating on the side herself. What's more, Emma always does the intelligent thing—if she stumbles into a dangerous situation, she turns and runs. And though it's Hank who sets out to be a detective, even he has to admit that it's Emma who really cracks the case.

Equally refreshing is the banter among Emma, Hank, Jeff and various policemen and reporters as they pour scotch and sit around the shop talking murder. These exchanges bring to mind similar repartee in the novels of Craig Rice or in Dashiell Hammett's *The Thin Man*, prompting a *New Yorker* reviewer to call *Murder is a Collector's Item* "fast

and funny," although a *New York Times* critic, in an otherwise compli-
mentary review, did suggest that Emma "drinks more than a nice girl
should."

When asked what made her books stand out from the pack, Dean
would always cite their spontaneity. She refused to work from either an
outline or a synopsis, knowing only the setting, the pivotal incident that
sets the plot in movement, and the identity of the murderer. To know
more, she said, would take the fun out of writing—and reading—her
novels. Her work habits were simple. "I sit down at the typewriter (posi-
tioned on a mid-1700 walnut slant desk) and stare at that blank paper
until I write something just to relieve the monotony."

Written on a dare, *Murder is a Collector's Item* was published in the
spring of 1939. Liz (as her friends called her) wasn't thinking about
writing a mystery when she met one day with a group of friends in her
Council Bluffs, Iowa, home. One of them suggested as a lark that they
each see if they could write 20,000 words of fiction in a month's time.
Only Liz met the deadline, at which point her friends challenged her to
enlarge it into an 80,000 word novel. A year later it was done and accepted by the prestigious Doubleday, Doran Crime Club, whose editors
proclaimed it "one of the best stories in the spring . . . list."

For the background of the mystery she drew upon her own experiences. After graduating from Pembroke College (now part of Brown
University) and obtaining a masters degree from Radcliffe, Liz worked
in the famous Boston antiques shop owned by George McMahon, who
provided the model for the irascible but tender-hearted Jeff Graham.
Much of the enjoyment of *Murder is a Collector's Item* lies in Dean's obviously authentic portrait of the day-to-day operations of an antiques shop.
Watch her as she maneuvers a difficult customer into a purchase or
tries to explain the financial aspects of the business to wide-eyed cops
who can't believe a dealer would pay a thousand dollars for an old desk
and then turn around and sell it for four times that amount.

She followed up that maiden effort with two more novels featuring
Emma, *Murder is a Serious Business* (1940), written at the encouragement of her editors at the *Saturday Evening Post* and once again set in
Boston, and *Murder a Mile High* (1944), set in Colorado, where Liz and
Abbott, her ophthalmologist husband, maintained a summer home on
a ranch near Evergreen because of Liz's severe hay fever. She used the
royalties from her first book to furnish her historic Council Bluffs home
with antiques, all purchased in New England except for one table which
had been transported by pioneers by oxcart to Boulder, Colorado. The
rest of her royalties went to buying purebred Aberdeen Angus cattle to
stock the ranch she called Buckshot. Liz approached the cattle business

with the same enthusiasm she had tackled other projects and in 1951 she finished first in the Jefferson County (Colorado) Angus field trials, with her entry scoring 193 out of a possible 200 points.

Her third and final mystery was published while she was living in Warrington, Florida, near Pensacola, where her husband was stationed during World War II. Her son William said the change in scenery disrupted her writing and though she continued to sell stories and articles to well-paying slick magazines like *Colliers* and *The Saturday Evening Post*, she was never able to recapture the spirit needed to create her Emma Marsh mysteries.

Upon her return to Council Bluffs at the end of the war, Dean threw herself into the activities of the local historical society, spearheading a drive to save the historic Squirrel Cage Jail with its revolving cylindrical cellblock. Born in New York City in 1901, she died in Council Bluffs in 1985 at the age of 84. Her career as a mystery writer was a short one, but in *Murder is a Collector's Item* she produced one of the most entertaining detective novels of the 1930s and in Emma Marsh she gave us a truly original character, a precursor of the independent women sleuths who finally came into their own in the last two decades of the century.

Tom & Enid Schantz
April 1998
Boulder, Colorado

For A.D. and G. McM.

Chapter

1

IT WAS ALMOST five-thirty. Jeff was yelling into the telephone. Hank was sprawled out in a wing chair. The shop of J. Graham, Antiques, was having a gratifying, if inconvenient, rush of customers. Emma, her brown hair rumpled and a harassed look on her face, was trying to attend to them.

"I said eleven o'clock, didn't I?" Jeff was bellowing. "Do you suppose I want to catch cold either? Damn it, I said I'd be there at eleven and I'll wait for you. Oh all right, all right."

The telephone banged up and there was a great scuffling of paper and jerking of drawers in the little office as Jeff prepared to leave.

"Your uncle," he remarked to Hank in a voice that paid no hushed tribute to wealth or position, "is a fussy old fool."

"Shall I deliver the message?" Hank asked, blandly extending his long legs well into the aisle between the rows of furniture.

A grin broke through the clouds of annoyance on Jeff's face.

"Don't bother," he said. "I'll probably do it myself. Chap'll drive me crazy." Then his voice rose again. "Come here!"

Emma abandoned a woman who wanted a pair of Hessian andirons and came running. Jeff pointed to a key on his desk and said more quietly, "Old Norwitch is coming in for it. Telephone the madam that I won't be home for dinner."

"Where are you going?" Emma knew perfectly well, having heard Jeff arrange to sit in on a game but she felt that she ought to indicate disapproval.

"None of your business," said Jeff, stepping over Hank's legs on his way to get his coat and hat. "Why don't you send this lug home?"

Hank did not move, Emma went back to her customer and Jeff, his hat cocked over one eye, slammed out the door. A man who collected patch boxes remarked to his tweedy companion that Mr. Graham was an amusing character. Emma thought to herself that the big sissy didn't know the half of it and wondered, again, how one man could be so cross and make so much noise as Jeff. Perhaps his wife had something on her side after all. Emma went back to the business at hand trying to explain, tactfully, that Hessian andirons were practically nonexistent and that the customer would do much better to abandon her search and take a wrought-iron pair with nice open hearts on the shafts.

Mr. Finegold, one of the competitors, came in. Having no glass chandeliers of his own to sell, he was bringing a woman from Schenectady in to look at Jeff's. He pointed to the glittering row that hung down the center of the shop.

"German, of course," he said, "but just like Waterford. Nobody can tell the difference."

Emma turned to glower at him and lost control of the andiron lady who slipped away with the oft-broken promise to be back later.

Hank ambled up. "This," he said, "is no night for a quiet chat. I'll be going. Have a good time with the boys."

"He doesn't have to say they're German, does he?" Emma muttered.

Unattended customers still roamed the premises; with a bright smile Emma told them just to look around and leaped to the defense of the chandeliers. A chandelier brought real money and she was not going to risk the sale of one merely to attend to a bunch of dallying females. She launched into a masterly dissertation on glassmaking that had Waterford blowers in Germany or Ireland largely peopled with the descendants of German glass blowers. She threw in a nice description of the impoverished nobleman's castle, unlocated, where "our personal representative" had purchased the chandelier under consideration and finally completed the sale. She also promised that Jeff would wire the chandelier for electricity, though she knew he hated to do it, would put it off until the customer threatened not to pay and would litter the shop for a day with wire and curses when he finally did the job.

On the way to the office to make out the sales slip, Emma sold a candy paperweight and blessed the customer for slipping it into his overcoat pocket without the formality of wrapping. She looked at the clock. It was nearly six now and it would take her a good hour to remove the marks of toil after she got home, if she ever did. Emma wrote down the address and said a polite good-by to the woman from Schenectady, adding, not too pointedly, that she would be glad to see her on her next trip to Boston.

Why, Emma thought wearily, did there have to be a crowd on the night when she had an especially good date and wanted to live up to it? If it were only Hank with whom she were going out, she wouldn't care. Put on your best clothes for him and he took you to a joint in South Boston where he had to see some lad just out of the pen; but two college boys who wanted to make the rounds deserved every encouragement to ask you again. Emma looked up and caught the eye of a woman who was standing by.

"Was there something?" Emma asked coldly.

"Tapestry, or something to put on a wall . . ." began the woman vaguely.

Emma was about to cut her off and get rid of her with a flat no, when her better nature triumphed and she thought of a large piece of needlepoint depicting the return of the Prodigal Son. It had been wrapped around a pair of Bristol doorstops in a bottom drawer for years but Emma tugged it out, thinking that you never could tell what people would buy. The woman, however, was not impressed by the charm of an amiable calf, all unaware of his impending fate, and wandered out. The other customers, discouraged no doubt, had gone too. Then Mr. Norwitch came in for the key, accepted it stiffly from Emma and hurried out.

Emma was marking "rush wiring" hopefully, in large letters, on the sales slip, when Mr. Petty came in. Mr. Petty was a New York antique dealer of some importance. Like Jeff, he had a flair for decorative ideas and he had progressed from providing the furniture for period plays, to the designing of complete stage sets. It was rumored that he had backed several plays so that he might have a hand in their mounting; not all of the plays had been successful. He knew a great many people and his recommendation was a thing to be desired.

"Was that Jeff I saw coming out of the store?" Petty wanted to know.

"Heavens no. Jeff's been gone for hours." Giving herself twenty minutes before she could ease Petty out, Emma sat down and lit a cigarette. "It must have been Mr. Norwitch that you saw, he was just in here."

"You mean Richard Minot Norwitch, Esquire?" Petty's tone was light.

"Sure," said Emma. "The great collector. One of our best customers. Don't you know him?"

"Not yet. What's he like?"

Did Petty, Emma wondered, have something special to sell Norwitch? She'd better be careful, Norwitch was Jeff's meat right now and she didn't want anything to go wrong. She was not surprised that Petty did not know Norwitch. Petty's trips to Boston were infrequent and one of Mr. Norwitch's peculiarities was a belief, often stated, that all New York dealers were crooks.

Mr. Norwitch had other idiosyncrasies. He would not, for example, own an automobile, he disliked taxicabs and usually walked or took a streetcar. Emma knew the place the Norwitch family had occupied in Boston history. They had come over in the Ark, or whatever it was, and had had a finger in the local doings ever since. One Norwitch, a wild young revolutionist, had participated in the well-known tea party; another, a stanch Tory, had denounced John Hancock. One had been a privateer, and another an abolitionist. There had been Norwitches in the China trade, and Norwitches whose essays had been published by the *Atlantic*. Norwitches were legislators and trustees and bankers and members of the Harvard Corporation. Norwitches founded symphony orchestras, museums and hospitals. As Hank rather vulgarly put it: squeeze a local event and out popped a Norwitch.

Emma was aware that Mr. Richard Norwitch, the last of the name, was quite in the best family tradition. He was director of this and trustee of that, but his wealth required no other effort. He was a bachelor, a proprietor of the Athenaeum, the author of a scholarly monograph on a Revere tea caddy and the possessor of a collection of silver and fine furniture, already famous, that would one day go to the Museum of Fine Arts. Emma knew all this, but she didn't like him. She disapproved of his unsympathetic treatment of Hank and she was thoroughly familiar with his reputation as a buyer of antiques.

Norwitch bought only the best, but he was a shrewd bargainer and possessed a vindictive tongue. Many a dealer, having failed to come to terms with Norwitch over a rare piece, found that the piece promptly acquired a bad reputation, could not be disposed of, had to be sold at a loss and was eventually acquired by Norwitch himself at a fraction of its value. His judgment was sound and he had an uncanny faculty for knowing when a dealer acquired something good. Some of the more superstitious races in the antique business credited him with a sixth sense but most of them claimed that he merely bribed the runners—those men with no shop who peddled what they picked up from dealer to dealer— to spot incoming rarities for him. Dealers with an expensive piece and a small clientele were more or less at his mercy but Jeff had once locked his shop for two days to keep Norwitch from seeing a Spanish-foot table before another collector got back from Bermuda. Jeff's reputation for knowledge and independence, some said downright cussedness, was the equal of Norwitch's. They had moments of friendliness—Norwitch had even sent Jeff to his tailor when Jeff admired one of his overcoats— they had times of not speaking but a rare find usually brought them together, for they esteemed each other's opinion and ability to drive a hard bargain. Mr. Finegold referred to them as the two thieves. Jeff's rank as a thief depended on his ability to take the competitors at Casino in the back room on rainy days and Emma resented the comparison.

Emma did not feel able to give an unbiased opinion of Mr. Norwitch, so she merely said: "Wouldn't you like a drink?"

Petty thought he would and went to the washroom with Emma to superintend the making. Emma washed the glasses carefully, knowing that Petty would make her do it over if she skimped because he was fastidious as a cat.

When the drinks were mixed Petty asked, "How old is Norwitch?"

"About seventy, but he doesn't look it. He isn't very tall"—Norwitch was exactly five feet six—"and he might be a little chubby if he let himself go." Emma brought herself up short; it would not do either to repeat Hank's hardly sympathetic description of the exercises and antics that his uncle labored through each morning, to say nothing of the rigid diet that he underwent to preserve his figure.

"But," Emma went on, "he's terribly fussy about his clothes and he has a little gray mustache and kind of a ruddy face "

"He sounds healthy," Petty put in.

"Oh, definitely. He'll live for years just to keep Hank from—" Emma stopped, felt herself blushing and was doubly furious.

"Hank would be his nephew, Henry Fairbanks? Haven't I met him in here?" Petty's tone was mildly curious.

"Yes," said Emma, too thoroughly annoyed with herself to wonder how Mr. Petty knew that Hank was Mr. Norwitch's nephew.

The twenty minutes had lengthened into half an hour. Emma refused a second drink, assured Mr. Petty, with her fingers crossed, that Jeff would be in early the next morning and had him at the door when an old, high-busted limousine swept up and Mrs. Endicott scuttled into the shop. Mrs. Endicott was short and dumpy, but she was twice an Endicott, having married her cousin; and she was a customer beside whom baths and cocktails and dinners and dancing faded to nothing. She had four houses and numberless relatives, on all of which she was constantly lavishing little things—to use her favorite diminutive. She had just bought a little cottage of fourteen rooms in Vermont, which was to be furnished with—"nothing but the best early American, my dear." Mrs. Endicott pounced on Petty and had purchased a scalloped pine cupboard and a maple day bed, sight unseen, before either Emma or Petty had got their breath. All she wanted from Emma was Sam, the cabinetmaker, wrapped up, tied with a string and ready for her to take back to Lennox the following morning.

"Because, my dear," she said, patting Emma, "I have just come down from there and the furniture is simply falling apart. And I wouldn't think of letting anyone but Sam touch it. Why, my dears," her voice became low with horror, "some carpenter in Magnolia put a nail in one of Great-grandmother Frothingham's chairs. Not one of the Chinese Chippendales, thank fortune, but it might have been. Now you have

Sam ready at nine o'clock."

"Whee—e," said Emma as they watched Mrs. Endicott being hoisted into the limousine. "And of course Sam's gone home by now, and I did have other things to do, but that is nothing in her young life. It's a good thing I wangled a fifty-foot cord for my telephone; I can search while I soak. Wait till I get my coat."

And then Jeff's wife came in the other door of the shop. Emma didn't like Martha Graham and the sight of the smart hat on the sleek dark hair, the mink cape and the short dress that revealed the sheer-clad curves of admittedly handsome legs, served only to increase her irritation. Mink cape indeed, Emma grumbled to herself. Did the woman think the depression was over? Jeff hadn't had any new clothes since the overcoat Norwitch's tailor had made him. Then Emma remembered that she had not delivered Jeff's message. She tried hurriedly to think of a likely place for Jeff to be. It would never do to admit that he was in a game. Gambling was another of the things Jeff did of which Mrs. Graham did not approve. There were so many of those things that Emma often wondered why Mrs. Graham had ever married him.

Mrs. Graham claimed to regard the antique business as only a short step removed from junk peddling but she was furiously jealous of Jeff's contacts with people whose names she saw in the society columns. She demanded expensive clothes and jewelry but she saw to it that any particular treasure that Jeff brought home for his own enjoyment was soon marred or broken. She was suspicious of the time and trips that the business required, but when Jeff did go home she complained and criticized until Jeff lost his temper and stormed out. In fact, a violent temper seemed to be the only thing that the two had in common, for physically as well as mentally they were an ill-assorted pair. Mrs. Graham was tall and dark and lissome, while Jeff was short, thick set and rapidly graying. Mrs. Graham sulked and held grudges; Jeff snapped at people and forgot about it.

Emma had tried to be friendly with Mrs. Graham, who was obviously lonely and unhappy, but Mrs. Graham persisted in treating her as though she were a combination of hired help and scheming minx and Emma quickly confined her sympathy to Jeff. She resented Mrs. Graham's attitude toward the business and she resented the guilty feeling she always had when she was forced to keep the peace by some elaborate lie as to Jeff's whereabouts. She was relieved that, of late, Mrs. Graham had uttered no protests when informed that Jeff would not be home.

"I'm terribly sorry," began Emma politely. "Mr. Graham has gone out to see some things. He told me to phone you but I was busy and I forgot. I'm afraid he won't be home until late because he has an appointment here with Mr. Norwitch at eleven, and you know how those things drag on."

"It doesn't matter, this time." Mrs. Graham was condescendingly forgiving. "I'll just go to a movie, alone. I'll need some money."

Emma wished that she had had time to make a deposit so that she could deny the request, but she handed over ten dollars without comment.

The door had scarcely closed behind her when Mrs. Arbuthnot appeared. Mrs. Arbuthnot lived in the apartment over the shop and was a customer in a mild sort of way. Jeff liked her because she was calm and quiet and played a sound game of bridge. She was looking for Jeff, now, to make a fourth but received the news of his absence with no expostulations, said a pleasant good night and departed.

"That other," said Emma, "was Mrs. Graham."

"Oh," said Petty. "You sounded very tactful."

"I'm the perfect buffer state," said Emma, "when I don't forget something. But this is positively all for tonight."

And grabbing hat, coat and Petty, Emma turned out the lights and fled.

* * * *

At quarter of eleven Emma was drinking a Ward Eight in the Gilded Slipper and feeling very pleased with herself. Sam had agreed to go to Lennox, for a consideration; a long row of cocktails and a pleasant dinner were behind her; she always had liked her green dress; the boys seemed to like both the dress and her ability to stay the course, and everything seemed pointing toward a large evening. She knew it was quarter of eleven because Joe Foster had just looked at his watch to see how long they had to wait for the floor show. Suddenly she clutched Joe's arm.

"Wait for me, I'll be right back," she said and was gone, tearing through the crowded room like a broken field runner.

Three quarters of an hour later the boys wandered out to the bar and found Emma, white and very shaky, drinking brandy with a cab driver. As they bore down upon her like two thunderclouds, they heard her say, "Jeff can't fix this," and saw something change hands.

"Woman," declaimed Bill Barton (he was the fat one), "you certainly flatter us. During this eon that you have been gone, we have done nothing but mourn your absence. My thin friend here," indicating Joe with a sweeping gesture, "has not taken his eyes or his mouth, either, off his liquor and I only pinched the cigarette girl once." He paused to order drinks; then continued:

"We thought, of course, that you had gone to the ladies' room to wash your hands; instead, we find you carousing in low company." With an effort, he focused his eyes for a glare at the cab driver but that worthy had disappeared.

"Shut up, rat," said Joe and pulled Emma away to dance.

"That one is drunk," he went on, startling a passing waiter.

"I'm going to be if I can arrange it," this from Emma.

"Hooray, my dove. Is Jeff in a jam somewhere?"

Emma looked relieved. "No. One of . . . Hank's friends. Wife and fourteen children, abandoned, right in the middle of the kitchen floor." Emma giggled.

"Oh, all right," said Joe, "I'm sure glad it's serious. When you were talking to that hack driver, you sure looked as though someone had left you a million dollars."

"I was afraid you'd discover me doing my good deed for the year."

"Let's have a drink."

At four o'clock they left the Royal Palms, another spot of glitter in the city's milk-punch way, to find Joe's car parked rather toward the center of Columbus Avenue and liberally sprinkled with tickets. Emma tore them all up, one by one, and threw them into the spring morning.

"Chums, this is nothing," she enunciated carefully.

"Home, Jameses."

On the way to work the next morning Emma let the roadster nose its own way through the traffic.

"You're too old, dearie," she moaned gently, half aloud, "to be going out with college boys; they go too many places."

Emma was twenty-six and usually considered herself a mere lass but right now she felt like an old woman.

"Dinner and a bottle of wine is about your speed," she continued to admonish herself. "And besides, you're the one who is supposed to be at the shop on time."

Emma stopped violently behind a truck at the Beacon Street intersection, felt her head to see if the jar had dislodged it and went on with her musing.

Perhaps Jeff would be late. Happy thought. It was all right for the boss to be late. She wondered if Jeff would have a hangover too. Anyhow, she hadn't been out with Hank and old Norwitch couldn't look down his nose at her if he came in about the secretary. Had he bought it? He'd better. There was only one other swell-front, tambour secretary in existence with the swell on both the shutters and the body and he wouldn't get that; not unless the Metropolitan Museum had a fire sale. Just like the old fool, though, after insisting on seeing the secretary first, and in the middle of the night too, to tell everyone that the inlay was new. Well, it wasn't; she personally could vouch for it. Good Lord! Jeff didn't have a key; he had given his to Norwitch.

Just then the traffic cop blew his whistle and, as Emma passed him, yelled consolingly, "You're half an hour late."

Emma made a face at him, took the next block in a jump and pulled into the "No Parking" space reserved for customers. Jeff's car was not in sight and the shop looked very calm and peaceful. The sign "J. Graham, Antiques," glittered, not too ostentatiously, in the morning sun.

In one window, a pink luster tea set, complete, sat decorously on a Pembroke table, American Sheraton, circa 1780; in another window, against a background of trotting horse and rooster weather vanes, stood two large pewter vases filled with pussy willows. As she got out of the roadster, Emma gave a moment of grudging admiration. Who but Jeff could sell slop jars for vases just by showing how well flowers looked in them; or shoemakers' benches for coffee tables? The benches had sold like hot cakes but they were dead now; all the decorating shops were full of reproductions.

Emma got out her key, wondering why there had to be two doors just because the shop was on a corner. The front door, opposite the office, was all right; push the gadget and the door locked when one shut it. To this door both Emma and Jeff had keys. The corner door, on the other hand, was definitely wrong. It had no lock and had to be bolted from the inside whenever one left the shop. The arrangement presented no difficulties when Jeff was the last to leave because years of habit made him remember to throw the bolt. Emma, however, frequently forgot and regarded the corner door as her pet peeve, her millstone and her cross to bear. For, she reasoned, Jeff could easily have a spring lock put on the door and save her the embarrassment of having the cop on the beat report, as he did with evident enjoyment, that he had found the door unbolted again. But Jeff steadfastly refused to change the bolt. He was used to it, he said, and anyhow, Emma ought to learn to remember something. Any argument between the two of them always ended with bitter references to the door; but, as their arguments were frequent and they still remained violently loyal to each other, no one quite knew whether to treat the matter as a joke or as something serious.

Jeff also claimed that he only let Hank sit around the shop because, if he were there at closing time, he reminded Emma to bolt the door. This annoyed Emma as Jeff intended it should. After two years, Emma wasn't yet sure that Hank sat around the shop because of her.

Henry Fairbanks, the only son of Mr. Norwitch's only sister who had married a Fairbanks and drowned with him in a squall off Egg

Rock, should have graduated from Harvard with a C average, gone into the woll and noils business and developed at least an appreciative taste in antiques. Instead, he graduated cum laude after showing an undue interest in psychology and ethnology and spending his spare time in police courts, rather than at Brattle Hall dances. In fact, he had met Emma in a police court whither she had been haled for driving through a red light at an outlying intersection. Her defense, that she had thought the cop who was lurking in the bushes to trap offenders, a prowler; that she had driven through the light to avoid being held up; and what she thought of such low practices on the part of the police as hiding in bushes, had so impressed Mr. Henry Fairbanks that he took her out to lunch. After graduation Hank had shown no inclination to do anything but continue his previous interests, to which he added that of sitting in Jeff's shop.

All this, or even a little of this, irked Hank's uncle, who felt that leisure was the prerogative of age after an industrious youth. He felt that it would be undignified to do anything so drastic as to disinherit Hank; so he contented himself with making his allowance as small, and their meetings as disagreeable, as possible. This was easy because Mr. Norwitch was Hank's sole means of support, the Fairbanks money having, apparently, also gone down in the catboat, and the two lived together in the Norwitch house on Chestnut Street.

Emma, who stood alone and firmly on her rather large but shapely feet, berated Hank for being a spineless sponge and frequently declared that she was through with him. Nothing ever came of this, however, because he always showed up at the shop and Emma always forgot that she wasn't speaking to him. His answer to her demands that he earn his own living was, simply, that he couldn't; and that, anyway his uncle would die someday, and then he wouldn't have to. To this Emma always replied that he shouldn't talk that way; someone might hear him.

Chapter
2

THE SHOP ON CHARLES STREET presented its customary appearance when Emma went in. A row of chests, bureaus and sideboards stretched away to the right and left, piled high with chairs, tables and lesser bric-a-brac; chandeliers, lanterns, kettles and fire buckets swung from the ceiling; pictures and mirrors lined the walls; bed posts stood in the corners; andirons and trivets were tucked under sofas; and Emma knew, although it did not show in the picture, that every cupboard and drawer was filled with needlepoint, hinges, brasses, odd prisms, paperweights, handwrought nails, picture frames, excelsior, old dolls or miniature tea sets. The wall of the office, a tiny cubbyhole marked off from the rest of the store with a five-foot partition, was ornamented with a row of ship models. The office itself managed to contain two desks, two chairs, two ash trays, a filing cabinet, the telephone, the clock, the typewriter, some choice miniatures, an ornate Italian mirror and on the shelf over the desk to the left, which was Jeff's, Kerfoot's book on pewter, a dictionary, back numbers of *Antiques*, and whatever else neither of them knew what to do with. The opening into the office faced the front door and was plainly visible from the street. To the left of the office, and hidden from the street by the row of highpiled furniture, was the door to a small coat- and washroom which had, besides the customary fittings, a shelf, holding ordinarily a can of cleaning powder, a bottle of scotch, a siphon, two cracked Stiegel flip glasses and a blackjack. Jeff had bought the blackjack after several local holdups but Emma claimed the only use she had for it was to keep the cops out of the whisky.

Bending over with a groan, Emma picked up the mail from where it had fallen through the slot in the door and started for the office. At first she thought it was Jeff, passed out there, between the office and the door to the washroom. Then she realized it wasn't Jeff. It was Richard Norwitch lying there on his back in a black pool. He looked very dead.

Emma shut her eyes. She was, she thought, either going to faint or throw up. If she didn't look again, maybe she could get to the telephone. She thought about the telephone and tried not to think of the other. . . . She became conscious of a loud knocking on the still-bolted corner door, turned slowly in that direction and opened her eyes. Hank stood there, grinning broadly and carrying a large bottle of tomato juice. Emma wanted to scream, she wanted to run to him for help, sympathy, protection, but no sound came from her mouth and her legs refused to carry her. Hank came around to the front door.

"What's the matter, honey? Got a hangover? Or," as he looked at her, "seen a ghost?"

Emma shut her eyes again because black and red spots were whirling before them. Hank thought she was going to faint.

"Cut it out," he said sharply, coming toward her.

Emma's eyes snapped open. "You needn't be cross," she said, pointing. "I thought it was Jeff."

Hank pushed past her and saw the body.

"Golly," said Hank. "Oh golly. Lock the door."

She wasn't, Emma realized, even going to be allowed the comfort of a good cry. Hank dialed a number on the office phone and asked for Lieutenant Donovan.

"Jerry? This is Hank. Somebody has stabbed my uncle. No, I'm not kidding. No, Jeff Graham's shop on Charles Street. Yeah, that's it." He leaned back in the chair.

"Now who," he asked mildly of Emma, "besides you, and me, and Jeff, would want to kill the old coot? And, by the way, where is Jeff?"

"I don't know," said Emma miserably.

The knowledge of the eleven o'clock appointment hung in silence between them.

"Go look in the washroom." It was definitely a command; so Emma stepped over the body into the washroom and was very sick for several minutes.

"The things I do for you," said she bitterly. Then she gave a little yelp like a terrier spying a rabbit. Hank came in quickly.

It lay there in the washbasin: a little ivory-handled dagger that Jeff had long used as a letter opener. There were pink stains on the basin but none left on the blade. The handle looked very clean. They stood looking at it till Emma finally voiced what they were both thinking.

"I wonder if we hope that handle was washed clean?"

She put out her hand as though to take it; Hank's fingers on her arm stopped her.

"Uh-uh," he said with emphasis. "Whoever was washing that knife was interrupted. If it was Jeff, we'll just hope he washed the handle first; but if it wasn't, you're not going to destroy evidence, if any. Unless," he added slowly, "you've already touched it. By gosh, not even then. If you touched it now, it wouldn't change last night's picture. You weren't here last night."

Emma thought she was going to be sick again. Hank was looking at her.

"But I was, I—"

Somebody was knocking on the door.

"Holy cow," said Hank. "Here's Jerry; you better tell the truth."

Lieutenant Jerome Donovan was square and red faced and looked intelligent. Sergeant Timothy Connerton was square and red-faced and looked tough.

"Hi," said Donovan as Hank let them in. "What you got here?"

"The body of the late Richard Norwitch and the knife that probably killed him. He's over there. But no fingerprints, I'm afraid." Hank led the way to the washroom.

"You didn't do it, I don't suppose?" asked Donovan.

"And why not? He cut off my allowance; so I stabbed him." Hank was trying to be casual but he was thinking of Emma's disclosure. "Of course I wiped the knife and, anyhow, it's really Jeff's paper cutter." Hank paused, not liking to have said that. But he had already decided that it would do no good to attempt to conceal the fact that the paper cutter really was Jeff's, or that Jeff had arranged to meet his uncle on the previous night. He explained briefly.

The sergeant, meanwhile, produced notebook and pencil. He bulked large and red in the little office doorway. Emma disliked him on sight.

"Well, sister, what do you know about this?"

"The name," said sister coldly, "is Emma Marsh, M-A-R-S-H."

"As in Fenway," said Hank who had just come out of the washroom.

The sergeant looked baffled, but continued, "Occupation?"

Emma thought she might as well joke too, and said, "Maid of all work."

The sergeant got red but before he could think of anything to say he was interrupted by the arrival of the medical examiner and a flock of technical experts.

"That reminds me," said Hank and picked up the telephone.

"Hey, chief, he's phoning," yelled the sergeant.

"No," said Donovan with irony and went on talking to the medical examiner.

"The press," said Hank in answer to Emma's questioning look, "will be here anyway but they'll be nicer if they're invited. I know most of the boys but as a concession to the dear departed, I'll call the *Transcript* first."

"Go ahead," said Donovan. "They'll do all our work for us."

Hank had barely finished his call when the telephone rang.

"After you, Sergeant," he said, offering the receiver.

Donovan stopped him.

"Who's it for?"

"Emma."

Donovan motioned for her to answer.

Emma took the phone.

"Yes?" she said.

"No. No. . . . No. No. . . . No. Oh yes."

She hung up slowly. Everybody was waiting. She caught Hank's eye, swallowed hard and said reluctantly, "It was Mrs. Graham. She wanted to know if Jeff was here . . . he didn't go home last night. But he never does when . . ." She stopped, she didn't have to explain, just tell the truth.

"Who is . . . ?" began the sergeant but he was interrupted by Donovan.

"Never mind, I know. Do you know where Jeff is?" he asked gently of Emma.

"No."

A flock of reporters were clamoring for admittance. After making sure that the photographers and the fingerprint men were through, Donovan told the sergeant to let the reporters in.

"Get in the office," said Hank to Emma, "and keep still."

"Well, watch the silverware for me," said Emma.

The reporters crowded in; flashlights popped; finally Donovan said, "Gentlemen, the deceased, as you know, is Mr. Richard Norwitch of Boston . . ."

". . . and Duxbury," said Hank.

". . . and Duxbury," wrote the *Transcript* man.

". . . well known clubman and antiquarian," went on Donovan.

"Harvard '89," murmured Hank.

"See Who's Who," said Donovan. "Who's robbing this train?"

"The body," he went on, "was discovered by Miss Emma Marsh . . ."

At this point the proceedings were interrupted by a loud laugh from the sergeant. Donovan glared and the sergeant, hastily covering his face with his handkerchief, stepped outside muttering, "I get it."

". . . employee in this shop," continued Donovan, controlling himself with an effort. "The deceased met death from a wound—you can have the medical examiner's first report in a minute—inflicted with this weapon." He displayed the dagger, which looked very small on the large white handkerchief.

". . . a toy weapon," wrote the man from the *American*, "seemingly not capable of the destruction it wrought."

"This weapon," the statement went on, "belongs in this shop. In fact, I am told by Henry Fairbanks, nephew of the deceased and second person to view the body, that this weapon was ordinarily used as a paper cutter by Mr. Jefferson Graham, proprietor of this shop, who cannot be located. You boys might be some use finding him. It is known that he had an appointment with Norwitch for eleven o'clock last night. Was that appointment kept? This weapon will be examined for fingerprints and traces of . . ."

Emma could stand it no longer.

"That paper cutter," she broke in, "has been lost for two weeks. Jeff has bawled me out every day for losing it but I didn't; and it's not fair to make a case out against him when he isn't here. Half a dozen people must have heard us fighting about it."

She looked accusingly at Hank but that gentleman disclaimed all knowledge with a shrug.

The flashlights popped again and the reporters scribbled madly: "Shop Girl Defends Boss."

"Gentlemen," said Donovan ominously, "if you want the medical report . . ."

Hank put Emma, still protesting the unfairness of the proceedings, back in the office, the reporters quieted down and the medical examiner stepped forward.

"Wound over the heart," he began, "one inch to the left of the center of the sternum, between the third and fourth ribs. From the length of the blade and the amount of blood, the wound probably continues downward through the heart or great vessels. Deceased has been dead about twelve hours."

Emma looked at the clock; it was just eleven. She shivered.

"Slight contusion," the examiner continued, "on the left temple, indicates that the head struck something as the body slumped to the left."

There was a great craning of necks from the reporters to see what the head had struck. Donovan helped them out, pointing to a small maple blanket chest that stood against the office wall to the left of the door.

". . . on a small bureau," wrote everybody but the *Transcript* man.

"All I can tell you now," said the examiner. "Take him away, boys."

For a moment, while the body was being taken to the ambulance, there was quiet in the shop. The reporters pushed back silently into the aisles to clear the passage to the door. Donovan fiddled with his cap.

The sergeant cleared the sidewalk of the crowd that was peering in at the windows. Emma, who wanted to cry, being a sentimental soul with a hard surface polish, looked at Hank. Hank was looking interestedly at the floor where the body had been. Emma looked too, but all she could see were faint scratches on the oiled surface, just below where the heels had rested. The door shut. Emma blew her nose. The silence was broken and the reporters surged toward the office.

Donovan barred the way.

"Get out of here. All of you. I'll talk to you at Stuart Street tonight."

When the sergeant had closed and locked the door on the last of them, Donovan turned to Hank.

"Now that your chums have gone, let's sit down and talk this thing over."

He was interrupted by the ringing of the telephone and stopped Emma as she reached for the receiver.

"I'll take it," said he. "Hello.... Hello." The click of the receiver, as it was hung up at the other end, was audible in the office. Keeping an eye on Emma, Donovan dialed a number. "Hello," he said. "Trace all calls to Haymarket 4444. No, nothing much."

He turned to Emma. "Are you expecting a call?"

"Yes," answered Emma, "about forty, but not what you mean. And I have no idea who hung up. Can we have a drink?"

Donovan looked at the tiny office, already filled by the two of them, and at the peering crowd outside the windows, grinned and said, "Well, not here."

"In the basement," said Emma.

"O.K."

Emma went to the washroom to get the scotch and the glasses.

"They're gone," she called.

"Fingerprints, lovey," said Hank.

"Some of the boys on the beat will be glad to hear that," said Emma, thinking tenderly of the one who always told Jeff about the bolt. "There's more below. Come on."

The basement was littered with lumber, old paneling, broken ship models and odds and ends of furniture. There was a couch on which Jeff took occasional naps, a wing chair with broken legs, several crates and an iron restaurant table. From a carpenter's chest Emma produced another array of bottles and glasses.

"This looks like a dive," said Donovan.

"It is," said Emma, handing him a glass. She offered one to the sergeant. He looked at Donovan.

"Don't look at me," said that arm of the law unbuttoning his tunic.

"If you drink at home, drink here."

The sergeant grabbed the glass.

"It doesn't look as though he got much to drink at home," said Emma reprovingly, pouring herself one and handing the bottle to Hank.

Emboldened by the unbuttoned tunic, the sergeant struck back.

"It's a fine way to investigate a murder, drinking in a basement and with them as might have done it." Ignoring Emma's gasp he went on: "Oh, I know ye know the lad and think he's going to make a great detective; but it's his uncle dead and him to get the money; and small respect for the dead he shows, either. And her," he went on stubbornly, "she found the body, and she's in love with him and you don't even ask her where she was last night." He drained his glass at a gulp.

"Tim, have another drink," said Donovan cordially. "You haven't said so many words since you learned your catechism."

"Me," said Hank, "I'm just drinking to hide a broken heart."

"Oh, stop joking," cried Emma, who was again near tears. "The sergeant's right; even if we didn't do it, it's all mixed up. There's Jeff, and the knife, and the bolt . . ."

Hank interrupted her quickly. "Pull yourself together, my pet. Jeff probably has seventeen alibis; but, if you hold out anything on me to protect him, I'll spank you."

He turned to the sergeant. "I didn't like my uncle very well when he was alive and I'm not going to pretend to like him just because he's dead, but I intend to find out who killed him. Unless," he bowed to Donovan, "you do it first. Now for Pete's sake, let's settle down and let Donovan ask questions."

"Let's see what we know first," said Donovan, "and then check on what we have to find out. I know that Jeff had an appointment with Norwitch. But what for and why at eleven o'clock?"

Emma explained about the secretary and Norwitch's anxiety to be the first to see it.

"He called first about five o'clock," she went on, "and wanted to come right down but Jeff wouldn't wait for him. He was sitting in on a game somewhere, but he didn't tell Norwitch that. Norwitch was going out of town the next day and wanted to see it that night. I guess Jeff found out later that the game was somewhere around here, because he called Norwitch back and offered to meet him at eight; but Norwitch was going to some meeting in Brookline at eight. They argued about it quite awhile, and then finally agreed to meet here about eleven if Jeff would leave his key for Norwitch, who didn't want to risk waiting in the night air."

Donovan asked if she got all this from the telephone conversations.

"Yes, Jeff was mad and you could hear him a block away."

"Were there many people in the shop while all this was going on?" asked Donovan.

"About a million," said Emma, "and Jeff was no help, and I was trying to tend to them alone."

"I was here," said Hank.

The sergeant looked at Hank.

"You always are," said Emma; "so I forget to mention it."

"Never mind that," said Donovan. "What time did Jeff leave?"

"About five-thirty, and nearly ran into Norwitch stopping in for the key."

"No," interrupted Hank, "you were in too much of a dither to know, but it wasn't that close. I didn't leave till after Jeff did and Uncle hadn't come for the key then."

"I guess you're right; it was after I sold the chandelier. I looked at the clock because I was late; it was almost six, and then he came in and hardly spoke and hurried right out."

"O.K., Tim," said Donovan. "Put down five thirty-five for Jeff, five forty-five for Hank and six for Norwitch; and maybe we can check with a customer who wasn't in a dither. Why were you in a dither?" he added.

"I had a date," said Emma.

"Dates," corrected Hank.

Emma ignored the interruption. "And I wanted to get home to dress and Jeff had gone and thousands of people kept coming in; Mrs. Endicott wanting Sam, and Petty wanting a drink, and traffic was bad, and Mrs. Graham wanting money, and Mrs. Arbuthnot wanting a bridge game; and I don't know when I left, because I finally pushed them all out and locked the door but it was seven-thirty when I got home," she finished triumphantly.

Donovan sighed. "Sergeant," he said, "when we get through, see if Miss Marsh can remember the names of her dates and of the horde who seem to have been in here."

Hank was watching Emma through the smoke of his cigarette.

"And that," continued Donovan, "was the last you saw of Norwitch until you found the body this morning?"

"Oh yes," said Emma, "I didn't see him when I . . ." Her voice trailed off.

"When you what?" asked Donovan quietly.

"When I came back here," said Emma in a very small voice.

"When was this?"

"About eleven."

Hank was smiling now. The sergeant was looking triumphantly at

Donovan but Donovan refused to catch his eye.

"You see," Emma rushed on, "I remembered that I'd probably forgotten to bolt the door. The other door; it hasn't any lock," she explained, "just a bolt; and I knew I'd been in a hurry and Hank hadn't been here. He usually remembers it for me. And Joe said it was quarter to eleven and I thought of the appointment; and then I wondered about the door and I thought I'd better come and see if it was fastened before Jeff got here and gave me the devil; and it was bolted and I needn't have come; and I wish I'd never thought of it, because now . . ."

"Just a minute, please," cried Donovan. "Let me see if I can sort this out. At quarter of eleven where were you?"

"At the Gilded Slipper, on . . .

"I know," said Donovan. "Who said it was quarter of eleven? "

"Joe Foster, he's quite tall . . ."

"Address?" fairly panted the sergeant.

"Gore, 13."

"There's no such street . . ."

"It's a building, not a street," yelled Donovan. "Put it down and shut up. And at quarter to eleven," he turned again to Emma, "you came hack here to find out if you had bolted a door? How long did it take you?"

"Not very long. I got a taxi right away and told the driver to hurry."

"Go on."

"That's all. I unlocked the front door and went down to the other, and it was bolted; and I thought I'd forgotten to remember I bolted it, and I went back out and tried that door; and—and went back to the Gilded Slipper."

"That's all?" exclaimed Hank and Donovan together, disgustedly.

"Did you turn on the light?" asked Donovan.

"Why didn't you try the door from the outside to see if it was locked, silly?" This from Hank.

"Why," said Emma, "I never thought of that. No, I didn't turn on the light. I know where things are in this place. I put most of them there. And besides, there's enough light through the windows to see by."

"Sometimes," said Hank, "she shows a grain of sense."

The sergeant was quivering with excitement.

"Think hard," said Donovan, "think again exactly what you did in the shop and try to remember whether or not you saw or heard anything that wasn't normal."

"Well," said Emma promptly, thinking out loud, "I know I rushed in, because I was in a hurry and I think I rushed right out. No, I remember now, someone had knocked over some chessmen that I had all set up in Evans' gambit and I set them up again. They're very good ivory chessmen; the knights are elephants . . ."

Hank laughed.

"Skip it," said Donovan.

"That's all," said Emma. "I went out and I know the door locked because I tried it."

"If you remember anything else," said Donovan, "call me up. Don't you realize that you've put yourself in a dandy spot? Nobody but a kind-hearted soul like me is going to believe that you came back to bolt a door. And every time you insist that the doors were both locked the spot gets hotter. Ivory elephants, phoney; if you have to remember something, why can't you remember a prowling figure or even a noise?"

"Come to think of it," began Emma.

"You mustn't put ideas in the witness' head," said Hank.

"I was scared when I went in," Emma continued.

Donovan looked at Hank.

". . . because, if the door had not been bolted, someone might have been in the shop; but, as soon as I found it was, I wasn't."

Donovan groaned. "My God, for a minute I thought you were going to say you'd seen someone skulking around with a knife but had forgotten it. I guess," he went on, "we'll have to take your word for it that the door was bolted."

"That's right," said Hank calmly, "I know it was. I bolted it."

For a moment there was astonished silence in the basement.

"I told you so," began the sergeant.

"I thought I forgot to bolt it," said Emma.

"Brother," said Donovan, "tell me more."

"I left here about quarter of six. See your notebook, Sergeant."

The sergeant looked seriously at his notebook and nodded.

Hank went on. "I bought a newspaper and some Camels across the street and walked up the hill. Once home, I shaved and took a bath. I heard Uncle come in but I didn't see him. He dressed and went out while I was still in the tub. I was reading the newspaper," he explained shamelessly. "Then I got dressed and read for a while and walked on up to the City Club for dinner. I had two drinks in the bar and a very good dinner. Later I had a brandy in the bar and talked to a couple of fellows, names on request; then I thought I'd go to a movie. It was nine-thirty, though, so I didn't. I went back home and started to read: Palmiston, on African tribes, if you must know. I suppose I read for about an hour. Then I got to thinking about you, my sweet," he looked at Emma, "and wondering how you were getting on and I wondered if you had remembered to bolt the door. Knowing that Jeff would be there about eleven, I looked to see what time it was; it was ten thirty-five; so I came down, it takes about five minutes, and tried the door. It opened. I went in, bolted it and went out the other door. Then I went home and read some more. I know it sounds pretty lame but Oscar brought me some coffee about eleven-thirty, if that's any corroboration."

"Who's Oscar?" the sergeant put in.

"He's the"—Hank grinned at Emma—"maid of all work," he finished.

"What about the old gent's not showing up for breakfast?" asked Donovan.

"Uncle and I," explained Hank, "did not eat breakfast together, for the simple reason that he breakfasted at the unheard-of hour of seven. Oscar brings me my breakfast when I wake up: a practice that Uncle thought slovenly. In fact, he told Oscar not to do it. Uncle, however, did not know that Oscar once served time for forgery and I do; so I get breakfast in bed."

"And he'd swear you were home at eleven o'clock whether you were or not," cried the sergeant exultantly.

"He might," said Hank, "but it wouldn't be to keep his past dark because I've already told you about it."

The sergeant looked crestfallen.

"Most nights," said Donovan disgustedly, "you'd be up at the station, where I could keep an eye on you; but the night your uncle gets knifed, just because your girl has a date, you go mooning off alone with nobody but an ex-con to alibi you. How much money do you get out of this?"

"I dunno," said Hank. "About a million, I guess. Uncle was quite bright."

Donovan groaned. "It's too bad you didn't take after him. The commissioner'd have me have you in jail if it wasn't that I can make out a better case for Jeff."

"But can you?" asked Hank helpfully. "Maybe I got there first; I knew Uncle expected to wait because he asked for the key. So I came down first and popped him off; then Jeff came and saw him and was scared he was framed and did a runout."

"You're breaking my heart," said Donovan. "How did you know the door was going to be unbolted?"

"The chances that it would be were about a thousand-to-one," said Hank, "much as I hate to mention it."

"But, Hank," cried Emma, "stop this clowning; the paper cutter has been lost for weeks."

"Oh," said Hank airily, "I stole it. I've been wearing it strapped to my arm, waiting for a chance to use it. After the murder I washed off the fingerprints and left it to incriminate Jeff. Only Emma fooled me; she remembered that the thing had been lost. Now all I can do is to throw myself on the mercy of the court."

"You fool," said Donovan fondly. "It's a good thing this court knows you."

"Hank," said Emma, "please don't talk like that. It all sounds so plausible; though I know you didn't do it because you wouldn't be so mean as to make it look as though Jeff did, if he didn't; and he didn't, either." She finished, somewhat confused.

"Aren't women wonderful?" asked Hank of the room at large. "I might stab poor old Uncle but I wouldn't be so mean as to make it look as though Jeff had done it."

"Hank, darling, you know I don't . . ." began Emma pleadingly but Hank ignored her interruption, asking, "Just how, my little duck, do you know that Jeff didn't do it?"

Faced with the burden of proof, Emma was silent. There was the fact of the appointment; she couldn't get around that. Jeff would keep it too, because he had said he would; but he would be in a bad humor, for he had left the shop already annoyed at Norwitch's insistence; and, if he had been losing money, he would become even more ill-tempered. Then, if Norwitch said anything against the desk, Jeff would really fly in a rage. Emma shivered, remembering the time he had punched the nose of a dealer who accused him of selling a faked mirror. And he always got into fights if he were drunk and he'd probably been drunk. But he wouldn't stab, not Jeff. She just knew he wouldn't but Donovan would laugh at her if she said that. Jeff was really kind, even if he was frequently cross as a bear. That was the trouble, Emma realized. Jeff had been cross to so many customers that some didn't like him. Some of the dealers didn't like him, either. He was successful because he was smart; and he was outspoken against dishonest practices; neither of these traits made for complete popularity in a business that perched precariously between a dwindling source of supply and changing public taste. Oh yes, a lot of people would gladly testify to Jeff's bad temper. Few knew about his kindnesses for Jeff kept them as hidden as an idiot aunt. Emma was the only one who knew that he practically kept little Kratz in business, sending him customers, just because Kratz was scrupulously honest and had a nice taste in scrimshaw work; or about Sam's youngest boy, who had tuberculosis.

Well, she'd tell 'em.... But she was in this thing too.... She'd need a couple of character witnesses herself.... Oh dear, why hadn't she been a better girl? . . . She'd never take another drink. . . .

Mechanically, she took a swallow from the glass in her hand. The sergeant coughed. Emma realized that they were waiting for her to say something.

"But proof," she burst out. "You haven't any proof that Jeff was really there."

"We may have, on the dagger," said Donovan. "And besides, Norwitch let someone in and he probably wouldn't have unlocked the door for a stranger."

"You're forgetting," said Hank, "that the other door was unbolted from sometime around seven until I bolted it at ten-forty. Anyone could have come in during that time; maybe a chance prowler happened on the dagger; then, surprised at his prowling by Uncle, up and stabbed him. You know, that doesn't sound so improbable. Really," he said consolingly to Emma, "it was a good thing you forgot to bolt that door; it gives Jeff a great big loophole that you fixed it so someone else could have come in."

"Yes," sighed Donovan, "it's probably just some such dumb thing. But, if that is the way of it, why doesn't Jeff show up? Where on earth is he?"

"Well," said Emma, who was immeasurably cheered by the prosaic turn matters had taken, "much as I hate to be disrespectful to the boss, he's probably somewhere sleeping off a drunk. He'll show up this afternoon with a head two sizes too big and be sore as a boiled owl because I said he'd wire a chandelier. Honestly, Lieutenant Donovan, Jeff wouldn't kill a man over a piece of furniture—even something as swell as that secretary. He'd be furious if Norwitch picked flaws in it and he'd fight like a wildcat over the price, but he wouldn't kill." Unless, she thought to herself, he were awfully drunk.

"By the way," asked Donovan suddenly, "where is this desk or secretary or what is it? Maybe the boys didn't examine it for fingerprints."

"I bet they didn't," said Emma. "We hid it. Norwitch was very fussy about being the first to see what he bought. A lot of collectors are," she explained. "They hate to have another collector say, 'Oh yes, I saw that,' implying that he could have bought it if he had wanted it. It's over there." She pointed to a pile of crates and paneling on the other side of the basement.

They all got up and went toward the pile. The sergeant started pulling at the barricade. The secretary was well hidden; no corner of it could be seen. The sergeant tugged away a huge six-paneled door that still bore its knocker and brass latch. Behind it were more crates and the basement wall.

"It's gone," screamed Emma. "It's gone; it's gone."

"We heard you," said Hank dryly.

"Now what kind of monkey business is this?" began the sergeant. "They say Norwitch came here to see a desk and there ain't no desk."

"When," asked Donovan of Emma, "did you last see the desk?"

"Yesterday noon, when it came in."

"Who saw it come in?"

"Nobody, it was covered up with an old sheet."

"The movers, dumbbell," put in Hank, "knew they were carrying something. There really was a secretary," he went on to Donovan. "They have been talking about it for weeks. Emma found it and seduced the old lady who owned it, and hated antique dealers, into selling it."

"And she wanted a lot for it," Emma broke in, "and Jeff had to borrow the money to buy it and now it's been stolen and I left the door unbolted and Jeff will give me the devil." Emma was crying real tears.

"If and when Jeff shows up," said Donovan grimly, "he'll have so many questions to answer that he won't have time to bawl you out. I don't suppose you have anything like a receipt to show for it?"

"Yes, I have too," said Emma. "I had to pretend I was buying it for myself; so Jeff gave me a bank draft made out to her and I got a receipt."

"Let's see it."

Emma led the way and they all trooped back upstairs. From the filing cabinet she produced a slip of paper and handed it to Donovan.

He looked at it and whistled. "You paid a thousand dollars for a desk?"

Emma looked at him in disgust. "It was worth four times that," she explained patiently. "Norwitch would have paid thirty-five hundred for it and have been glad to get it. Whoever stole it will sell it down the river for about two thousand, which is just like giving it away."

"My God," said Donovan. "How much profit do you expect in this business?"

"It isn't a question of profit," Emma continued to explain, "it's what a thing is worth and that's based on rarity and condition. Only one other secretary with the swell-front tambour and body has ever turned up, and that's in a museum with a cracked leg" (Emma meant the secretary); "this one was perfect, though, with gobs more inlay than the other; and Jeff was going to make a lot of money."

Donovan cut her off, "This isn't in my department, but give me a description of the thing and I'll start 'em looking for it. You know so much about this business," he added, "would you have any idea who took it?"

Emma shook her head. "If I could tell you, even the competitors would give me a medal. It goes on all the time, this stealing; why, last fall, somebody backed a truck up to Steinmetz's rear entrance and cleaned out every good piece he had—which wasn't much," she put in, just to show what she thought of Steinmetz. "It's not the cops' fault," she went on, not wanting to be unjust. "We all move furniture at all hours of the night, customers being that way; and only the big boys carry insurance."

"But who'll buy stolen . . . ?"

"How do we know it's stolen? I've probably bought stolen stuff myself," Emma went on airily. "Somebody drives up with a load of stuff, says they bought it in New Hampshire and we buy what we want. Antiques don't grow on bushes. Pieces from here are trucked to Connecticut or New York and sometimes back again." She giggled reminiscently. "Steinmetz bought back one of the chairs that had been stolen from him and never knew it till he found his own price mark on it."

Donovan looked aghast. "It sounds like a nice clean business," he said. "Thank God I'm in the homicide department."

"If there is no more business to come before the meeting," said Hank plaintively, "let's go eat. It's two o'clock and I'm hungry."

The sergeant, who had been hungry for some time but hadn't dared mention it, quickly put away his notebook and pencil.

"What do I do?" asked Emma meekly. "Do I go to jail, or can I keep the shop open?"

"Yes, no," said Donovan on whom Emma's method of answering questions was beginning to tell. "What I mean is, you don't have to go to jail, at least not yet, and you better keep the shop open; Jeff might come back or call." He looked at her firmly. "No tricks, now. The ghouls and the reporters will probably drive you crazy but you'll probably drive the reporters crazy too. If you remember anything else, tell 'em; I'll read the papers."

"Oh, thank you," said Emma, ignoring the slurs. "You see, business has been terrible for the last few years and it's just beginning to be good again and Jeff's gone and maybe I can sell the ghouls something and I ought to get money for a lawyer and there is that thousand dollars and . . ."

"Good-by," said Donovan firmly. "Coming?" he asked of Hank.

"Not yet," said Hank. "I must feed the girl friend and see that she locks the doors. I'll see you later."

"Good-by, Sergeant," called Emma kindly but the sergeant had gone, plowing in Donovan's wake like a barge after a tugboat.

"Call the Greek," said Hank, "and have him send over some food;

we'll be mobbed if we try to eat out now. By tomorrow most folks will have forgotten about us, except the reporters and a few benighted souls who'll carry off cups and chairs and tables for souvenirs."

Emma wrung her hands at the prospect but did as she was bidden.

They ate in the basement, washing down the corned beef hash with the rest of the whisky.

"I suppose," said Emma, "we might as well be drunk as the way we are."

"How true," murmured Hank. He leaned back comfortably in the wing chair. Emma was sitting on a crate. "I, myself, find that, at a certain point—only at a certain point, mind you," he waggled an admonitory finger at Emma, "alcoholic beverages not only stimulate but actually sharpen the perceptions; after that, the deluge." He waved his half-empty glass. "Right now, before I finish this drink, I'll tell you what happened last night."

He took a long swallow.

"You'll have to hurry," said Emma, "or it'll be too late."

"Hush," said Hank, closing his eyes. "About seven-fifteen you went home, forgetting to bolt the door. Came the dark. Unknown horse thieves crept up; everyone," he said, opening one eye accusingly, "knows your favorite shortcoming. They dig out the desk. I come and bolt the door. This gives 'em a scare; so they wait awhile. You come and bolt the door. This panics 'em; they think the house is haunted." Hank took another drink. "Then Uncle comes. I can just see the old buzzard high-tailing it downstairs to get a peek at the desk before Jeff gets here. Discovery, ruin, two months in jail for the horse thieves. They chase him upstairs, faster, faster; he's down; he's up. They stab him. It's a knockout. They flee with the payroll. Jeff comes." Hank emptied the glass. "He's drunk; he thinks he did it . . . he jumps in the . . . river . . . only where . . . did they find . . . the knife . . ."

With a jerk, Emma kept from falling off the crate. She looked at Hank; he was breathing gently, the empty glass clasped to his stomach. The suggestion was too much for Emma. It had been a hard night and an impossible day. She groped for the couch, lay down and shut her eyes just for a minute.

It was completely dark in the basement when they awoke. Upstairs, the telephone was ringing wildly. Emma staggered to her feet, trying to drive out of her brain sleep and a terrible dream in which Hank was chasing her with a knife while the sergeant cheered him on. She turned on the light. Hank was regarding his empty glass.

"Here it is Sunday," he said sadly, "and not a drop of whisky in the house."

"The trouble with you," said Emma haughtily, "is that you drink too much."

Hank eyed her with cold disfavor. "That," said he, "is probably the funniest thing you ever said. Go on upstairs, if you can make it, and answer the telephone."

The call was for Hank. Donovan had been trying to get him for two hours. Hank was impeding the wheels of progress. The police wanted to see Norwitch's papers. They wanted the family lawyer. They wanted the will. Oscar, in Hank's absence, had refused to let them in the Chestnut Street house without a search warrant. Where had he been and up to what?

Hank was grandly noncommittal. He had been doing a little private research. No, it hadn't amounted to anything. He'd get the lawyers and wills and things arranged for in the morning. No, they couldn't get into the house tonight. Because he was going to bed. No, he wasn't crazy; he was sleepy. Yes, he knew it was only eight o'clock. All right, all right. He bet it was the sergeant who was so hell-bent to be doing something. Sure, sure. All right, he'd let them in but he had to take Emma home first. Yes, she'd been with him all the time. No, not very far. O.K. In half an hour.

Hank hung up with a yawn. "Such energy," he informed Emma, "I have never seen; no thought, no contemplation, no assimilation of facts."

"Well," said Emma consolingly, "you let them get the facts and you just sit and think it out. It will probably come to you in a dream."

Hank regarded her meditatively. "You know," he said, "I think that's just what I'll do."

Chapter

3

THE FIRST EVENING QUIET had fallen on the city as they started toward the apartment where Emma lived. An occasional truck lumbered by, bound for the market or the warehouses near the North Station; a few taxis, carrying belated theatergoers, screeched at the corners; but the hustle and clamor of the day was gone. From the tulip beds in the Public Gardens came the smell of fresh-turned earth. Somewhere, out in the harbor, a steamer whistled. The roadster, with Hank at the wheel, wound to the south, into a maze of tiny streets in a forgotten corner of the city. Here, between a square where the subway cars came up for air and the back of a big hotel, rows of two-story brick houses continued a placid existence begun some hundred years ago, when the waters of the bay lapped at their very steps. Hemp and tar were still sold there; in fact, several nearly lost little businesses seemed to exist there on the remote chance that someone might find them again. Emma's apartment was over a grocery store run by a very old Frenchman who, Emma thought privately, had been washed ashore in the great storm of '71, before the bay was filled in. The grocery store was handy and not too smelly; the fireplaces in Emma's two rooms had light, delicate mantels; the floorboards were wide and painted pumpkin yellow; and the tiny attic above was occupied by a harmless soul who practiced Yoga and decorated greeting cards. Emma liked the house, she liked M. LeBotien who owned it and she liked the little alley, beside the house, in which the roadster could be parked. True, the numerous sons of the house of Mahoney, across the street, kept the assortment of trucks used in their multifarious businesses there too; and on some mornings Emma had to arouse the house of Mahoney before she could extricate the roadster from its tightly wedged-in stable mates.

Hank parked the car, patted Emma's arm and said goodnight. Emma would have liked to ask him to go upstairs with her to look under the bed, but she thought of M. LeBotien in his little back room and the Yogi lady upstairs and decided not to pamper herself. So she only said, "See you in the morning," and watched his lanky figure swinging toward the corner. Once there, she knew he would hail a cab, instead of riding the streetcar to the station. Well, he could afford to encourage his laziness now. She sighed and got out her latchkey. The street was poorly lighted, boasting only the street lamp at the corner, just now illuminating Hank's disappearing figure. The shadow in the doorway of an unoccupied house caught Emma's eye. She had seen that shadow every night for three years, but tonight it looked larger and blacker than usual.

"This is pretty silly," Emma thought out loud, wishing for Hank, "next thing you'll be thinking it moves."

The shadow seemed to grow bigger; it seemed to be bending toward her. Emma flung herself and the key toward the lock, whirled into the hallway and leaned against the door, eyes and ears strained to catch any further disturbance. There was none. The clock in the grocery store ticked steadily along; and, taking comfort from its familiar sound, Emma mounted the stairs. For the first time since she moved in Emma regretted the square old lock with the brass knob on her door; it had no key. She pushed open the door and hastily switched on the light. There was no body on the floor and nothing sprang at her from behind the sofa; the room looked just as she had last seen it, comfortably untidy and slightly in need of dusting.

Tossing her hat on the table, she went into the bedroom. From her window she could see the shadow in the doorway opposite. It looked the same as always. Emma watched it for several minutes but it did not change or move. Thoroughly disgusted with herself and firmly resolved to say nothing to Hank about her foolishness, Emma turned on the light. She did, however, look casually under the bed as she went by. She was too tired to eat and she couldn't remember that there was much of anything in the icebox. She walked loudly into the bathroom, brushed her teeth, took two aspirins and stalked back to bed. The bureau was heavy but she pushed it in front of the door. Tomorrow she'd take off that lock and have a key made. She knew she wouldn't sleep a wink. She did, though, but for the first time in her life Emma slept with both windows shut.

Next morning things looked better. Emma woke early, ravenously hungry; the shadow was gone; so was the coffee. She got some hard rolls, of which she was inordinately fond, and some coffee from M. LeBotien, picked up the morning paper from the steps and retired to bed to read in the sun, while the coffee began to bubble amiably over the electric plate on the night table. The sun went under a cloud and Emma shivered. There it was, all over the front page, ANTIQUARIAN KILLED IN SHOP; Proprietor missing; pretty secretary says employer in-

nocent; Mr. Henry Fairbanks, the heir, also at scene of crime; continued on page nine A." There were pictures of the shop, the body, and
Hank, looking rather handsome; and a dreadful one of her, years old.
Emma wondered when on earth it had been taken and if she had really
ever done her hair that way.

Without turning to page nine A, Emma drank the coffee and ate
two rolls. She was still hungry but she remembered suddenly that she
had many things to do. She dressed hurriedly, hoping that Hank would
be at the shop when she got there. She had to do it right away; she'd
promised she would; she wondered if the police . . . She shut her mind
resolutely on that. No, the police wouldn't, not if she could help it; and
she couldn't tell Hank. . . . Well, she'd better get to the shop and take
things as they came. Perhaps Jeff would be there with the murderer, in
whose capture he had spent the night and the preceding day; and everything would straighten itself out.

But Jeff was not at the shop. The door was still locked and it was
Hank who stood outside waiting for her. Emma had never been less
glad to see him and then she remembered that she wanted him there.

"Good morning, my early bird," said Hank. "Have you read the
papers?"

"Have you seen my picture?" groaned Emma.

"There is," said Hank, "a beauty in the *American*. Your mouth is
open and I'm holding you and Donovan is glaring. You look," he went
on affably, "like a gangster's moll defying the G-men."

Emma flounced into the shop and answered the telephone.

"It's Mrs. Graham," she said, turning as she hung up. "Jeff hasn't
come home, and the pol— Why, what on earth—?"

Hank was lying full length on the floor, between the door and the
office, peering under the furniture. "You don't seem," he began, "to
clean very well around here. There's one of your rubbers and that toddy
iron Jeff was yelling for last week and a nice ball of string and an awful
lot of dust."

"Well, I wondered where that—" Emma picked up the yardstick
and was about to retrieve the rubber, when Jeff stopped her.

"Don't," he murmured, "disturb the patina." He rolled over to look
under the opposite pile.

"Unless," said Emma, brandishing the yardstick, "you tell me, this
instant, what you're doing, I shall hit you."

"Tut-tut," said Hank. "Mustn't let Donovan see such a display of
temper." He fished out a sales slip, not unused, and held it up to Emma.
"The books will balance better if you have this."

Emma snatched the slip and put it in the drawer. Hank got up and dusted himself off. "It's not there."

"No?" asked Emma politely, refusing to be baited.

Hank grinned. "The key," he said.

"What key?" asked Emma, unable to control her curiosity further.

"Jeff's key, the one Uncle had . . ."

"Why, of course," said Emma, getting down on hands and knees to take a look herself.

"Of course nothing," said Hank, "it should have been in Uncle's pocket, but it wasn't. The house keys were there," he continued reflectively, "a handkerchief, his billfold, two tickets to the policemen's ball," he chuckled, "I'm surprised he didn't use them—some change, a streetcar transfer, his fountain pen and checkbook; but not this key. I thought maybe he dropped it. I hoped he had. You see," he went on slowly, not looking at Emma, "Donovan will think that's a clue against Jeff. If Uncle dropped the key, Jeff would automatically pick it up because it was his key; anyone else would be apt to leave it alone."

Emma was pushing furniture about and hunting wildly. "Oh, we must find it," she cried, "we must." A gleam came into her eye. "We'll take mine and have another one made."

Hank laughed out loud but stopped at the sight of Emma's face. "Darling," he said, "you know I don't want Jeff to have done this any more than you do, but don't think for a minute that you're going to help him out by mixing things up. You couldn't put Uncle's fingerprints on your key and Donovan would know within twenty-four hours where you had the new one made. I don't have the whole picture yet; all I can do is to look at the scraps. The lawyer and the police are going over Uncle's papers today and they may find out that he was being blackmailed or keeping a mistress. Although," he added seriously, "I regard that last as highly improbable."

Somewhat mollified but still not thoroughly convinced that her idea about the key wasn't a good one, Emma took a last look around before turning her attention to some people who had just entered the shop. The morning turned out to be a busy one. Finegold and Kratz came in to offer sympathy and help; some of the other dealers just came. A female reporter got most of Emma's life story before Hank came to the rescue. The woman who had bought the chandelier telephoned and Emma blithely told her that Jeff would be back in a few days. Mrs. Graham phoned again.

"Some women," said Emma, "make me tired. Just because the police keep calling her up to find out if she has heard from Jeff, she has a complete case of the jitters." Emma caught Hank's eye and had the grace to blush. She gathered up the checks from the morning's mail,

made out a deposit slip and told Hank to mind the shop while she went
to the bank.

When she came back she was surprised to find the shop locked.
Through the door she could see Hank, Donovan and the sergeant, sitting in a grim-faced row. Without a word the sergeant let her in.

"Tell me, have you found Jeff?" asked Emma anxiously. "Oh, tell
me. He's not dead, is he ?"

"No," said Donovan, "we haven't found Jeff. Sit down and tell me,
again, just what you did last night."

Emma sat down. Hank knew from the angle of her jaw that she was
going to be stubborn about something, but he could not make her
look at him. Calmly she repeated, almost word for word, her story of
Thursday night's events.

"Learned that story pretty well, haven't you," said Donovan. There
was no question in his voice. "Perhaps I can help you remember a little
more if I ask you why it took you three quarters of an hour to go six
blocks and back in a taxi and bolt a door."

"I'm sure you must be mistaken," said Emma politely. "I couldn't
have taken that long."

"Oh, mistaken, is it?" mimicked the sergeant.

Donovan held up his hand. "Fortunately, for us, you remembered
the names of the men with you. They both say that you had been gone
forty-five minutes when they found you in the bar."

"I had been in the bar quite a while," said Emma, "and besides,
they were both drunk."

"You were drinking with a taxi driver," Donovan went on, "and both
Foster and Barton say that you were badly upset about something. Are
you accustomed to buy drinks for taxi drivers ?"

"Yes," said Emma blandly, "I am; especially when I've been sick in
their cabs. I certainly was upset; so I had a brandy to quiet my insides. A
brandy is very good for that. You see, I was drunk too."

"She's lying," said the sergeant, "by the minute."

"You may not know," said Donovan, "that among Mr. Norwitch's
effects this was found." He handed her a slip of paper.

Emma took it; then laid it quickly on her lap because her hands
were beginning to tremble. "Received," it read, "from Richard Norwitch,
$1,000, with interest at two per cent." It was dated during the previous
week and signed: "J. O. Graham."

So that, thought Emma, was where Jeff had borrowed the money.
All the horrid implications crowded into her mind. Norwitch had
guessed what Jeff had bought with the thousand and had refused to pay
Jeff's price. Worse yet, he might have demanded the secretary in pay-

ment of the debt. But the secretary was gone. What if . . . ? Petty, what was Petty doing in town that night and why hadn't he been back to the shop? Suppose Jeff had sold him the secretary; and Norwitch had found out about the money and accused Jeff of doublecrossing him? But Jeff wouldn't do that; well, why not? He hadn't promised the secretary to Norwitch, although Emma knew Norwitch thought he had. She looked at Hank but there was no reassuring look on his face. She looked at Donovan helplessly, but Donovan's tunic wasn't unbuttoned and his red face looked very grim. She didn't have to look at the sergeant; she could imagine the triumph in his eye.

"Suppose," said Donovan, "I help you remember. You knew about this money and you knew Jeff was selling the secretary to someone else. We can't find this Petty you say was here and it may have been to him. You left the door unbolted so that the secretary could be moved; then you remembered that Hank sometimes locked up after you and you rushed over to make sure nothing had gone wrong. Well, the secretary had gone all right, because we found a woman who saw a truck leaving here about eight o'clock. But something else went wrong." Donovan was standing now, towering over her.

Emma couldn't see Hank; all she could see was a shiny button on Donovan's tunic.

"Look at me," said Donovan.

Slowly Emma raised her eyes to his hard blue ones.

"When you came in here last night, you saw the body; and you saw Jeff. You agreed to discover the body in the morning, to give Jeff time to get away and you bribed the taxi driver to disappear. The boys you were with saw you giving him money and we can't find any driver who admits to bringing a fare here." Donovan paused for a moment. "What kind of a cab was it?" he asked suddenly.

"I don't remember," said Emma composedly.

Donovan needn't think he could bully her.

"And furthermore," she went on, "there isn't a word of truth in what you've been saying—except about the money. I didn't know where Jeff got his money or anything about the secretary; I didn't see the body or Jeff; but I did give the driver money in the bar. I paid him off there, because I'd left my money in my coat...."

Damn, thought Emma. She couldn't say that because he'd check up with the coatroom girl.

"No, I remember; I thought I'd left my money in my coat, and I asked him to come in; and then I remembered I had it in my bag all the time—you know I do things like that." She actually laughed up at Donovan in a deprecatory sort of way.

Hank looked at Emma in amazement. Why, the little brat! He couldn't tell, himself, whether she was lying or not. He had the feeling, now, that she was telling the truth, in her own circuitous fashion, of course; but he would have sworn that at the start of the questioning she had intended to deny or conceal something. He'd see her privately.

Donovan was plainly stymied. He had hoped to startle some admission out of Emma by means of the disclosure of the source of the borrowed money. He had hoped that it would be an admission, damaging to Jeff, that would not involve Emma too much because he was fond of Hank; and he was sentimental enough, being Irish, to wish to solve the murder and promote a wedding at the same time. Now it looked as though the verdict of the inquest would be "murder, inflicted by person or persons unknown." He couldn't ask for a charge against Jeff on circumstantial evidence and a missing key. Donovan sighed and unfastened a button in the middle of his tunic where the fit was the tightest.

Emma controlled an exclamation of relief. That was over, and she hadn't . . . She almost liked Donovan again, and she favored the sergeant, who was looking very glum because all his carefully collected dynamite had produced only a faint pop, with a friendly smile.

"Now," said she, "if you boys will get out of here or down cellar or somewhere, I'll get back to work." She bustled into the office. "Oh, by the way, Sergeant," said she bustling out again, "will you leave this lock down the street and have some keys made for it. It has suddenly become very spooky in my neck of the woods."

Blushing furiously, the sergeant took the lock. Emma wondered if she had offended his dignity but was reassured by Donovan's laughter. She bowed them out without hearing Donovan tell the sergeant that he must be a noisy spook and turned her attention to packing a blue and white overlay glass lamp that she had managed to sell during the morning. Hank called a cab and went off to an appointment. Two women came in; Emma, who was feeling like a balloon released from its moorings, sailed to meet them. One of the women wanted to buy a footstool and one wanted to talk about the murder; Emma, to whom the customer was always right, because, to Jeff, the customer was usually ninety per cent wrong, set herself to accommodate them.

"Yes, the footstool with the square legs was Chippendale, very good."

"No, Mr. Graham hadn't returned. He was probably upstate and hadn't seen the newspapers."

"Of course the cover wasn't in very good shape, but the frame . . ."

"Yes, she had found the body; yes, simply horrified . . ."

"This Empire one has lovely needlepoint, if you like Empire . . ."

"No, no clues . . ."

The footstool lady was walking away. See here, thought Emma, she'd better concentrate on business. Allowing time for the woman to unearth a mongrel little structure from under a lowboy, Emma pursued her victim, put on a brave display of reluctance to part with the footstool, convinced her that she had unearthed a little treasure and made a sale. The woman who had wanted to talk about the murder was slow in following her companion out of the shop and Emma, still in a gracious mood, was about to offer her more details of the crime when some new arrivals distracted her. The newcomers didn't want to buy anything but they put up a great show of interest in glass paperweights and kept Emma busy.

Hank's appointment was with the family lawyer, Mr. Butterby. Mr. Butterby, of Butterby, Butterby, Schultz, and O'Hara, had felt that Donovan's haste to get at the will and Mr. Norwitch's private papers was most unseemly. He was the senior Mr. Butterby and moved slowly and legally among the last testaments of his sedate clients. Income taxes and the escapades of younger sons he left to the junior Mr. Butterby. Messrs Schultz and O'Hara made money for the firm by a discreet handling of divorces. The Norwitch affairs were all in order, Mr. Butterby was well aware of that; but he also knew that in the will he had a minor bombshell to explode. He regretted it, as he regretted the violence and attendant sensationalism of the taking off of Richard Norwitch; most of his clients died in bed, decently bereft of their boots, instead of being stabbed to death in secondhand shops. The whole affair had quite upset him; so he put the reading of the will as close to the time of the inquest as he dared.

When one o'clock came and Hank had not returned, Emma gave up waiting for him, ate a hasty lunch at the Greek's and went back to work hoping that he would come in time to take her to the inquest, which was set for two o'clock.

At quarter of two a taxi drove up and Hank tore into the shop. His hat was more than ever on one side and there was a look of pleased surprise on his face.

"Hurry and get your hat," he called to Emma, "and guess what?"

"What?" said Emma dutifully putting on her hat and coat.

"Uncle," began Hank, bolting the door and putting Emma into the cab; "he's been holding out on me. There is a skeleton in the family cupboard, a smell in the drains and a baby at the wedding."

"My God," said Emma, "don't tell me that Uncle had five illegitimate children and left his money all to them and that you have to go to work?"

"Sorry as I am to disappoint you," Hank replied, "I am still rolling in wealth. I can keep you in gardenias without turning a hair. Remind me to start doing it."

"Oh, get on," said Emma, "we're almost at the courthouse."

"It is a long, sad story," said Hank in a doleful voice.

Emma shut her eyes and prayed for patience.

"Uncle and my mother had an older sister who brought gray hairs to the name of Norwitch by eloping with a piano tuner named—but wait, that's the surprise. My grandfather cast her out, erased her name from the family Bible and so on; the family pretended that she had gone abroad and died of malaria or chicken pox. My mother knew nothing about it, having been a babe in arms at the time, but Uncle remembered her. He finally looked her up but by that time she and her husband had both died, leaving a son. As long as Uncle lived he did nothing for the boy, who was getting along all right anyway; but he figured that once he was dead I'd disgrace the fair name of Norwitch anyway and the old scandal might as well come out; so he left him a thumping big slice of the money."

"How swell," Emma exclaimed. "For the boy, I mean. Only he wouldn't be a boy now, would he?"

"No," said Hank. "He's a good bit older than I am. Don't you want to know who it is?"

"Why," said Emma in surprise, "is it anybody I know?"

"None other," said Hank, thoroughly enjoying himself, "than your friend Petty. R. N. Petty stands for Richard Norwitch Petty."

"Well, I'll be a son of a gun," said Emma, quite illogically.

"He seems like a nice enough feller," Hank went on, "but consider the complications. He shows up here just as Uncle gets the gong and then vanishes. He finally shows up in a hotel with the flu. He's been there all along, but the cops missed him. Butterby wired his shop in New York and Petty's hired help wired back that he was here, giving the name of his hotel. He was on hand for the reading of the will this morning; and, when it came out that he got two hundred thousand, you should have seen the sergeant's face. He wanted to arrest him on the spot. Donovan calmed Tim down, but not before old Butterby nearly had a heart attack. Oh, it was a merry session. You would have enjoyed it. Donovan is mad at Butterby for not telling him sooner and mad at me for not knowing I had a cousin. He'll probably bite chunks out of people at the inquest. Well, here we are."

Chapter

4

EMMA HAD NEVER been to an inquest and she had looked forward to this one with considerable curiosity not unmixed with apprehension. The Suffolk County courthouse had been to her merely a big gray building put most inconveniently in the middle of the street and magistrates and district attorneys were officials with whom an ordinary person had no contact. Only thieves and murderers aroused the D.A. to action and were bound over, whatever that meant, to a Grand Jury. Thieves and murderers, eh? Here she was, all tangled up with courts and justices. What would people think? She knew she wasn't a criminal but she wouldn't give a plugged nickel for the opinion the sergeant held of her. As the taxi pulled up at the courthouse, Emma put on some lipstick, tucked up her hair and got out, trying to look unconcerned before the cameras and reporters.

The courtroom was crowded and dingy. Emma didn't think much of the decorations, which consisted of a dusty flag and pictures of dour-visaged men. Emma thought maybe the men were criminals sentenced by the court.

Hank and Emma were escorted to a row of seats reserved for the witnesses. Donovan was there, the sergeant, Oscar, Mrs. Arbuthnot, Petty, Mrs. Graham and, to Emma's great surprise, Blanchard, Morton Blanchard, an antique dealer with whom Jeff had a feud of long standing. Emma nudged Hank, and was about to ask him what Blanchard was doing there when the clerk pounded for order.

The magistrate, a little man with thin brown hair brushed carefully over a large expanse of yellowish skull, stood up and peeked around his glasses at the jury. He began to talk in a thin, crackling voice which so fascinated Emma that she forgot to pay attention to what he was saying. He sounded, Emma decided, like a shortwave radio getting Berlin very badly. She wished she had a shortwave radio; it would be so handy to be able to get the police reports.

Emma came to with a start; Hank was pulling her to her feet. The District Attorney had requested that the witnesses be segregated, so that they might not hear each other's testimony.

Damn, thought Emma, she'd never be able to find out half what was said.

She went out reluctantly and came back almost immediately, for she was the first witness called.

Hank patted her arm. "Take it easy," he said, "and just answer the questions."

Emma needed his reassurance. From the witness stand she looked at a sea of craning necks and hostile faces. Not all were unfriendly faces, though; she saw little Kratz smiling at her and felt better. Someone was asking her name, now, and she turned her attention to the questions. The ordeal wasn't as bad as she had feared. Donovan, glaring at her in the shop, had been much worse. She gave her name, age, residence and occupation; and described the finding of Norwitch's body.

Then the questions changed to Jeff. How long had she known him? Was he easy to work for? Did customers like him?

Emma could sense what these questions were leading to and she resolved not to deny so much that her testimony would be discredited by the subsequent witnesses. These questions were easy; she had worked, she said, five years for Mr. Graham; if he hadn't been easy to work for she wouldn't have stayed that long. A ripple of amused sound ran over the courtroom. In answer to the third question Emma produced a slip of paper from her bag.

"This month," said she, "we sent bills to the following people."

She started to read a long list of well-known names and managed to get as far as that of the Lieutenant Governor before the magistrate stopped her.

Wasn't it true that Mr. Graham had a violent temper?

She might as well say yes, Emma thought, or they would start citing instances that she would have to admit.

"Yes," she replied placidly and waited for the next question. From the ensuing pause and the shuffling of papers she realized that she had kept examples of Jeff's temper, probably including the punch in the nose, from appearing on the record.

The attack shifted slightly. How much salary did she receive ?

Emma told.

Hadn't she refused the offer of a much larger salary from another dealer?

Emma wondered who had been tattling and what difference it made for whom she worked.

"That dealer," she said quickly, "went broke six months after he made the offer. Wasn't I smart?"

The clerk rapped for order. Didn't she, the question was put very slowly, frequently accompany Mr. Graham on trips?

So that was it! Emma glared at the magistrate. Trying to blacken her character, were they? Why, the dirty scoundrels!

"Do you mean," asked Emma sweetly, "did we stay all night at hotels?"

The District Attorney leaped to his feet. "Will the court," he shouted, "please instruct the witness to answer the questions?"

"Will the court," Emma shouted back, "please stop insinuating?"

Mr. Butterby moved that the question be stricken from the record.

When order had been restored, the subject was again changed, this time to Richard Norwitch. Were the deceased and Mr. Graham on good terms? The magistrate was trying to put his questions carefully. Women were impossible witnesses anyway and the inquest would never be over at this rate.

"Yes and no," Emma replied and then shut her lips firmly.

"Answer the question," roared the D.A.

Emma shrugged her shoulders.

"Let the witness answer in her own words," said the magistrate in a resigned voice.

Emma smiled at him sweetly. "Sometimes," she said, "they were and sometimes they weren't. I mean," she went on casually, "they always agreed about period and style, but they always fought about the price. Mr. Norwitch was . . . er . . . tight."

"Mr. Jefferson Graham frequently gambled for heavy stakes, did he not?"

Emma didn't think that Casino, at a penny a point, was heavy gambling.

Did the witness know of an appointment between the deceased and Mr. Graham for the night of March eighteenth?

The witness did.

Would the witness state the time and place of the appointment?

The witness would.

What was the purpose of the appointment?

Emma began an elaborate description of the secretary that Mr. Norwitch had wished to see, intending to convey the impression that Jeff was doing a great favor in permitting a sight of it; but as soon as she had stated the rarity and value of the piece she was cut off by another question.

Where had Mr. Graham obtained the secretary?

Emma had purchased it herself, she said proudly, from a woman in Natick.

And the price?

A thousand dollars.

Of her own money?

No, Emma admitted, she had merely acted as Mr. Graham's agent. She could see where the questions were heading, but she could think of no way to stop them.

Had she known, the question was put very slowly, that the money with which she purchased the secretary was borrowed?

Yes, Emma had known that.

Did she now know from whom that money had been borrowed? She did.

Would she tell the court the name of the lender?

Emma said the name of Richard Norwitch as casually as she could.

Had the deceased known of the use to which the money was put?

Emma didn't know.

Wasn't it possible that he did know and that the buying of the secretary was a direct commission?

Emma thought it highly unlikely, since they were asking Mr. Norwitch thirty-five hundred for the piece; a price he would hardly be likely to give if he knew what they had paid for it.

But suppose, the question was very bland, that the deceased had found out about the purchase and demanded either the secretary or his money.

Emma thought they would get him his money when the note was due, which wasn't for nearly three months.

Would the secretary be easily salable to someone else?

Answers whirled through Emma's mind. If she said yes, she strengthened the idea that Jeff might have sold the secretary elsewhere; if she said no, then Mr. Norwitch loomed as the logical customer, whose knowledge of the transaction might enable him to drive a hard bargain. Either answer left a situation full of possibilities for argument and quarreling between Jeff and Mr. Norwitch.

The question was repeated.

"Well," Emma began, not yet certain what she was going to say, "any collector would be glad to buy it, if he had the money. Of course," as she temporized, the thought of Petty flashed through her mind, "Mr. Graham could always sell it to any big dealer, though he wouldn't want to, because his profit would be less."

That, she thought to herself, is as near as I can come to saying nothing. It will probably put wrong ideas in the D.A.'s mind and he'll go for Petty, which is perfectly safe, because Petty didn't know about the secretary. She resolutely put away the thought that Petty's visit might have been instigated by Jeff.

If, another question was beginning and Emma turned her attention to it, Mr. Norwitch, who cared enough about the secretary to make an inconvenient appointment to see it, found that the secretary was sold, what, in the witness' opinion, would be his reaction?

"He'd be mad," Emma opined frankly, "as a hornet."

And where was the secretary now?

The legal method of bringing facts into the open was strange to Emma; she looked at the magistrate in surprise. He knew as well as she did that the secretary was gone.

"I wish I knew," she said sadly.

Oh, the secretary was missing?

Yes, said Emma, it certainly was.

When had she last seen it?

Emma told.

Could the secretary have been removed from the shop without her knowledge?

Not while she was there.

Then the secretary had not been removed with her knowledge?

No, Emma insisted, it hadn't.

At what time had she left the shop?

She did not remember exactly, ten or fifteen minutes past seven.

Had she returned to the shop again that night?

The words dropped like leaden bullets into Emma's consciousness. The question she had been dreading was uttered and she would have to answer it.

Yes, she said, she had returned about five or ten minutes to eleven.

A rustle ran over the crowd.

What had been the purpose of her visit?

Emma explained, as briefly as she could, about the door and her fear that she had left it unlocked.

She had not, then, been told to leave the door unbolted?

Surprised at the turn of the question, Emma answered with a flat no and waited, dreading what was to come next.

Were her own relations with the deceased always friendly?

Relieved, but bewildered by the sudden change of subject, Emma said tentatively that Mr. Norwitch was a valued customer and that she was the shop assistant.

Had she ever referred to the deceased, here the magistrate consulted his notes closely, as a "stingy old stuffed shirt?"

Emma thought it very likely.

Was her reason for considering the deceased stingy that he refused

to provide his nephew, Mr. Henry Fairbanks, with sufficient funds to
entertain her at night clubs?

Mr. Fairbanks, said Emma, seemed to be able to take her to night
clubs whenever she wanted to go.

So, she frequented night clubs, did she?

That was not, Emma remarked pointedly, what she had said.

Did she drink at night clubs?

There was obviously nothing to say but yes, and so Emma said it,
feeling that the garments of her good character were being plucked
from her one by one and that she would soon stand revealed to the jury
as nothing but a brazen hussy.

Had she considered Mr. Fairbanks to be the sole heir of the deceased?

Yes, Emma admitted that she had, until . . .

"Confine your remarks to the question," barked the District Attorney.

Oh well, thought Emma, if they wanted to keep Petty for a surprise
she wouldn't spoil their fun. What was this?

Would she please give the court a full account of her actions on the
night of March eighteenth?

Here it was again, the question that she dreaded. She would have
to tell the same story and run the risk of having them produce the taxi
driver to make her out a liar and perjurer. Did they put one in jail for
perjury? If she went to jail, who would run the shop? Egad, she had
never let anyone down yet and she wasn't going to begin now. Once
again, she decided to take things as they came and to pray for rain
although, she thought, nothing short of a cyclone would save her now.

"Where," she asked pleasantly, "shall I begin?"

"Begin with the arrival of the deceased at Charles Street for the
purpose of obtaining the key," said the District Attorney, who had not
yet been favored with a sample of Emma's narrative style and could not
realize the length to which she could go.

Emma lowered her eyes demurely to hide the feeling of elation
which came over her. She'd make them sick of letting her tell her own
story and get them back to questions. Then, if they didn't ask her directly, she wouldn't have to lie. "I was very busy," she began, "because
Mr. Graham had gone. . . ."

Around and about she wound, through the events of the late afternoon. Backward and forward she went, amid details of customers and
sales, with asides on characters and personalities, until the magistrate
writhed on the bench and the District Attorney wished he had never
spoken. When urged to get on, Emma asked, wide-eyed with wonder-

ment, if they didn't want all the details, because if they didn't . . .

By the time she had described the advantages of a long telephone cord, her failure to understand why the telephone company objected to them and her fervent hope that this confession would not cause the removal of hers, the District Attorney threw in the sponge and requested the magistrate to continue the examination by question.

Emma danced a jig of joy inside, but the only outward manifestation of her inward grace was that she answered the magistrate briefly and accurately. She had left the Gilded Slipper at quarter of eleven; it had probably been ten minutes later when she reached the shop; she had entered, bolted the door and left without seeing anything unusual. No, she had not seen Mr. Graham or the body in the shop. No, she had not seen Mr. Graham at all. She had returned to the Gilded Slipper by the same route as she had come, Charles to Beacon to Berkeley. She sounded, she thought to herself, like a double play. She explained, in a low voice, about being sick in the cab and buying the driver a drink. The questions switched again to Jeff and Emma's spirits danced a wild fandango. She was through the worst, and she hadn't lied. She didn't care what they found out now; they could look at the old record and see that she hadn't told a thing that wasn't absolutely true. Thank Heaven the sergeant was a witness and not one of the examiners.

Emma answered the rest of the questions perfunctorily.

Yes, business had been bad, but it was growing better.

Her gaze wandered out over the courtroom, spotting familiar faces among the crowd. There was Finegold again; he was always popping up of late. His business was none too good, either; he'd better stay at his shop and tend it.

No, she didn't think Mr. Graham had any other sources of income.

That face was one she'd seen before. Emma stared at a woman wearing a small black hat; probably she'd been in the shop some time. Sure enough, she had come with the woman who had bought the footstool. Emma hoped the footstool was still staying together. This woman had wanted to know all about the murder; well, she'd come to the right place.

What? What were they showing her? Could she identify the signature? Emma forgot all about the courtroom; she could no longer see the faces; she could not see the magistrate; all she saw were the little slips of paper that the District Attorney was spreading fanwise under her nose. "J. O. Graham, J. O. Graham, J. O. . . . ." There seemed to be thousands of signatures. "I promise to pay, in thirty days, sixty days, ninety days, one hundred, three hundred, five hundred, two hundred, three thousand." The dates covered a period of four years; some of the notes were canceled, but the last three, for the largest amounts, were not; they were due now and they were all made out to Richard Norwitch.

Emma looked at the notes in amazement. She had never seen them before. Where had they come from? Norwitch's papers? Then Donovan and Hank had held out on her, had let her think that the thousand for the secretary was all Jeff had borrowed; a dirty trick if she ever saw one. But the canceled notes? Jeff would have had those but she had never seen them at the shop. It occurred to Emma that she did not know as much about her employer as she had thought. Or about this case either. The police hadn't cared, Emma could see now, about where she had been on the night of March eighteenth, unless she had seen Jeff. Everything was to point to Jeff; and, if she would not incriminate him, they would destroy the good she had said about him by discrediting her as a witness.

"Where . . . ?" began Emma.

The District Attorney held the reins, now, and would have no interruptions.

The signatures? Emma supposed they were Jeff's; after all, she wasn't a handwriting expert. Yes, she was familiar with Mr. Graham's signature. Yes, these looked like his. All right, they were his, to the best of her knowledge.

Let the witness step down.

It was over but she no longer felt elated. As she was escorted from the room by the bailiff, Emma tried to think of what she had said but questions and answers were a confused whirl in her mind. Little Kratz looked very solemn. The woman in the black hat smiled at her but Emma could not smile back. She didn't think she had done Jeff any harm by her testimony, plenty of others would do that; but she hadn't done him any good and she was the one who should have helped him. She was taken to a small, unoccupied room and told to wait.

She waited a long time. She thought of all the things she could be doing at the shop; she thought about Jeff and the murder and the notes. Where had all the canceled ones been? Jeff's house? Of course, and Mrs. Graham had found them and turned them over to the police. That woman was up to something. Oh, come now, just because Emma didn't like her was no reason for suspecting her of deliberately incriminating her husband in a murder. The police had been to Jeff's and had probably searched the house and found the notes. The notes had been paid and Jeff hadn't, undoubtedly, felt it necessary to sew them into the mattress.

The time passed slowly.

Joe Ossip! That was the cab driver's name! She had been trying to think of it for days. Where had he dug himself in? Perhaps he had left town. Emma leaped from her chair and then sat slowly down again. She hadn't done what she promised. Why didn't she ever remember things? It was such a little thing but so important. Well, she couldn't do anything about it now; she'd have to wait till the next day. Emma began to fidget. Was she going to be kept here all day? Habeas corpus? Writ of mandamus? Who would stop her if she walked out? The janitor? She would not be humiliated by any janitor; she'd stay.

Emma recalled the day she had gone to work for Jeff. His hair hadn't been gray then but his disposition had been just as bad as it was now; and she had been scared to death. A week later her appendix had burst and she had been in a hospital for two months. Jeff had loaned her the money for her bills and kept her job for her and now they were trying to accuse him of murder.

The door was opened and Emma was told that she might go. A very sober Hank was waiting for her outside the courthouse, with a cab in leash.

"Get in," he said, "we're going to eat with Donovan."

The taxi wound its way down hill, through a section where the names of the streets contrasted oddly with the dark eyes and skins of those who lived there. It came to a halt before an Italian restaurant that had been a famous speakeasy in the days of prohibition and still maintained its reputation for good food and discreet surroundings. The proprietor greeted Hank as they went in, took them to a corner booth and spoke highly of a new shipment of sherry.

"Sherry," said Hank, "is a little mild for the way I feel; but, considering the amount of sensible talking I have to do, it's probably the only thing I ought to drink. Make it two. Donovan will be here in a minute but I can't answer for his palate."

Emma waited quietly for the sherry; she knew she wanted to know, had to know, what had been said in the courtroom after she left; but she dreaded the long flow of talk to come, with the speculation and suspicion and argument about the significance of testimony and the recapitulation of facts that she hated to face because it all pointed so damagingly to Jeff. She wished that Donovan might never come and that she might go comfortably to sleep, never to wake up till the whole horrid business was solved.

The sherry came, a lovely pale brown, in clear, plain crystal; it did not taste at all like brown paper. Donovan came, looking like a healthy broker in his gray suit. He would have sherry too.

"Well," said Donovan, "Petty walked right into it, didn't he?"

"Petty?" asked Emma coming out of her meditation with a bang.

"What has Petty to do with it?"

"Only this, my pet," said Hank. "He, too, had an appointment with Uncle on the fatal night. Uncle had a bad heart, according to the medical examiner; and perhaps he knew it, for he seems to have put all his affairs in order, including Petty, whom he had never seen. He had Butterby write him to come to Boston to be looked at and introduced to me. But to get back to Petty's story: he says that Uncle was to come to his hotel, which is on Charles Street, at ten-thirty but that he didn't show up. Petty had overheard you tell Mrs. Graham that Jeff was to meet Uncle at the shop at eleven; he waited until eleven and then walked over to the shop. That probably took him two or three minutes. The shop was dark and he didn't see anyone. He walked up and down the street until quarter past, decided that he was catching cold and went back to the hotel wondering what had upset all Uncle's plans."

"What had?" asked Emma. "I mean why didn't he meet Petty at ten-thirty? Was he dead by then? Because if he was, he was in there when I . . ." She broke off, not liking the idea.

"Uncle was late for his appointment with Petty," Hank explained. "Connerton checked up on him. He went to a meeting of the Numismatic Society at Arthur Richards' in Brookline. Mr. Richards reports a very interesting meeting—he has just acquired the octagonal Panama Pacific fifty-dollar piece that makes his U.S. gold type set complete, if that interests you. He says that sometime after ten, about quarter past, he thinks, Uncle jumped up and said that he was late and had to go. The length of time it would take him to come in depends on how soon he caught the subway, whether he got off at Arlington Street or went to Park and changed for Charles and how fast he walked. Connerton tried it three times and it took him thirty, thirty-seven and forty minutes."

"Of course he wouldn't take a taxi," said Emma.

"Certainly not. Richards even offered to send him in his car but Uncle would have none of that. Now you see," Hank leaned his elbows on the table, "giving him the minimum half-hour, he would be late for Petty. But Petty would wait. Jeff, on the other hand, might not. So Uncle, with that fine disregard of other persons which was one of his most endearing qualities, would go directly to the shop in order not to miss Jeff."

"Just a minute," Donovan put in. "Say Mr. Norwitch got to the shop at a quarter of . . ."

"But he couldn't have," Emma interrupted, "because then I'd have seen him. Unless," she repeated, "he was already dead."

". . . or ten minutes or five minutes of." Donovan ignored her for the moment. "What then? Did Petty come over and kill him?"

"Petty," Hank reminded him, "says he wasn't in the shop."

"He says." Donovan was skeptical. "Why couldn't he have been? Petty knew Jeff, if he saw someone else in there he'd assume it was Norwitch and knock. Or maybe," he added, giving his fancy free rein, "Norwitch left the door unlatched for Jeff and fell asleep."

"But Petty says the lights were out."

"Petty says," Donovan repeated. "Maybe they were on, maybe Petty went in, killed him and turned them off, or other way round. Who's to corroborate his story that he stood outside the shop for fifteen minutes? You say you didn't see him. It beats me how all you people kept from tripping over each other. That corner must have looked like a traffic jam but nobody saw anybody or heard anything, to hear them tell it. I think," he ended gloomily, "that they're all a bunch of liars and that includes both of you. Let's eat."

The salad was green and fresh, the meat balls were hot and spicy and the spaghetti was firm and round, cooked just to the point where it was something to chew and not a poor substitute for mashed potatoes. They fell to hungrily but they were too concerned with the events of the afternoon to let the flow of conversation die. The idea that there was someone to share the burden of guilt with Jeff lightened Emma's spirits and brought her curiosity back to its normal high.

"I suppose," she said, winding up her spaghetti, "if Petty knew he was going to inherit some money, he has as good a motive as anyone. The night he was in the shop, before the murder, I mean, he asked me a lot of questions about Mr. Norwitch, what he looked like and how old he was. I just thought he had something to sell him."

Hank waved his fork excitedly, but his mouth was full and it was Donovan who exclaimed, "Why didn't you say so? Now we're getting somewhere. Petty finds out from you what Norwitch looks like and overhears about the appointment for eleven. He probably planned to kill Norwitch at ten-thirty, but when Norwitch didn't show up, he goes over to the shop a little before eleven, gets in by making himself known to Norwitch and kills him there, knowing that Jeff will be blamed for it. The crafty devil!"

"He wasn't very crafty on the stand," Hank reminded him.

"He admitted that he knew he was going to inherit the money, said he could use it—I hear his new show is a flop—and confessed that he thought Uncle had been unjust to his mother. That doesn't sound like a crafty dissembling of motives."

"Just the same," said Donovan, "I'm going to have him tailed so he don't get out of town. If Charles Street wasn't dead as a morgue at night maybe I could find someone who saw him hanging around before eleven. Blanchard seems to have been the only person who was alive down there."

"Blanchard?" asked Emma, who had been thinking that Donovan's description of Charles Street was very apt. "I might have known it. What did Nosey see?"

"Nothing." Donovan felt for his middle vest button and undid it. "But he came around with the story that about eleven-twenty he thought he heard a shot."

"That's a help. Nobody was shot."

"He says he knew that and that what he heard might have been a backfire but he thought he ought to report anything suspicious. Say, what kind of a duck is he anyway?"

"Is it so unusual for a citizen to evince a spirit of friendly coopera-tion?" Hank wanted to know.

"Only the nuts do it." Donovan was disillusioned.

"He's an old Betty," Emma began. "He lives over his shop and puts the peek on everyone. Fortunately he's on our side of the street and he can't see everything."

"Why fortunately?" Donovan was casual.

"Because he tells everything he sees."

"Wouldn't it have been a help if he had seen something Thursday night?"

"Oh," said Emma, "I was thinking of business."

"Take it from another angle," Hank changed the subject. "Emma left the door unlocked around seven. I locked it at ten-forty." He looked at Donovan. "Anyhow, Peterson, the night cop, says it was locked at ten forty-two and three quarters. Emma was back at ten-fifty and must have missed Uncle by inches, whether he came just before or just after. Say he came at ten fifty-five. Petty says he was there from eleven to eleven-fifteen. That leaves just five minutes for Jeff to come, kill Uncle, wash the knife and get away. Petty, on the other hand, had an uninter-rupted quarter of an hour."

"Suppose Jeff came while Petty was in there?"

"Petty would just keep still. Jeff didn't have a key, would think Uncle was late, wouldn't give a damn and would go away."

"Or perhaps," Emma went back to the most neutral possibility, "who-ever got in there before ten-forty just stayed on and killed him."

Donovan looked at her pityingly. "A Mrs. Arbuthnot, know her?" Emma nodded assent and Donovan continued, "Mrs. Arbuthnot says she saw a truck backed up to the store when she went out about eight. There were no men in it but she thinks the motor was running, because she saw it jiggle as she walked past it. Isn't that something? Only a dame would say that a motor was running because she saw the car wiggle instead of because she heard the engine."

"That's perfectly sensible," Emma came gallantly to the defense, "because she wouldn't care whether the motor was running or not; but if she passed close to the truck and it shook, she'd notice; thinking that maybe it was going to back up on her; or perhaps just because it was there under her nose moving."

"All right," said Donovan patiently, "that's what Hank, here, would call psychology. What I'm getting at is that those guys who took the desk wouldn't take any three hours to do it. Now, suppose Norwitch came at ten-fifty and Jeff came in a couple of minutes and killed him. If Petty is telling the truth, anyone who was in the shop then would have to wait until Petty left. They would be safe enough, because Petty didn't have a key either, but it would take up quite a bit of time."

"Oh," said Emma. "I think I see what you mean." Her omission from Donovan's reconstruction had been obvious.

"But," Donovan smiled at Emma, "right now I think Petty looks like the best bet. He has two motives: gain and revenge; he stays at a dinky little hotel that's handy and he knows about the appointment."

"Of course, there is the bare possibility," said Hank, "that everyone is telling the truth, which leaves us just about where we started."

They all sipped thoughtfully at the brandy that came then.

"It's a queer thing," Hank went on after a pause, "but I can't get used to this murder. I don't mean that I can't get along without Uncle. I'm really bearing up very well. Let me put it differently. A lot of people seem to have had a motive for killing him, including myself, but I can't get up any enthusiasm for suspecting them. Possibly Petty did it, maybe Jeff; but somehow I think it's just as likely that Emma, here, did it. More logical, in fact, if she did, for that blasted dagger gums up the whole works. I don't mean that 'woman's weapon' stuff; a man will kill with anything handy, beer bottle or chair, if he's going to kill in a rage; but the dagger was gone, according to Emma, whom we will believe for the nonce; and, as I see it, that can mean but one thing: somebody stole the knife and planned the murder. Now I can't imagine Jeff planning a murder; killing, yes, if he got good and mad, but not scheming and conniving. Petty, now, looks like a planner, if his testimony was as meticulous and precise as you say; but he didn't have the opportunity to steal the dagger. That's why the picture—pardon me, my dear," this to Emma, who had put her hands over her ears at the word picture, "why the picture looks all lopsided. I keep waiting for it to come into focus or clear up."

"Maybe," Emma interrupted him, "it's like one of those puzzle pic-

tures that looks like a horse but has the old oaken bucket and Greta
Garbo hiding around in it."

Donovan chuckled; but Hank gave Emma a withering glance and
went on.

"That's why I say I can't get used to it; I can't put on the slippers and
get out the old pipe and settle down cozily to clear up the mystery,
because I catch myself waiting for something else, expecting something
to happen."

"You don't mean," Donovan said sharply, "you expect another murder?"

Hank waved his cigarette. "Maybe that's it. I don't know. All I know
is that this setup is the wrongest thing I ever went to bed with."

"You had me worried," said Donovan. "I thought you were going to
say that this patricular murderer belonged to the long heads, or the
square heads, and always killed in pairs. Let's stick to facts and cut out
the psychology and don't have any more murders, if you can arrange
that picture of yours without them. I got a hunch that Jeff is the missing
piece of the puzzle; maybe he didn't do it but I'd sure like to say a few
words to him on the subject.

"By the way," he turned to Emma, "what do you know about Mrs.
Graham's boy friend?"

"Nothing," said Emma. "I didn't know she had one but, now that
you mention it, that explains a lot of things. She used to raise particular
hell when Jeff didn't come home, in addition to grabbing all the money
she could; lately, though, she has just been after the money and hasn't
yelped about his absences. A boy friend is the logical answer and it was
dull of me not to see it. How," she asked, "did you happen to think of
it?"

"The Police Department," answered Donovan, "doesn't think but
it can spare a lot of men, just to find out things."

"Well," said Emma, a determined light in her eye, "I'm glad you
told me. I'll cut her allowance down to where it won't support a spare
canary. But I don't see what connection Mrs. Graham's boy friend has
with Mr. Norwitch's murder."

"No more do I," said Donovan. "It's just one of the freak fish that
come up in the net sometimes."

"What did she say in court?" asked Hank casually.

"Yes," said Emma, "I knew I'd never find out what was said if I
couldn't hear it myself."

"Patience, dovey," counseled Hank.

"Nothing much," answered Donovan. "She was called before Petty
and at that time all the D.A. wanted was a case against Jeff; so all they let

her say was that Jeff wasn't home on the night of March eighteenth and that she hadn't heard from him since. If she had been you," Donovan gave Emma a dark look, "she would have managed to convey the idea that there was nothing to his not being home on that night because he never came home most nights. She agreed that Jeff had a bad temper, in fact, she told the court that he frequently 'laid hands on her' when they quarreled." Donovan fluttered his eyelashes and spoke in a half-choked voice that was such a good imitation of Mrs. Graham in the role of injured wife that Emma giggled. She was not, however, going to be diverted from the rest of the story.

"Did she," she asked, "give you the notes?"

"No," said Donovan; "found them in a desk."

"Uncle," said Hank, "must have regarded Jeff as a good investment."

"How," Emma asked, "did Hank get along?"

"All right," said Donovan, "with the audience. He looked so handsome with his hair combed that the gals sighed like he was Robert Taylor." He turned to Hank. "You answered the questions O.K., but," he sighed, "the D.A. is none too happy about you. He's got a dandy new notion that you and Petty planned the thing together to get the money."

"The District Attorney," said Hank, "must be taking dope. I never saw Petty until this morning."

"Says you," was Donovan's moody comment.

Emma was gazing at Hank in mild surprise. Yes, she supposed he was handsomer although she had come to take him so much for granted that she never thought of it. His lean brown face was well shaped, his nose was straight and his wide-set gray eyes were straightforward and intelligent. Just now the eyes were half shut in a familiar pose of contemplation and Emma could see the dark lashes which, while they did not have the luxuriant curl of Donovan's, were more than adequate. So, the gals in the courtroom liked him, did they? Emma decided to inaugurate "Be nicer to Hank" week. Aloud she said:

"We did draw a nice crowd, didn't we?"

"Uh-huh," said Hank.

Then, to Donovan, "Was Oscar all right?"

"Sure, Oscar was all right; it's just that you spent so much time wandering around that bothers the D.A. That, and the million dollars. Oh well," Donovan looked regretfully at his empty brandy glass, "we'll find Jeff pretty soon and that'll help."

"Do I dare ask," said Hank, "how Emma affected the District Attorney?"

Donovan pushed back his chair. "You can ask me," he said, "but I wouldn't mention it to him. She wouldn't even admit that Jeff's signatures were his, just said they looked like it. She'll get along. Good night."

Emma got up reluctantly; she was sure they hadn't told her everything but she couldn't think of any more questions to ask and she was very tired.

"Good night, Jerry," she said with a smile.

Donovan resolved to tell the sergeant he was a fool to keep her shadowed but before he got around to doing it something changed his mind.

Chapter

5

THE NEXT DAY was Sunday. Emma woke at about her customary hour, realized what day it was and went luxuriously back to sleep. Two hours later she awoke again, stretched all over and decided that, since it was a nice day, she might as well be up and doing. She put the coffeepot on and thought longingly of the Sunday paper on the front step. With an effort she wrenched herself out of bed, found her slippers and padded softly downstairs. A seedy-looking man in a derby watched her as she gathered up the paper. Emma wondered, idly, what he was doing there; loafers were not common in her street. She let in Minnie, a large, dog-eared, yellow tomcat belonging to M. LeBotien and paused to drink in the peaceful, sunny quiet of the morning. Emma decided that no matter how long she slept she could always tell if it were Sunday when she woke up. The city had a special quiet then, a prolonged absence of noise that surprised the mind and made it listen for the little noises that reechoed strangely in the empty streets. Minnie rubbed against Emma's bare ankles, emitting wide, soundless miaows. The man in the derby hat stirred. Emma went inside and shut the door.

Upstairs again, she poured herself a cup of coffee and rummaged through the icebox. The only thing she could find that remotely resembled breakfast was part of a box of figs; so, munching one philosophically, she went back to the bedroom. She fished out the sporting section and the funnies, threw the rest of the paper firmly under the bed and settled herself to read about the annual hope for a ball team and the daily mischances of Uncle Willie. She would not read about the murder; she would not even think about it; and when Hank came she would not let him talk about it. She was wishing sadly that she had seen Rabbit Maranville and had lived in the good old days when the city was not permanently at the bottom of the league standing when she heard a loud knocking at the front door. She looked at her watch; it was later than she thought; the funeral would be well over by now. She padded downstairs again and admitted Hank, who was laden with a large bundle and a green wrapped pot of daffodils.

"Why, you little God-love-it," said Emma, seizing the flowers and eying the bundle. "If you tell me there is anything like a human breakfast in there, I shall die of joy."

"I have seen your icebox before," said Hank, following her upstairs, "and I haven't eaten yet; the Norwitches don't go in for the funeral baked meats. By the way, have you seen the papers?"

Emma turned to face him on the landing. "Please, Hank," she said seriously. "It's such a nice day, and you're here, and I feel good, and let's pretend there isn't any murder at all. Let's eat, and take the car, and go out in the country somewhere, and look at the spring before they find Jeff and something dreadful happens."

Hank looked at her standing there in the brown bathrobe, clutching the daffodils. She didn't look as tall as he remembered; it must be the slippers. In fact, she didn't look a bit tall; she seemed small and rather pathetic. She was a silly little goose but he loved her very much. He wondered, with a pang, just how much it would hurt her if Jeff really had done it.

"O.K., baby," he said.

Hank, Emma decided, was a good provider. There were eggs, sausage, butter, cream and a fresh pineapple in the bundle, besides her favorite rolls. She made a new pot of coffee and puttered around in the cupboard that served for a kitchenette. She divided the pineapple in sections and set it neatly around piles of powdered sugar; she washed plates that were dusty because her domesticity did not include frequent meals at home; she set a little table in front of the sofa, putting the daffodils in the center and admiring her handiwork, until Hank, who had not had his hunger assuaged by so much as a cup of coffee, decided to take steps. He scrambled some eggs, cooked the sausage and had everything ready before Emma had finished putting the butter and cream on the table.

"You didn't," said Hank, "learn arithmetic in school; so I thought perhaps you took domestic science." He was about to add that he wondered why Jeff kept her around when he remembered that he mustn't mention Jeff.

"I was quite good," said Emma meekly, "in geography."

"Huh," said Hank, "I bet you don't know the capital of California."

"San Francisco," said Emma promptly. "Don't be silly."

It was early afternoon when they finished breakfast. Emma dressed while Hank put away the scanty remains of the food. He piled the plates and cups in the sink, mentally resigning himself to seeing them there until chance should prompt Emma to use them again.

While Hank backed the roadster out of the alley, they bickered amiably over whether spring would be nicer on the South Shore or out toward Bellerica. Emma and Bellerica finally won. As they turned out of the street, the man in the derby hat sprinted madly toward the nearest call box.

The Basin sparkled in the sun as they crossed Harvard Bridge. A few single shells were being oared about by hardy souls from the boat club, but almost all of the Basin's small craft still wore their winter covering of brown canvas and rocked, undisturbed, at their moorings. Cars flashed by along the Parkway, but Hank kept straight ahead through Cambridge on Massachusetts Avenue. He looked down at Emma, wondering at the unaccustomed silence. She was leaning back on the cushions, half dozing in the sunshine. Feeling his gaze, she opened one eye, saying as she did so, "Ugliest street in the world."

Hank laughed. "You wanted to come this way. Have you ever seen 13th Street in St. Joe?"

"Travel," said Emma, "has never broadened me but nothing could be plainer than this stretch of warehouses and cheap stores and apartment houses."

"Come now," said Hank, "think of Harvard Square."

"Pooh," said Emma, "a graveyard on one side and a brick wall on the other."

"I didn't mean there," began Hank, "and besides, the graveyard isn't on Massachusetts...."

"Don't bother me," said Emma, "I'm sleepy."

They drove on in silence through North Cambridge. In Arlington Hank decided that Emma really was asleep and wove as smoothly as he could among the Sunday traffic. At East Lexington the country was just ahead but the city did not relinquish its hold gracefully. It died in a great convulsion of tawdry movie houses, rickety wooden tenements and secondhand automobile yards. As Hank speeded up to pass an ancient sedan loaded with yelling children, Emma sat bolt upright.

"Stop," she yelled in Hank's ear, "stop quickly! It's Jeff's car. I saw it."

Hank looked back at the rickety sedan. "You're asleep," he said, "and dreaming."

Emma shook his arm. "I'm not either. You passed it back there in a junk yard."

"Go on," said Hank doubtfully, slowing down. "You couldn't spot Jeff's car that quickly out of a bunch of others. I thought you were asleep."

"Hank Fairbanks," said Emma, "I would know that Packard in China. I've seen it every day for five years. I helped Jeff pick it out and made him get green when he wanted black. I have ridden in it and driven it.

The front bumper is rusty on one end and there is a big dent in the left front fender; I know, I put it there. Furthermore, there is a tear in the upholstery of the back seat made by a nail in the back of a miniature desk. Now will you stop this automobile?"

Hank pulled over to the curb. "Toots," said he, "maybe you got something."

"Turn around, quick," said Emma, beginning to bounce with excitement.

Hank shut off the motor and got out of the car. He walked around to open the door for Emma.

"Get out," he said. "If we were a couple of newlyweds looking for a secondhand car, we'd be walking."

Emma wanted to hurry; she tugged like a dog on a leash against Hank's casual sauntering. It was a good two blocks back to the place they sought and, unrestrained, she would have run all the way. The ramshackle garage and the motley collection of all makes of automobiles that stood or leaned in the adjacent lot were no more disreputable in appearance than others of the same kind. To Hank it did not differ from several that they had passed but Emma turned in unerringly, having spotted the Packard in the front row of cars in the lot.

The man who came forward to attend to their wants was very dapper, in contrast to the general decrepit air of the place. Hank took command of the situation with the remark that they were in the market for a secondhand sedan—something classy but not too expensive. The dapper gentleman, with that perversity which is the caste mark of all salesmen, promptly led them to a yellow roadster with orange wheels. Hank admired it extravagantly. Emma, however, insisted that her hair would blow too much in a roadster and that she thought a sedan more elegant. After several false starts and considerable talk of transmissions and valves from Hank, who actually knew nothing about a car except how to drive it, they maneuvered themselves into the neighborhood of the Packard. Emma pounced on it with squeals. It was just what she wanted. It looked so rich. She did hope it wasn't going to cost too much. She walked ecstatically around the car and finally climbed inside. She just loved it, she announced, and the dapper person mentally raised the price. Of course, the upholstery was a bit torn. The mental calculations came down somewhat, but not much, for Emma promptly decided she could sew up the tear herself.

Hank retreated, ostensibly out of earshot of the little woman, to discuss the price; and Emma continued her investigation in a saner key. She ran her hand down between the cushions, thinking that she might find something of hers or Jeff's to further identify the car. With a muttered "Damn," she withdrew a pricked finger for inspection. A tiny sliver of glass was still stuck to the skin. Emma looked around. The interior of the car was too clean not to have been recently swept; but, by running her hand over the upholstery at the risk of more pricks, Emma found several more particles of glass. The windshield was intact and so, seemingly, were the windows. All but the one by the driver's seat were rolled to the top; that one, however, was either missing or cranked down. Emma had her hand on the crank when Hank came back, beaming and full of conversation. The Packard, it seemed, could be theirs for a mere three hundred dollars; a bargain, too, mind you; but the deal had to be cash; and they had only two hundred and fifty with them. Could she think of anyone—here Hank fixed Emma firmly with his eye—to whom he could telephone to borrow fifty dollars? With an effort, Emma calmed herself and got back into character. Telephone, she thought to herself, he wants to telephone, probably to Donovan. She turned a demure countenance to the dealer.

"Maybe Papa would loan us the money," she said. "My papa, or Jerry. Jerry Donovan, he's my brother," she explained, using Donovan's name on the chance that Hank's call might be overheard. "He's a contractor, he and Papa both; and they both want us to have a car, especially now that we, I mean I, am going to have . . ." Emma stopped. Clearly her life story was getting out of hand. Hank was trying not to laugh but the dealer, who was congratulating himself on having caught a complete pair of saps, nodded understandingly and led Hank away to the telephone.

Emma's hand flew to the crank. The window was there all right; it began to appear above the frame of the door. A long crack began to appear also; then a flurry of little cracks that surrounded a tiny round hole. Emma's hand dropped from the crank. Jeff was dead, then; she'd felt all along that perhaps Jeff had not come back to the shop at all. Once before, in the days when hijacking was almost a legitimate business, Emma had seen a hole like that. She and Jeff had been taking a short cut back from Hingham and had come upon an empty truck by the roadside. There had been just such a hole in the window and the state police had been removing the body of the dead driver. Emma wished Hank would come back. He'd stall as much as he could, though, to give Donovan time to get there. She cranked the window slowly down again, wondering if she looked as heartsick as she felt. Poor old Jeff. He had been sitting right there where she was sitting. Emma got out of the car suddenly and looked at the seat. There was a shiny, scrubbed spot near the edge that she did not remember. Emma touched it tentatively with a finger and found it slippery, almost greasy. Sniffing at her hand, she thought she detected a faint odor of oil and gasoline. Donovan would cut a piece out of the seat and have it tested for this and that but Emma thought she knew what he'd find. If you wanted to cover up a blood spot, you put grease or crankcase oil on it and then cleaned the mess up with gasoline.

Where on earth was Hank? Probably regaling the dealer with the story of their courtship. Let him. She wished Donovan would come so that she wouldn't have to put on any more of this silly farce. If he kept the siren wide open and didn't stop for anything, how long would it take him to get there? Maybe he wasn't at the station; maybe he was at home. She supposed that Hank knew where Donovan lived but what if he couldn't find him? Perhaps Donovan had the children out for a Sunday afternoon ride, if he had any children. What if they had to stay there for hours, pretending to be a couple of lovebirds? They'd better buy the car and take it away. Using what for money?

All at once Emma saw Donovan, the dealer and Hank, walking quietly toward her; she realized that she had been expecting at least a fleet of armored cars. Donovan was wearing a soft hat and the gray flannel suit. Emma thought, for a frantic moment, that he was pretending to be her brother and that she couldn't tell him, yet, about the bullet hole and the stain. However, there was no doubt in the dealer's mind about Donovan's identity. Looking considerably less dapper, he was very busily explaining how the Packard had come into his possession.

He had, he said, bought it from a couple of fellows on Friday. Oh no, he had never seen them before but the registration and the plates had seemed all right. The fellow who had said he owned the car had given a plausible story about going back to his regular job as ship's cook and not needing the Packard any longer. He didn't think there was anything wrong with a ship's cook having a Packard. It was an old car and he'd paid a hundred for it, cash; and where was he going to get his money? Business was terrible. Identify them? No, he hadn't noticed them especially. Well, maybe one had on a cap and a leather jacket, the one that did most of the talking; the other had on a blue suit and just a hat, maybe brown, maybe gray. No, the feller in the blue suit didn't limp and he'd never heard of Shorty DiVoto and what was the police trying to do? Trying to pin something on him?

Donovan walked over to Emma. "Hello," he said. "You're sure this is Jeff's car?"

Emma pointed out the bump and the torn seat.

"O.K.," said Donovan. "I'll drive it in. The plates have been changed and the registration is forged; but it was sold so quickly the engine numbers probably weren't touched. All we have to do now is find the guys that stole this."

"Look," said Emma. She had been cranking up the window while Donovan was speaking.

"And look," she pointed to the stain. "It's oil and gas but I bet there's blood there too."

Donovan whistled. "Kid Sherlock, himself," he said. "You didn't find a confession tied to the steering wheel, did you?"

"But don't you see," Emma said, "this means Jeff had nothing to do with Norwitch's murder. He never went to the shop; he was held up; maybe Blanchard did hear a shot; and his body was put somewhere, and the car sold."

"And you and Hank killed Norwitch?" asked Donovan.

"No, no," Emma went on, "the men who stole the secretary killed him, just as Hank said. It's all so clear and simple now."

"Simple, is it?" said Donovan. "You mean all I have to do is to find the secretary, and the mugs that took it, and Jeff's body, and the guys that stole his car, and then prove who did which. It's too bad we can't get the fire department in on this case somehow, then we'd have the whole city working on it."

"Don't be so cross," said Emma, "or I'll claim I never saw this car before. Here I spoil a perfectly good day finding you the first real break in this mess and you snap at me. I ask you, is that gratitude?"

"I didn't snap," denied Donovan. "And as for spoiling a good day, Hank woke me out of a sound sleep. And precious few of 'em I've had lately."

"Children, children," said Hank, "stop quarreling and Papa'll buy you both an ice-cream cone."

"That reminds me," said the dealer. "Are you two really married? Because if you are, I got a nice little Buick . . ."

Emma began to laugh and Hank joined in. Donovan looked at all of them with disgust. "For God's sake," he said, "shut up and let's get out of here."

Chapter

6

MONDAY IT RAINED. A slow steady spring rain came down deliberately, as though it had plenty of time to do a thorough job of saturating the city with moisture. The trees dripped rhythmically and a gentle tinkle of water came from the downspouts. There was a fine mist on Emma's hair when she got to the shop and she was thankful that, last night, Hank's weather eye had prompted him to put up the top on the roadster. All too frequently she rode to work sitting in a puddle. It would doubtless rain for a week now. Then the weather would turn hot, the leaves would come out over night and spring would be gone before she had had a chance to enjoy it. She sighed, thinking what a nice day yesterday had started to be and how dismally it had failed. But, in spite of the spoiled day, she was glad they had found the car. Finding it was at least a step forward toward the solution of their difficulties, even though she hated to think of what it must mean about Jeff. Did Blanchard's story of the shot fit in somehow with the stolen car and the bullet hole? It was all too complicated for Emma so she decided to leave the speculation to Hank and Donovan, who seemed to like it, and to devote herself to the next problem at hand which would be last month's bills.

Emma was rattling away on the typewriter when Hank came in about noon. There was no spot of rain on him and Emma was about to lecture him on the subject of his extravagant use of taxicabs when he forestalled her by saying that he had hurried down to tell her the news. She had been right about the spot. Traces of blood had been found mixed with the oil and gasoline on the seat and the bullet that made the hole came from a .32-caliber gun. Donovan asked that she say nothing about the finding of the car. He hoped to catch the thieves through some other robbery and didn't want them warned off. Would she like some lunch?

After they had eaten, Emma returned to the bills. Hank smoked quietly, leaning back in Jeff's chair with his feet braced against the office wall. The rain continued its monotonous patter and no customers came to disturb them.

"Tell me," said Hank suddenly, "everything that happened in the shop the day of the murder."

Emma looked up from her work. She was nearly through and a little inclined to resent the interruption but decided that a moment's rest and a cigarette would do no harm. There was a long afternoon ahead. "Of course," she began patiently, "you have heard all this before but I'll tell you again."

"Begin in the morning," said Hank.

Emma racked her brain. That morning was a little vague but she couldn't see that it made much difference. She repeated the customary day's routine, throwing in a few customers that she remembered having seen around at some recent date. As she talked, the hustle and confusion of the afternoon came back to her; she told of the telephone conversation, Jeff's ill-humor and the rush of buyers with which his departure had saddled her. The story of the lady and the Hessian andirons was set forth in great detail and that brought her to Finegold and the chandelier.

"What shall I do?" she wailed. "It was a swell sale and Mrs. Graham needs the money." She paused for a moment, realizing that she was speaking as if she knew that Jeff was dead. "And the woman who bought it is going back to Schenectady tomorrow."

Hank was not interested in the chandelier. "There's nothing there," he said glumly. "You omitted Petty and a couple of other details but you didn't add anything that would help. It's like a picture with holes cut in it and I can't find the scraps. Uncle led a blameless life—well almost, I don't care for that business about Petty's mother—and somebody stabbed him. Petty is in the picture, but how? He says he was never in the shop and there's nothing to prove that he was. I may have a motive but I really don't think I did it. The bullet hole in Jeff's car and Blanchard's shot might go together except that eleven-twenty is too late for the goings on here and Connerton can't find anyone else who heard a shot."

"Maybe," Emma suggested, "Petty shot Jeff."

"Please," said Hank, "don't smear the picture."

Rebuffed, Emma lost interest; she had heard about the picture with holes in it before and regarded it as a mild hallucination on Hank's part. She turned again to the bills. As she was sealing the last envelope, the telephone rang. She picked it up quickly.

Hank, lost in a cloud of speculation, thought that the shrill voice that came over the wire sounded like that of a child.

"My God," he heard Emma say. "I forgot all about it; yes, yes, I'll do it right away."

"Do what?" asked Hank.

Emma was putting on her hat and coat. "Mind the shop for me," she said. "I have to see a man about a dog."

Her laugh as she went out the door had a jarring note in it. Hank was suddenly disturbed. The feeling that he had had once before—he couldn't remember just when—that she was concealing something, came back to him. He wished he had made her tell him where she was going. He tried to think back to the time when he had felt the same way. He hadn't heard her at the inquest but the record showed the same story she had told Donovan. Hank's feet came down from the wall with a bang. That was it. There had been something wrong when Donovan taxed her with the length of time it took her to return to the Gilded Slipper the night of the murder. Her story had been reasonable enough but he knew he had been afraid for her at the start of it. It was queer too, that the police had not been able to find the taxi driver. What if she had seen the murder done? He thought of her almost fanatical devotion to Jeff and wondered to what depths it would carry her. Why, the dirty little tramp! If she were double-crossing him! Hank went to the washroom and poured himself a drink. He supposed he was silly to care so much that she hadn't told him the truth. It didn't do to care too much for people or things. He remembered a fox terrier he had had as a child and the pangs its roving disposition had cost him. He poured himself another drink and surveyed the shelf. The bottles and glasses had been returned but something familiar was missing. Pondering what it could be, he started back to the office.

A woman was standing in the aisle, facing him. She was tall and dark. Hank liked the smooth black hair that showed underneath her black hat. She did not look at all like Emma. Hank smiled at her. She seemed to be gazing at the glass in his hand. Probably she was thinking that he was not attending to business. Emma had left him to mind the shop. To hell with Emma. He'd show her.

"Won't you," said Hank, "have a drink?"

Chapter

7

EMMA CAME BACK to the shop feeling almost jubilant. The job was over now; she had done all she could; and the thing she had forgotten would no longer return to plague her in the night. If Jeff were really dead, what she had said didn't matter. She could take care of herself; the inquest was over and now she need never think of it again. She shook herself and threw back her shoulders, as though casting off a load.

Hank was pacing excitedly up and down and began shouting at Emma before she was through the door. In his enthusiasm he forgot, for the moment, that he was angry with her.

"They caught them," he exclaimed, "the fellows that stole Jeff's car. It was Shorty DiVoto and a pal. The dealer who had the car was part of the ring and he tipped Shorty off to leave town; but the dummy tried to get away in another stolen car that the police were looking for and they picked him up. Donovan told DiVoto they were going to accuse him of Jeff's murder, so he squealed on the pal. DiVoto's story is that the pal found the car on Chambers Street, with the motor running and the keys in it and just drove it away. DiVoto, who's the boss, changed the plates and went along out to East Lexington to see that there was no crossing up between the dealer and the pal. Your friend, the sergeant, found Jeff's plates in the garage the ring uses for headquarters. And the police have been trying to bust them up for a long time and everyone is very happy and they think you're a smart girl.

"DiVoto and the pal both swear that there was no one in the car, or near, when they found it, although they admit seeing the bullet hole in the window and cleaning off the bloodstain. What might have happened, they thought, was none of their business but the car was just so much gravy."

Emma's thoughts were racing. Chambers Street? What did she know about Chambers Street? She couldn't concentrate because Hank was going on, saying something about Jeff. Jeff was dead. The police had decided that. Why did Hank seem to delight in telling it to her? He was saying it again. They had put a cop about Jeff's height in the car, cranked

71

up the window and figured, from the height of the hole, that the bullet would have hit him in the head. There was no bullet hole in the car, so the shot must have found its mark and .32 shots in the head were, it seemed, fatal. Donovan was working on DiVoto and the pal now, trying to make them change their story and admit the shooting; and Hank was going down to headquarters.

They stood looking at each other in the dim light of the fading afternoon. The light from the street lamp, falling through the rivulets of water on the windows, cast strange shadows on Hank's face. He was stern, Emma thought, too stern, standing there telling her that Jeff was dead. She needed a little sympathy very badly and Hank had never failed her before. She stood still, holding her pocketbook tightly in both hands and trying not to cry. It was no use; her face worked; and the tears spurted from her eyes, as from a child's that is suddenly hurt.

All Hank's anger vanished; he put his arms around her and patted her gently while she sobbed comfortably into his breast pocket. She was just a baby, he thought. One didn't get angry with children when they were hurt as a result of their own actions; one comforted them and hoped they had learned a lesson. He smiled wryly to himself; tomorrow, probably, she'd remember to tell him something that would explain everything. He fished around for his handkerchief.

"Listen, pigeon," he said, wiping Emma's eyes, "I want to see Donovan. Will you shut up the shop and let me take you home before I go ?"

"No," said Emma, sniffling, "I'm all right now. You go along and call me right back if you find out anything more."

After the door had closed behind Hank, Emma sat down in the office to think over what he had told her. She wondered if she ought to call Mrs. Graham but decided against it. After all, Jeff's body hadn't been found and he might yet come back to surprise them all, especially Mrs. Graham. She thought of DiVoto; she hoped, ferociously, that Donovan was beating him with a rubber hose. Chambers Street? Why couldn't she recall what it was she knew about that place? The memory of the Merry-go-round Bar flashed incongruously through her mind. But what did that gilded place have to do with the sordidness of Chambers Street? It had been something funny, too. Dr. Smiley! That was it, not that it had any importance. She went on remembering, just for the practice. Dr. Smiley had joined them at the bar—he had been a classmate of Hank's. After three manhattans she had thought his name a great big joke and had kept harping on it, up to the very door, when they finally drove him to the rear entrance of the hospital on Chambers Street. The time would come, she supposed, when she'd be amused again at names like Smiley but that time seemed immeasurably remote. If Jeff were dead, what would happen to her and to the shop? For five years, now, the business of buying and selling old furniture and knickknacks had been her chief consideration. Life would be pretty dull without the daily contacts, the trade gossip and the battle of wits that every sale or purchase involved. Perhaps Mrs. Graham would let her carry on the business. But things wouldn't be the same without Jeff there to share the minutiae and humor of situations and events. She thought she was smart but Jeff was the one who really knew things, who had a sixth sense for spotting fakes and who had imagination and taste. Could she support herself and Mrs. Graham without him? Emma looked at his empty office chair and wished she could see him sitting in it, ragging her about forgetting the door. She shut her eyes but, instead of seeing Jeff in the office chair, she saw him sitting at the wheel of the car, with the ugly little round hole in line with his head. What was wrong with that picture? Was she catching the picture idea from Hank? What had Hank said about the car window? If the window were cranked up, the shot would have hit him in the head. But how could Donovan and Hank be silly enough to think that Jeff would be driving with the window shut on a mild spring night? Emma sat up straight with excitement. If the window were half open, the shot would not hit the head, but the body. Well, one was just as dead from a shot in the heart as in the head. But put the hole up a little higher and the bullet would strike the shoulder. Why, Emma thought suddenly, Jeff wasn't dead at all. She was almost certain she knew where to find him. Her hands shaking with excitement, she fumbled through the telephone book until she found the number of the hospital where Dr. Smiley was an interne.

Minutes, hours, it seemed to Emma, went by before Dr. Smiley was on the wire. Certainly he remembered her. Yes, he'd be glad to do something for her. Days, as Emma reckoned time, passed before she got the answer to her next question; and when it came she was disappointed. No, the hospital had no record of a man named Graham with a bullet wound in the shoulder. Did he have to be named Graham? Because they had a lovely case with just such a wound, named Oakes, who had been out of his head for four days. Yes, he came in Thursday night. An orderly had found him, in a faint, just inside the rear door. What? Yes, he supposed she could. Yes, he'd meet her at the main entrance.

In spite of the haste of her departure, Emma took time to bolt the door. She would never, she thought, forget that again. As she went out, she saw someone standing, looking at the snuffboxes in the window. It was a woman who, although her face was turned away, seemed vaguely familiar. Probably a customer, but Emma had no time for the best customer just then. She jumped into the roadster and tore recklessly down the slippery street. She did not have to stop at the Cambridge Street intersection and slithered to a stop in front of the hospital, having gone the seven blocks in something under three minutes.

Dr. Smiley, full of questions, met her as she hurried in. Wasn't Graham the missing man in the Norwitch case? Did she think Oakes might be Graham? What made her think so and what was she going to do if he were? Emma asked him to please hurry and to stop talking. She also extracted a promise from him to say nothing about the whole situation until after she had seen Oakes. She learned that a reporter had been there, following up the hospital's necessary report to the police. The reporter had seen Oakes, who was delirious at the time and had looked at his record, which listed his wound as self-inflicted and accidental.

By the time they got to the private ward, Emma was beginning to lose confidence in her hunch. Mr. Oakes and his troubles sounded too well-authenticated to turn into Jeff. If Mr. Oakes had been unconscious when he got to the hospital, his name must have been obtained from his papers. Jeff's pockets would hardly have yielded the name of Oakes, unless he had gone to his game more thoroughly disguised than Emma would have thought necessary. And how did the hospital know the wound was self-inflicted? Her trip was doubtless nothing but a wild-goose chase but, just to satisfy herself, she was going to take a look at Mr. Oakes.

"Here we are," said Dr. Smiley, pausing before the closed door of a private room. "The nurse says he's asleep; so go in quietly and take a look. I can't wait for you, I have to give a blood transfusion, but let me know the verdict."

Emma opened the door gently and stepped inside, feeling pretty silly. Mr. Oakes would probably wake up and break into loud screams at the sight of a strange woman. She shut the door and stood looking at the man on the bed. He was apparently bald, but Emma knew him instantly.

"Jeff Graham," she said, "what have you done to your hair?"

The figure on the bed opened one eye and looked at her.

"Go way," it said. "I'm unconscious."

"You look," said Emma, "simply hideous but I was never so glad to see anyone in my life. What do you mean, driving everyone crazy with worry ? The hospital thinks you're Oakes; the police think you killed Norwitch; and I thought you were dead. Are you really shot or did you make that up too?"

"I'll say I'm shot," said Jeff. "The damn doctors have dug for the bullet until I feel like a subway excavation. How," he changed the subject abruptly, "did you know where I was?"

"The police," Emma explained, "found the men who stole your car. . . ."

"What a break," said Jeff. "I couldn't eat the damn thing and I've been expecting it to give me away any minute. Go on."

"Well," Emma continued, "I remembered that there was a hospital on Chambers Street and I thought that, if you weren't dead, you'd be in the hospital."

"My," said Jeff, "how you do jump to conclusions."

"Suppose," said Emma, "you jump to some explanations. Norwitch is dead, as you seem to know; though how you managed to read the papers when delirious, I couldn't guess. Jeff, I know you didn't do it. But what on earth are you hiding in here for and who shot you? You know I won't give you away. . . ."

With his unbandaged arm Jeff pulled Emma to a seat on the bed.

"Listen to me," he said. "I know you won't give me away, but the jig is probably up now. The police may not have your woman's intuition but they will get to the same place finally. Who's on this case? Donovan? He's a smart mick. I'll tell you all you need to know and then I want you to do something for me. Somebody, never mind who," he said grimly, "shot at me when I was in the car just outside the store. I managed to drive the bus here and get inside. There was an orderly hanging around. I gave him a phony name, bribed him to report the shooting accidental and told him to get rid of all the papers I had on me. It was lucky I'd won a lot in the game. He got me into a private room and shaved my head—he also tells me the news. Then I went delirious on 'em. It wasn't hard. It's no joke to have a slug nestle in your shoulder and I kept seeing Norwitch looking at me. . ."

"Jeff, you were there," cried Emma wildly. "Jeff, Jeff."

"Yes," said Jeff, "I was in there all right. Shut up and pay attention. Get me a lawyer, quick; Sullivan will do; and tell that smart guy of yours to get the police after a feller named Dunn. I think he stole the secretary and he may have killed Norwitch for all I know."

"Jeff," said Emma, "listen to me a minute. Did you take the key?"

"What key?" asked Jeff. "Where?"

"Your key, the one you loaned Norwitch. The police can't find it and they think that Norwitch dropped it and that you picked it up without thinking."

"Well, maybe I did," said Jeff. "What difference does it make?"

"It makes," Emma replied, "a very great deal of difference. Donovan thinks you were there but he can't get any proof. What would you have done with the key if you had taken it?"

"I don't know; put it in my pocket, probably," said Jeff wearily. "Now will you get out of here and do what I told you?"

Jeff, Emma decided, was still too sick to realize the seriousness of the situation. She would have to take care of him in spite of himself.

"Where," she asked, "are your clothes?"

"I don't know," Jeff repeated. "The orderly put 'em away. Will you just . . ."

"What," Emma kept on, "is the orderly's name?"

"Pissano." Jeff yelled it at her. "Scram!"

Emma found Pissano, who seemed, at first, to doubt her right to question him. Emma decided that Jeff must have given him a lot of money. Pissano had found a bunch of keys, he finally admitted, in the pocket of Jeff's trousers and had left them there. He grudgingly took Emma to the locker where the clothes were kept. With trembling fingers, Emma pulled out the keys. There were no car keys, those had been left in the Packard. The ring contained only Jeff's house key and an assortment of keys for luggage. The shop key was missing. Emma searched the pockets of the suit coat and vest, thinking that Jeff might have slipped it in and that it had escaped Pissano's notice. There was no key to be found. She stepped back, relieved but wondering, and surveyed the pile of clothes. Her eye fell on the hat. Why, it wasn't Jeff's hat. It looked like it but the band was narrower and the bow was different. She picked the hat off the hook and looked inside. The initials R.M.N. met her anguished gaze. What was Jeff doing with a hat that belonged to Richard Minot Norwitch? This was worse than finding the key. She must do something, but what? Oh, he had been there; perhaps he had killed Norwitch in self-defense; but she had to help him; she couldn't let Donovan find this hat. The orderly was saying something. Emma turned the hat over quickly to hide the telltale initials and listened.

The orderly, it seemed, was getting belated qualms of conscience. He would lose his job if he were found out and he had an aged mother.... He wants more money, Emma thought to herself, and I haven't any to give him. I can't ask him to destroy the hat, because then he'll look at the initials. It's a wonder he hasn't spotted them already. She ran her hand over the top of the hat.

"My," she said aloud, "this hat is dirty. It must have fallen in the gutter. Mr. Graham will be leaving the hospital soon and he wouldn't wear it like this. If it's all right with you, I'm going to take it out to have it cleaned. Thank you," she said, "for being so nice to Mr. Graham. He will see you again before he goes." She hoped that Jeff had some more money with which to make good her hint.

It was a poor bluff but, surprisingly, it worked. Emma tried to be casual as she left the hospital but she felt as though the hat were the size of an umbrella, and bright red. She fervently hoped that Dr. Smiley was still busy with his transfusion. Once in the roadster, she stuffed Richard Norwitch's brown felt down behind the seat. He wouldn't need it again.

Chapter
8

EMMA HAD ALWAYS BEEN pretty much of a fatalist but the next few days
surtaxed her particular brand of composure. Days started out well and
then turned out very badly. She sold a Liverpool pitcher and then broke
it during the packing. She forgot about the hat until it was too late,
after successfully removing it from the hospital. Black days turned suddenly rosy; an old gentleman with a plaid waistcoat insulted everything
in the shop and then bought four hundred dollars worth of this and
that. Life was like the Fun House, where one stepped into holes or went
backward with every step forward, only it wasn't fun because she quarreled with Hank.

She had meant to tell him about Jeff, she really had, but he had not
called her after he left to see Donovan; and after she talked to Sullivan,
the lawyer, she decided not to. Jeff was still weak, Sullivan had said, in
no shape to face a police grilling or go to jail; a few more days in the
hospital would not delay justice too long and would help Jeff. In a few
days, perhaps, Donovan would have found proof against Petty. Emma
rather liked Petty but she would cheerfully throw him to the wolves to
save Jeff. She did not consider herself in the light of potential wolf bait.

It was still raining on Tuesday but people had become reconciled
to the wet and were going about their business as usual. It was a fairly
busy morning in the shop. Emma sold four brass trivets that she had
been stumbling over for years and bought a good blue plate from a
stout housewife with a string bag. When Hank came in, red-eyed and
glum from his futile all-night session with Donovan and DiVoto, she
acted on Jeff's suggestion and told him of Dunn. She remembered, she
said, that a man by that name had been suspected of having something
to do with some robberies on the Cape; she knew it was only a hunch
but he might be the one who had taken the secretary. It could do no
harm to look him up. Hank telephoned the detective, who was grateful
for any hint in a matter with which he was getting nowhere rapidly.

"Tell him," said Emma, "that there are a lot of men on the Connecticut and New York force, too, that can be spared just to find out

things. Tell him to advertise in the papers."

"He wants to know," relayed Hank, "will you pay for the advertisement?"

"Hell yes," said Emma, "tell him we'll give a reward—of not more than a hundred dollars," she added cautiously.

Hank laughed and told the detective to go to it.

"It's a funny thing," Emma fumed, "that they can't find a big thing like a secretary, one that would be a sensation wherever it turned up."

"Precious," said Hank, "that secretary may be a sensation to you but remember that to some people it's just a roll-top desk; and, besides, probably the person who got it isn't anxious to tell about it."

Just then Sergeant Connerton came in, looking almost jovial, with Emma's lock and keys.

"Thank you so much, Sergeant," Emma said graciously, much relieved at the prospect of having protection on her doors, "you really needn't have gone to the trouble of bringing them back to me after I put you to the bother of taking them."

"Sure it was a pleasure," said the sergeant. And Emma decided that Irishmen were all chivalrous at heart, after all.

Hank and the sergeant fell to talking about the inquest and Emma was relieved to note, putting the adhesive tape sticker on her new blue plate, that Connerton seemed to have transferred his affection for the likely murderer to Petty.

She went about the business of marking the price on the adhesive tape sticker before putting the plate in an advantageous position.

"By the way," said Hank after the sergeant had gone, taking, in an excess of gallantry, Emma's lock to put on for her, "did you see your friend, Miss Mathews, at the inquest?"

"Mathews?" said Emma wonderingly. "I don't know any Miss Mathews."

"Please," said Hank, "try to remember the customers' names; first principle of success, remembering names. You do so know her, she was in the shop---" Hank recalled that Emma hadn't been there and that he had been angry with her.

"I forgot to tell you," he went on, "she came in the other afternoon while you were out. I was having a drink and she caught me at it; so I gave her one. Anything to keep the customers happy. And we had a nice visit." Hank swallowed, thinking of how nice he had been while his anger at Emma had lasted.

"She said she had been in before. She's a nice-looking gal, maybe a little oldish, but I like 'em dark and sleek like that," he finished defensively.

"Oh, her," said Emma, calling to mind the woman who had smiled at her as she left the courtroom. "She's damn near forty and keep your hands off the customers. I was sure I'd seen her but I don't think I ever knew her name; so she can't be much of a buyer. We only serve drinks to the best customers."

"And another thing," said Hank, "what used to be on the shelf in the washroom that isn't there now?"

"Is this a game?" Emma asked. "I don't know. What's there now?"

"Two cracked glasses," Hank checked the items off on his fingers, "a bottle of soda, half full, and a can of Dutch Cleanser."

"I know, teacher," said Emma, "the bottle of scotch is gone. It was empty and I threw it out. If that is a hint, there is some more down cellar."

"I never," Hank threw in, "drink before lunch on rainy days. No, seriously, isn't there something else missing? If you'll forgive my mentioning it, the picture of the shelf is incomplete."

Emma groaned, then went to look at the shelf. "It's the blackjack; the cops must have forgotten to bring it back. You'd think they'd have enough of their own without depriving a poor girl of her only weapon."

"That's queer, that's very queer," mused Hank, "because I saw the junk down at the station and I don't think the blackjack was there."

He turned to the telephone and finally got one of the fingerprint men on the line.

"Hello," he said, "this is Hank Fairbanks. Did you have a blackjack down there? No, no, I don't want a blackjack. I said, did you test a blackjack for fingerprints? Yes, in the Norwitch case. No? Thank you, that's all."

He swung around to Emma. "When did you last see that thing?" he asked.

"When Petty was here," Emma said slowly. "I mixed him a drink. I washed the glass because he's fussy that way, and I know it was on the shelf then."

"Did Petty go to the washroom?" Hank's eyes were open now with excitement.

"No," said Emma, "I don't think he did. Yes, he did too. He watched me make the drinks and he let me go out first. I noticed that because I'm not used to such politeness. Do you think he took it? But what would he want of a blackjack? Mr. Norwitch was killed with the paper cutter."

"I don't know that he took it," said Hank, "but it'll be interesting if he admits that he did. Say, you don't suppose the knife was hidden under the blackjack, do you? It could have been. And he took the blackjack and then saw the knife and took that too. Or didn't take it but used it later?"

"You're just saying words," Emma remarked; "he wouldn't take the blackjack and the knife both; and, if he took the billy, he'd use that and not go groping around for the dagger; and I don't think it was there anyway; I'm sure I would have seen it if it had been."

"Somebody took it." Hank clung stubbornly to his idea. "Maybe you'd rather Jeff took it?"

"Oh, but he didn't," Emma began, then stopped, panicstricken at what she had been going to say.

"How do you know he didn't?" asked Hank.

Emma shifted quickly into reverse and hoped the noise of grinding gears was not audible. "I'm not sure he didn't," she admitted, "but he carried one in the car. He wouldn't want one in each hand, would he?"

"So," said Hank, "you've decided that Jeff was in here. I thought you were sticking firmly to the notion that he never came here at all. What made you change your mind?"

"I haven't; I mean I didn't say that." Emma was dodging desperately in heavy traffic now. "Do I have," she went on, "to put in all the qualifying clauses? I said he didn't take it; and, if I thought he wasn't here, he couldn't take it, could he? But, if he had been, he wouldn't, see, because he had one."

"Don't," said Hank, "strain yourself. I think I know what you think you mean. I guess it's not important anyway."

"That," said Emma, but not out loud, "is what you think."

Again Hank telephoned, this time to Donovan. He told him of the missing blackjack and when Emma had last seen it. He suggested that Petty be questioned about it and his room and luggage searched. Donovan thanked him for the tip and added that the idea of the search occurred to him at once. Hank said he was surprised and hung up.

After lunch Hank asked Emma to repeat, again, the events of the day before the murder. He was fast becoming discouraged with himself as a detective. So far Donovan had done all the work, Emma had found the car and even the sergeant was busily running around checking up on stories. Of course, Donovan hadn't discovered anything that wasn't right out for anyone to see. Even finding DiVoto was just a matter of police routine. He, Hank, was the one who was supposed to see through walls and around corners by virtue of reasoning and superior intelligence, and his intelligence seemed to be letting him down badly. Only he didn't think it was. He could not work the problem out because his intelligence told him that some of the figures were missing. If he could only feel that he knew all the facts, he could go ahead. Probably by that time, he thought bitterly, Donovan would get a confession or analyze a piece of rope and the case would be over. He'd have to risk it, though, because, if your head worked a certain way, that was just the way it worked and it was no good trying to turn a bulldog brain, for example, into a greyhound one. He ought to go see Petty and find out something about the half of Petty that wasn't Norwitch, but he didn't want to walk the three blocks to Petty's hotel in the rain and Emma would scalp him if he tried to take a cab for that distance. He'd content himself with Emma's story and wait for Donovan to phone him what Petty said about the blackjack.

"Go on," he said to Emma, "I'm listening."

Again Emma went patiently over the events of the fatal day, specifying even the details of Mrs. Graham's costume. "I don't know why," she remarked plaintively when she had finished, "you make me keep telling this; you must know it by heart by this time."

"My darling," said Hank, "if you'd ever tell it twice alike I'd let up on you, but you never do; so I keep hoping you'll put in a vital bit that will cut the knot, open the safe and save the American standard of living. See how important it was that you remembered that Petty went to the washroom? You've never mentioned that before or that Mrs. Graham had a mink cape on. Now if you had only told me about the cape, I could have saved you the embarrassment of having Donovan surprise you with the boy friend. Why, anybody could deduce him. Mink and boy friends are like ham and eggs or gin and jitters, yet you make Donovan spend the taxpayers' money—and let me tell you—that as a newly arrived taxpayer I feel this very keenly—on a dick to shadow Mrs. Graham, just by leaving out important details. Sometimes I wonder what I see in you."

"Worry," said Emma, "is undoubtedly unbalancing your mind. Psst. Here comes a customer."

"Psst yourself," said Hank. "It's Miss Mathews."

"Remind me," said Emma quickly, "to tell you something."

But Hank was on his feet, greeting the newcomer. "Hello," he said. "How are you? Emma, this is Miss Mathews; Miss Mathews, Miss Marsh."

He needn't, Emma thought, purr quite so loudly or keep hold of her hand so long. Mink and boy friends, huh? She could deduce a little herself.

"Hello," she said. "I do hope you dropped in for a visit. Hank has been telling me about you," she went on blandly. "I'm sorry I wasn't here the other day. And how did you like the inquest? It's such a foul day we were just talking about having a drink to cheer us up. Will you have one? You do drink, don't you?"

Miss Mathews let Hank take her coat and sank smoothly into the wing chair that he pulled up for her. She was, Emma thought to herself, a knockout, with her pale ivory skin and her black dress against the faded rose brocade of the chair. Miss Mathews took a cigarette from Hank and smiled up at him as he lit it for her.

"Hussy," thought Emma but aloud she said, not too sharply, "Run down cellar, Hank, and get the scotch."

Miss Mathews turned her slow smile on Emma. "He's very nice, isn't he?" she said. "And so devoted to you; he was telling me about you when I was here the other day."

Emma was somewhat taken aback, possibly she had been deducing too rapidly; Miss Mathews wasn't such a bad sort after all. By the time Hank came back with the drinks, they were visiting merrily away about the antique business, about which Miss Mathews knew very little but seemed pleasantly curious, and their favorite actresses. Miss Mathews was thoroughly conversant with the theatrical world, having been, she said in answer to Emma's question, a costume designer. No, she wasn't a Russian, she just looked like one; she cultivated a slow manner of speaking to increase the impression that she was a foreigner and hence, in some people's minds, a better designer.

The talk turned to the inquest and Miss Mathews wanted to know if Hank wasn't disappointed to have to divide his uncle's estate with a stranger. No, Hank said, it was plenty large for two; but, if Petty didn't look out, he wouldn't get to enjoy it. They all agreed that Petty had not acquitted himself well on the witness stand. He had, said Miss Mathews, an even better motive for the murder than Mr. Graham. Hank conceded that he had and added that the police had him where they could get their hands on him, which was a great comfort to them, since they could neither find Mr. Graham nor any direct evidence against him. Hadn't, Miss Mathews wanted to know, anyone any idea what had happened to Mr. Graham? Emma lit a cigarette while Hank said no.

The telephone began to ring, and Emma stepped into the office to answer it. When she heard the voice on the wire she pressed the receiver close to her ear. Why, oh, why, had Jeff picked that very minute to call her? If the police were still tracing incoming calls they'd go right to the hospital. But it seemed that Jeff was no longer in the hospital. Emma couldn't ask where he was or what he was up to. All she could do was to say yes and no at all the wrong places in the conversation, until Jeff realized that there was someone in the shop and that he would have to explain from his end of the line. He had just, he said, become damn sick of staying in the hospital while nobody did anything about the secretary. What was the idea, not finding it? And where, in heaven's name, was his hat? Emma could have slapped him, as if she didn't have troubles enough without having him jump on her about the secretary and the hat. He was staying at a hotel, he wouldn't tell her where, and Emma was seriously handicapped at finding out; he was in touch with a chap who knew where Dunn was and he wanted some money. Emma said no, she didn't think she could deliver it today and the line crackled with Jeff's expletives. In about a minute, Emma thought, I'm going to hang up on him. But she couldn't do that, he'd just call back and perhaps Hank would get to the phone first. What? Was there a hundred dollars in the cash drawer? No, said Emma, not possibly. Fifty? Emma thought yes, she could deliver the pitcher tomorrow. She was not to bank the money and was to leave the corner door of the shop unbolted. She had forgotten it the night of Norwitch's murder, she could forget it on purpose for once, Jeff supposed, and Emma boiled with unspoken rage. If anything went wrong, he would call her tomorrow; so she was to be at the shop on time. Emma hung up with a bang. How could she get rid of Hank and Miss Mathews in order to leave the door unlocked? And why did Jeff have to make a bad matter worse by leaping off somewhere and refusing to tell her about it? Hank was leaning toward Miss Mathews, laughing softly at something she had just said. Men, Emma decided, were impossible.

Hank turned casually to Emma. "Are deliveries," he asked, "a week late as usual?"

"It sounded," said Miss Mathews, "like a man's voice. I didn't think men were that fussy."

Did Emma imagine it or did Miss Mathews have an unbelieving gleam in her eye?

"Miss Mathews knows Avery Cartwright," Hank went on, "the one who did the costumes for *Sense and Sensibility*. Funny thing," Hank mused, "when I knew him he was a good squash player. They use real antiques, you'll be glad to hear. We ought to go see it."

"If Miss Marsh has to deliver something," said Miss Mathews, "I'd better be going. You are nice to let me stay so long." She looked wistfully at Emma, who realized that she had been standing glowering silently at both of them.

"Oh don't," Emma said impulsively. The poor thing was probably lonely, or out of a job; Emma recalled that she had always seen her in the same black outfit. Just because she was upset about Jeff was no reason to be disagreeable to people. An idea came. She'd get rid of Hank and take Miss Mathews out with her. Miss Mathews wouldn't notice the unbolted door. Fortunately, she had sold a pitcher that morning.

"Hank," she asked in her sweetest voice, "if I do up a pitcher, will you take it out to the Blains? I know it's way out in Watertown but you can take my car. They want it for a present and I said I couldn't deliver it tonight but they'd like it very much. You wouldn't mind, would you?"

Hank was used to Emma's sudden reversals of form; so he said that he did mind but that he'd do it, if she'd let him keep the car, because he was taking a man out to dinner.

Emma said he could. But why didn't he buy himself a car, now that he was so rich, and whom was he taking to dinner?

Why should he, Hank wanted to know, when he could use hers and it was none of her business. He took the bundle and left.

Emma and Miss Mathews had another drink and decided to call each other by their first names. Miss Mathews' real name was Anna, she said, but she called herself Stephana because it sounded more foreign. Emma thought well of the improvement; her own family, she felt, had been a trifle too conservative in the matter of her name but they were dead now, poor things, and you couldn't do much with Emma except change it to Emmie, which was worse.

At five o'clock Emma decided that it was time to go home. It was still raining, the chance of more customers was remote and she didn't know when Jeff would decide to come for the money. She rather thought he'd be keeping an eye on the place to see when she left, in order that the door wouldn't be left open too long. For, of course, he could fasten the corner door and leave by the other. Emma went over and fiddled with the bolt and saw no reason why Stephana should notice that she hadn't shot it. She asked Stephana to eat with her but Stephana sadly declined, saying that she had to see a woman about some work.

As they were saying goodnight in front of the door, Donovan drove up. He jumped out of the car and took Emma by the arm.

"Get in," he said, leading her to the car, "I want to talk to you."

Chapter
9

SERGEANT TIM CONNERTON'S intelligence was of the bulldog variety. He was slow in mind and movement, he was unimaginative but he was thorough; he could search a place systematically and not leave the slightest trace of his passing. In the Norwitch case he had done the necessary checking of alibis and times with the utmost accuracy. Donovan appreciated his care in details and had laughed at his fixed idea that Emma had anything more to do with the murder than she had said. Tim couldn't have told, himself, why he was suspicious of her. His mistrust probably came from the doubt put in his mind by the story told by the two boys, Barton and Foster, whom he had interviewed first. Once there, the doubt remained; and neither Emma's relation to Hank of whom, indeed, Tim was none too sure, nor her friendliness with Donovan could dislodge it. To humor Tim, Donovan had let him shadow Emma, until her half-told fright had made Donovan see the misunderstood surveillance as a joke on Tim and an unnecessary annoyance to Emma. Tim still brooded, however, on the idea that he would like to search Emma's apartment. He could have done it easily enough by getting a warrant but Donovan had laughed at him so much for his failure as a shadow that he was half ashamed to ask for one; and as time went on, and no further evidence against Emma appeared, he did not think his request would be justified. For several days he puzzled over how to get into the apartment. He could not walk in during the day even though there was no key for Emma's lock because M. LeBotien, who had a fine view of the front door from his grocery, would have been sure to ask him his business. He could not get in at night, for then the entrance to the little house was locked; and, had he cared to trust his bulk on the fire escape, he would have been observed again because Emma had developed, since the publicity attendant on the murder, a most unhandy habit of staying at home in the evenings. After the inquest, the finding of the car and the concentration of suspicion on Jeff and Petty, he would have given the whole idea of the search up but by then he had the lock and it seemed a pity not to use it. Tim hadn't realized, until the locksmith asked him how many keys he wanted made, what a bit of luck Emma had unconsciously put in his way. He had a duplicate key made for himself and, to avoid her finding that out, called for the keys and the lock and brought them to her. In the meantime he had realized that the keys really didn't help him any because he still had no key to the front door and couldn't enter without explaining himself to M. LeBotien.

Emma had thanked him so nicely for his kindness that he had felt very guilty standing there, deceiving her, with the duplicate key in his pocket. She was about the size Martha Grady had been when he married her and much more soft spoken. He sighed, thinking of Mrs. Connerton's sharp tongue. Emma was a nice little thing and quite guilelessly, to make up for his unwarranted suspicions, he offered to fix the lock to the door for her.

It was not until he had explained his errand to M. LeBotien and seen that worthy retire, with a grunt, behind his newly arrived copy of *L'Intransigeant*, that Tim realized that his opportunity for a search of the apartment had come. The chance was too good to miss. Upstairs, he rattled the lock and the screwdriver that he had borrowed from the shop and started to unlace his shoes. He stopped almost at once, though, because he heard M. LeBotien padding up the steps. The old frog, thought Tim in disgust, would probably stay and watch to see that he didn't put a scratch on the lovely paint.

M. LeBotien, however, who certainly did not think of himself as an old frog and who did consider a policeman a public servant, wanted to know if the very kind lieutenant would keep an eye on the shop for him. He would not, he said, dream of inconveniencing the lieutenant and ordinarily he simply locked the door when he went out; but this day a Mrs. Silene was coming in for her groceries and there were the vegetables for the soup—the lieutenant appreciated that a good soup had to cook a long time. If she had to wait for her groceries until he returned, there would be no good soup for the little Silenes. The bundle was all wrapped, the lieutenant could lock the door after passing it over and need not be further troubled.

Ordinarily, the sergeant would have expressed himself forcefully in the vernacular at the suggestion that he tend any such-of-a-suching store. This time he blessed the luck of the Irish and agreed to take care of the matter of Mrs. Silene's groceries. It took M. LeBotien so long to put on his many coats and mufflers that Tim almost got the lock in place before he finally had the house to himself. The front door had hardly clicked shut before he was in the kitchen, his nose raised in disdain at Emma's casual housekeeping, his big hands moving quickly and surely

among china and glassware and pans. The icebox was a mess; Tim re-
sisted an almost uncontrollable impulse to set it to rights, to empty the
sour cream and the moldy cheese into the garbage can. Mrs. Connerton
might be the devil's own for tongue-lashing but she was an angel for
neatness. It was lucky young Fairbanks would have plenty of money and
would not be caring about the waste of good food. With relief, the sergeant moved on to the living room.

If it hadn't been tucked down in the back of the sofa, under the
cushions, he probably wouldn't have taken it because he hadn't then
talked to Donovan and did not realize its significance. He did think,
though, that a blackjack had no place under a lady's sofa cushions.
What'd she do, hit the boy friends with it? Or maybe it had been in
some lad's pocket. Maybe Hank would like to know about this. Perhaps
Miss Wasteful wouldn't get the Norwitch money if she also had boy
friends who carried blackjacks.

The sergeant laid the implement out on the table for further consideration, found a box of candy and forgetfully munched a piece. Then
he slammed down the cover and looked hastily around to see if anyone
had caught him in such an unethical practice. He was still quite alone.
He thought of Mrs. Silene and went into the bedroom where he could
more easily hear any noise below.

Emma's bureau drawers drew another sigh from Tim; and, when
he saw the clothes closet, he decided that Hank was a fine young man
who was making a serious mistake. There were clothes on the floor and
stockings on the hooks. Emma could have told him that the clothes
were dirty, that if she didn't put them on the floor she never remembered to have them cleaned and that she hung up her stockings because the rough boards snagged them; but she was to have trouble
enough explaining the dark stain that the sergeant found on a pale
green slipper unearthed from the heap on the floor. Tim had seen
bloodstains before; he pawed around for the mate to the slipper, found
it and compared the two. The second slipper was clean, but he put
them both on the table beside the blackjack and regarded them fondly.
Donovan had laughed at him, had he? Well, he'd laugh out of the other
side of his mouth now. And Miss Can't Remember, let her think up how
that blood got there, if she dared. Gathering up his booty, he went
downstairs and wrapped a neat bundle with M. LeBotien's best paper.
He waited awhile, fuming with impatience, for Mrs. Silene; then he
went back upstairs and finished screwing on the lock, more to be doing
something than out of any kindliness, now, toward Emma. He called
Donovan, told him that he had made a find and to stay where he was
and was about to deprive the little Silenes of their good soup when Mrs.

Silene came in. She was quite flustered at being waited on by an officer and it took Tim several minutes to explain to her that everything was all right and that M. LeBotien was neither dead nor arrested. Tim glanced at the clock; the hands pointed to nearly four. Grabbing a banana as no more than his rightful due, he ushered Mrs. Silene out, threw the catch on the door and went, half-running, toward the subway.

* * * *

Lieutenant Jerry Donovan sat and looked at the trophies that the sergeant laid before him. He was not, as Tim had suspected, laughing now; and, to Tim's amazement, he seemed to consider the blackjack more important than the slippers. He repeated to Tim what Hank had told him over the phone. He had, he went on, telephoned Petty who admitted that he had seen a blackjack in the washroom but denied that he had taken it.

"Now," said Donovan, "if we can prove it's the same one, and that ought to be easy," he pointed to one side of the billy, where a deep but not fresh-colored gash indicated that at some time contact had been made with a sharp object, "Miss Emma Marsh's story goes all to pieces. Petty and Emma herself say the thing was on the shelf when they left the shop; we know it wasn't there when we took the other things to the station in the morning. Now it shows up in Emma's davenport. According to her story, she walked in the shop, bolted the door and walked out. The washroom is not on that route. Catch on? If she got the blood on her shoe just from stepping over Norwitch to go to the shelf and get the billy because she was scared someone was after her, too, why didn't she tell us about it? Get me that Joe Foster on the phone."

Joe Foster, when reached, thought that Emma had worn "kind of a light dress" on the occasion of their evening at the Gilded Slipper but Bill Barton proved more observing. He was certain that she had had on a green dress and volunteered the information that her slippers had been of the same color. Donovan thanked him, not without a certain regret, and hung up.

"Perhaps," Donovan said to Tim, "she's worn these shoes since that night?" But Tim thought not; he had kept, he admitted, a sort of an interest in her goings and comings; and, except for the night of the inquest, when she had been with Donovan himself, she had not been out in the evening.

Donovan sighed some more and chewed moodily on the end of his cigar. He wondered if Emma had been fooling him all along. If she had, she had been deceiving Hank too. They were both, probably, just a couple of saps who had let her get away with something because they liked her and thought that that meant she was innocent of any connection with the murder. Donovan couldn't yet bring himself to think that Emma had actually committed the crime but he was dead certain that she knew who had. Tim, he thought, would be all for charging her with the murder at once but then she'd get a lawyer and refuse to talk; Hank, too, would probably go off the deep end, refuse to believe the evidence against her and be very angry with him. An idea began to take shape in Donovan's mind. He'd get her to talk and he would fix it so that Hank knew nothing about it.

"Listen," he said, "I'm going to try something and I don't want you butting in. You go home, or stay here, or go watch Mrs. Graham make whoopee with the boy friend; but don't say a word to a living soul about what you have found out. I gotta go somewhere, and don't try to find me because I don't want to be found. Get me?"

Connerton didn't; he had looked forward to more sensational results from his work; he had even hoped that he might have the pleasure of arresting Emma himself. He felt that it was distinctly unfair of Donovan not to let him in on the plans but he only uttered a hopeful, "I'll be around if you want me," and departed.

Donovan cleared his desk, made a few telephone calls and went out.

As he and Emma rode away from the shop on Charles Street, Donovan was very silent. Emma tried several conversational openings; she asked what he wanted to talk to her about, how he was coming along with Petty and if he knew what Hank was doing that evening. When she had got down to the subject of the weather without receiving any response, Emma asked suddenly, "Are you kidnaping me?" This bow, drawn at a venture, scored a bull's-eye. Donovan grunted, "Something like it. Shut up."

A cold sweat broke out on the palms of Emma's hands; a sick feeling, starting somewhere in the pit of her stomach, spread slowly over her. She touched Donovan's arm.

"Tell me," she said. "Have you found Hank somewhere? Is he hurt?"

"No," said Donovan shortly, "he's O.K., far as I know."

Emma relaxed with relief in the corner of the seat; then, suddenly, her nerves were tense again. They must have found Jeff or perhaps the orderly at the hospital had squealed. She remembered the hat. Why, oh, why hadn't she burned it up, or put it in the garbage can or simply thrown it into the street in the midst of heavy traffic, instead of leaving it under the seat of the roadster? At any rate, Hank had the car; so Donovan didn't have the hat, for he had admitted that he didn't know where Hank was. Or had he? She guessed he just hadn't said. Maybe it was all part of a scheme—Hank's borrowing the car and this gloomy abduction—and at the station they would confront her with Jeff and the hat. And what would she say? Why hadn't she at least removed the initials from the hat; then she could swear that it was Jeff's? But if there weren't any initials in the hat, she wouldn't have to swear anything because then no one would have paid any attention to it. Emma gave the whole thing up, deciding to tell the truth, since she was definitely not cut out for a life of crime.

At the police station, Donovan led her past the sergeant on duty and past the benches full of drunks, bums and shoddy women awaiting official attention. Emma remembered the time she had walked through Franklin Square Park, a notorious hangout for loafers, between two policemen. She had been going to identify her stolen car which had been found, stripped, in a nearby alley but the tramps had assumed that she had been picked up by the cops and had leered at her all the way across the park. She caught the same look in the eyes of those waiting in the station and a feeling of discouragement welled up within her. Had she been poorly dressed, she knew that the attitude of the other unfortunates would have been one of sympathy but her neat tweed suit, which did not bag in the seat, the short silk mackintosh, the Tyrolean brush at the back of her felt hat and her well-cared-for shoes brought forth a bitter expression of class hatred instead of an attitude of commiseration toward a fellow sufferer. And the worst they can get, thought Emma, is thirty days.

At the end of a long, bleak corridor Donovan and Emma were met by a stony-faced, gray-haired woman. Donovan stood silently by while the police matron searched Emma's clothes and pocketbook. Emma spluttered indignantly.

"You can't," she said, not very originally, "do this to me."

"Oh, can't I?" said Donovan. "Take a look at these."

From his pockets he produced the blackjack and the bloodstained slipper.

"What," said Emma, "are you doing with my slipper and Jeff's billy?"

"That's fine," said Donovan. "I'm glad you recognize them. These," he pointed to the dark smear on the sole and the spots on the light fabric, "are bloodstains; and this," he waved the blackjack at her, "was found in your sofa."

"Lock her up," he said to the matron.

Turning on his heel, he walked away. In the morning, he thought, maybe she'd talk. In the meantime, the shoe would go to the laboratory for a test.

Chapter

10

SUDDENLY HANK WAS wide awake and, for an instant, feeling fine. Then a blinding throbbing shut down on his head and he became conscious that his mouth had a bitter, furry taste. With a groan he rang for Oscar. He lay with his eyes closed, breathing very gently in order not to jar his head. When the sounds of slightly asthmatic breathing and the clink of china announced the presence of a second person, he said very softly, "What day is it and where am I?"

"Today is Wednesday and you're in bed, thanks to me," said Oscar primly.

"Could I," said Hank doubtfully, "have acquired this head in one night?"

"No doubt you could, sir," said Oscar, "by diligent application."

"Oscar," said Hank, opening one watery eye, "I don't like your attitude."

"Yes sir," said Oscar, pouring a cup of coffee.

"No sir," said Hank, "I don't like it at all. I resent your implications; at least I would if I had my strength."

Hank propped himself up on one elbow to drink the coffee but shut his eyes with a shudder as the lead weight that seemed to have taken the place of his brain hit his forehead with a bang. "All right," he said resignedly, "I'll believe anything. Tell me the worst."

"About four o'clock," said Oscar sternly, "I was awakened by a loud pounding on the front door. Descending, I found you, supported with difficulty," Oscar put in with evident relish, "by a woman, a man and a taxi driver."

"Did the lady," asked Hank, the mist beginning to rise from his brain, "have on a mink cape?"

"The woman," Oscar seemed certain of the word, "had on some kind of a fur wrap. I really did not notice; I was too concerned with getting you inside before the whole street was aroused. The man was quite noisy; he fancied that I was the one needed for a quartet. The late Mr. Norwitch would have been most displeased."

92

"Oscar," said Hank sharply, "speak no ill of the dead. Uncle had no ear for music. Proceed."

"The taxi driver was a most helpful person," Oscar went on, "between us, we got you to bed. I trust the occurrence will not be repeated, as I find that I am becoming too old for er—ar—rassling, I believe you call it."

"It's nice of you, Oscar, to make me feel at home," said Hank dreamily. "With you here, I shan't miss Uncle a bit. Seriously, though, I'm sorry about getting you up and being such a general ass. Don't ever," he went on admonishingly, "put your trust in princes or princesses or feel that you must drown your sorrows when your friends desert you. Alcohol is a poor adhesive for a broken heart. As a matter of fact, I wouldn't have thought my heart was broken if I hadn't had so many drinks while I was waiting for that yap."

"Yes sir," said Oscar, who hadn't the faintest idea what Hank was talking about. "Shall I draw your bath?"

"Do," said Hank, "and fill the tub. I can drink every bit of it."

Hank poured himself more coffee, nibbled weakly at a strip of bacon and ruminated on the sins of the night. His suggestion that Petty dine with him had been in the nature of a friendly gesture. Petty had been a little stuffy about accepting but Hank hadn't expected to be left waiting in the bar of Petty's hotel for more than an hour, to discover finally, upon inquiry, that Petty had gone out without a word to him. It had taken him a few more drinks to reconcile himself to the notion that his cousinly invitation had not been appreciated or, to put it more bluntly, that he had been slapped in the face. He had tried to call Emma but had received no answer. He had put in a call for Donovan and had had a quick one while the desk sergeant was unable to locate him. About then he had begun to feel sad and lonely. He had driven past Emma's apartment but there had been no light in the window and he had gone on, increasing his melancholy by imagining Emma and Stephana Mathews together, laughing at him, as they let down their hair or washed out stockings or did whatever women did do when they were together. Seeing a corner pub, he had yielded to the urge for companionship and gone in but had found neither the drinks nor the company to his liking. Because it was handy, he had stopped at the Royal Palms, still feeling the need to tell his woes to someone and there he had found Mrs. Graham and the boy friend. Looking back on it, he decided that they had probably been considerably surprised at his sociability but, all things considered, they had enjoyed a very jolly evening. The boy friend was undoubtedly a heel of darkest hue but he had possessed a fine tenor voice and knew all the songs Hank liked. The band, Hank recalled a little wryly, had been most helpful in their rendering of "Old Uncle Jack." Events became confused after that. He thought he had left the party at some point, he couldn't recollect just when, but he must have rejoined it because, by Oscar's account, Mrs. Graham and the boy friend had brought him home. He wished he could remember the subject of the long argument he had had with Mrs. Graham. At the time he had felt it very important to the case and had flattered himself by thinking that, while she was drunk and didn't realize what she was saying, he was perfectly sober. Where, where had he put Emma's car? He would have to get to the shop and make apologies and institute a search. Without doubt the police had the car by now and Donovan would regard him as not fit to be left alone. Cautiously he got out of bed. The bath felt good and the subsequent shave improved his appearance. By the time he was walking toward the shop, he was whistling softly to himself and wishing he had eaten more breakfast. The shop was not open and there was no sign of Emma; but, as it was only about nine-thirty, Hank was not greatly surprised. He bought a paper and stood reading it, leaning comfortably against the doorway, in the pale sunlight. According to the press, the Norwitch case was at a standstill. "Press hunt for missing man," on page two, indicated that the reporters were having a hard time keeping up their enthusiasm. When half an hour had passed, Hank went across the street and called Donovan. He gave his name, but he was told that the lieutenant was busy. He left word for Donovan to call him and was back in the doorway before he realized that he couldn't get into the shop to answer the phone if it rang. Did Emma expect him to take her to work just because he had borrowed her car? Let her walk; walking would be good for her. But he knew that Emma would no sooner walk to work than he would; she would take a cab and she certainly should be there by now. Hank began to get a little worried. Too many people had been disappearing on him of late. He'd have to call and see what had happened to Petty. A passing cab made him decide to attend to Emma first.

Minnie gave vent to his soundless greeting as Hank ran up the steps and M. LeBotien called an amiable goodmorning, but Hank continued up the stairs, barely noticing the salutations.

The sergeant had not troubled to lock Emma's door. Hank pushed it open and went into the empty living room.

"Hey," he called, more hopefully than he felt, "it's time to get up."

There was no answer to his hail and Hank rushed into the bedroom. The bed was neatly made. Emma rarely did that before going to work. Growing more frightened by the minute, Hank looked in the bathroom, the closets and even in the tiny kitchenette. There was no trace of Emma. M. LeBotien, coming up to see what was the matter, was filled with dismay. No, he had not seen Emma that morning nor, he recalled, had he heard her come in on the previous night. He did not always hear her come in but he usually was made conscious of her presence by some sound during the evening. Last night there had been no noise of the radio or conversation. He was truly disturbed and was hopeful that Hank did not think any ill had befallen her.

Hank hastily picked up the telephone and again tried to get Donovan but that officer was just as firmly busy as before. With an unaccustomed oath, Hank dashed from the house, sprinted to the corner and tried to get a cab. It seemed to him that he waited hours; when he got one, the driver took one look at his face and moved off rapidly in the direction indicated. On the way to the station, Hank cursed himself for all kinds of a fool. He had had the feeling all along that something was going to happen; so, instead of taking care of Emma, he had got himself blind drunk; and now she was gone. He would never forgive himself if she had been hurt and if she were dead . . . his mind refused to entertain the possibility. He had to find her, that was all, and Donovan had to help him.

He flung a bill at the astonished driver and did not wait for his change. He tore up to Donovan's office and burst in the door, shouting, "My God, she's gone. Emma. Her bed hasn't been slept in. You must help me find her."

Donovan remained seated. On the desk, in front of him, was a battered, brown felt hat. He picked it up and tried to smooth out the creases. The look on Hank's face troubled him.

"Don't worry," he said gruffly, "Emma's all right. She's here."

The relief was almost too much for Hank. He wanted to cry, but he managed to say quite naturally, "Thank goodness. But what," he added, "is she doing here?"

"Sit down," said Donovan. "It's a long story." He sat so long, creasing and uncreasing the hat, that Hank twitched with impatience.

"Put that thing down," said Hank, "and get on with the tale. I want to see Emma. She's not hurt, is she? You're not trying to let me down easy?"

"No," said Donovan. "She's not hurt. Wait a minute, can't you? Since you've mentioned it, we might as well begin with this hat." He shoved it across the desk. "Know whose it is?"

Hank picked up the hat and looked at it curiously. Inside he saw the initials "R.M.N."

"I suppose," he said, "it's Uncle's but where did you get it? From the dirt, you must have fished it out of a dump."

"That hat," said Donovan, a tired note in his voice, "was found under the seat of the car belonging to Miss Emma Marsh, which you so carelessly left all night over by the Royal Palms. At least I guess it was you. She said you had her car."

"I did and I'd wondered what I'd done with it, but I didn't put that hat in it."

"No, the hat had been there long enough to have dirt on top of it. Don't you realize that a hat was found beside your uncle's body? It was assumed that it was Mr. Norwitch's hat, which only goes to show that you should never take anything for granted. This hat," Donovan pointed to the one in front of him, "is size seven and one eighth; the hat found at the shop is seven and three eighths, a rather large size. This morning Mrs. Graham obliged the sergeant with one of her husband's old hats. It is size seven and three eighths. Now you tell me how Jeff Graham's hat came to be picked up for Norwitch's, and why Emma Marsh had your uncle's hat under her car seat."

"What does Emma say; have you asked her about it?"

"Miss Marsh," Donovan's voice had the same flat tone, "says the hat was under the seat because she put it there. She refuses to say where she found the hat or to admit that the other one belongs to Jeff. She says she won't say a thing until I let her out and I say that I won't let her out until she does a powerful lot of explaining."

Hank could see that Emma was probably being very tiresome and felt sorry for Donovan.

"I know," he said, "how you feel but I also know Emma, and she'll do as she says. After all, you can't keep her here indefinitely just because she had Uncle's hat; though I'd give a good deal, myself, to find out where she got it."

Donovan leaned back in his chair and fiddled with the button on the front of his tunic.

"Wait a minute, I'm telling this all backwards." He explained about the sergeant's desire to search Emma's apartment and the chance that replacing the lock had given him. Opening a drawer of the desk, he produced the blackjack and laid it beside the hat.

"This," he went on, "is the missing billy. Tim found it under Miss Marsh's sofa cushions. Hold on," he said as Hank was about to interrupt him. He reached into the drawer again and produced a green slipper. "He found this in her closet; it's the slipper she wore on the night of the murder and on the mate, which is in the laboratory, are bloodstains."

Hank looked at the three objects on the desk before him. He hated them; he hated Donovan. He hated the picture that came all too clearly to his mind. He could see Emma stepping over his uncle's body and scrubbing at the telltale smears on the knife. He could see her start at some sound, glance furtively around and seize the blackjack. He could see her waiting for Petty to abandon his vigil outside the door. He raised his eyes dully to Donovan's. The next morning she had realized that her fingerprints would be on the weapon and had hidden it, probably first at the shop, and then later in the sofa, where she had forgotten it. And she had lied; she had lied to Donovan and to him.

"I guess," he said tonelessly, "you've got her. I'll pay for the lawyer." Donovan looked at Hank quickly. He had expected more display of emotion and bitter denial. He moved restlessly on his chair. It was much easier for him to have Hank take it this way but the hard, disillusioned voice bothered him. He had seen the relentlessness of the evidence against Emma but he had not imagined that Hank would accept it so quickly. Hank, he had thought, would make more of the hats and would at least try to turn the facts into an attempt on Emma's part to protect Jeff. He pushed at the hat and wished bitterly that he had studied for the priesthood, where he could cure the troubles of others with a word.

Hank looked at the hat and a faint flicker of reason shot through the pain in his mind. What, in the picture that tortured him, was Emma doing with the hat? He had omitted Jeff from the scene entirely and Jeff had to be there somewhere, because he had left his hat—perhaps he was the motive. After all, what reason did Emma have for killing his uncle? The little devil in the back of Hank's brain whispered that she would rather marry a man who was independently wealthy than a poor loafer, dependent on another's bounty. Other women had killed their husbands for insurance in order to marry their lovers. But not Emma. Even in the depths of his hopelessness, he could not imagine Emma killing for money; and, he recalled, she had never said that she'd marry him, anyway. But she had always been after him, until lately, to earn his own living. He turned his back on the devil and thought of Jeff. He could see Emma, interrupting a quarrel between Mr. Norwitch and Jeff, leap to Jeff's defense if she thought he were threatened with bodily violence. Norwitch, or Jeff, had had the paper cutter and, in grappling with them, Emma had, perhaps unwittingly, struck the fatal blow. Then Petty had come and they had waited together for his departure. But, if that were true, why hadn't she told him the whole story? He would have believed her and a defense under those circumstances would have been easy. Perhaps Jeff's disappearance and the loss of corroboration of her story had prevented her from telling the police but, surely, she could have trusted him. Or again, Hank thought, Jeff had wielded the knife, had fled in a panic and left Emma to wash the dagger and dispose of the blackjack with which, perhaps, Norwitch had armed himself. In his panic Jeff had taken the wrong hat and Emma had secreted the other; no, both hats had been left behind and Emma had supposed that she was hiding Jeff's hat until Donovan faced her with the incriminating initials. That, Hank's tired brain decided, was the logical explanation, as Donovan would inevitably see for himself. It did not alter the fact that Emma had lied about what she had seen in the shop and her knowledge of Jeff's guilt. Boiled down to the dregs, it simply meant that Emma cared more for Jeff than she did for him. Instead of asking for his help and giving him her confidence, she had lied and betrayed his trust at every turn. Very well, since she didn't want his help, she wouldn't get it. Of course, he'd see that she had a lawyer but he hoped to God that he never had to look at her again. The lying little cheat! No wonder she had appeared upset when she got back to the Gilded Slipper; she had never been able to give a satisfactory reason for the length of time she had been gone; no doubt she had bribed the cab driver to clear out of town. And her own carelessness had given her away. If she had cleaned her shoes or disposed of the blackjack, a dimwit like the sergeant wouldn't have caught up with her. Served her right. He was through with her; he was finished with the case; his ambition to be a detective had vanished. He guessed he'd go around the world, as soon as Donovan would let him go. Emma had accomplished one thing; he no longer needed to work for his living in order to be independent. He'd go to Australia and raise sheep or kangaroos or yellow dogs.

Donovan could bear the silence no longer. He cleared his throat.

"And another funny thing," he said. "Last night, while I was gone, a call came in, saying that if we'd go to the General Hospital we'd find news of Jeff Graham. A woman made the call and we traced it to a drugstore on Boylston Street. But that store has half-a-dozen booths and around seven o'clock there are dozens of women telephoning that they are going to stay in town and go to the movies and nobody pays any attention to them. Tim went over to the hospital and our bird had been there all right but he skipped out yesterday morning. An orderly by the name of Pissano helped. We've got Pissano down here now and I'm going to get after him pretty soon. He's in bad at the hospital because he helped Jeff get away and it seems that he was the one who let him in and put him down on the record as Oakes. When Tim started yelling round for a feller with a bullet wound, the hospital produced Oakes' record and this guy Pissano. He admitted that he had known Oakes was Graham but said Jeff had given him a lot of money to keep it quiet."

Donovan felt that he must say something more to get the look of

blank apathy off Hank's face. He went on, blaming himself for not checking up on the hospital's report of the bullet wound more thoroughly
and promising to find Jeff, if he had to string Pissano up by the toes to
do it, but his words had no effect.

Hank stood up and held out his hand. "Don't blame yourself," he
said. "You're so close behind Jeff now it will probably be only a question of hours before you get him and then your case is practically sewed
up. Good-by."

Donovan got to his feet. "Good-by," he said. "What do you mean,
'Good-by'?"

"Why, just this," Hank explained slowly, "that I'm through, finished,
washed-up, no longer necessary and let out."

"So," said Donovan hotly, still trying to break through Hank's icy
calm, "you're sore because you think I held out information on you
and you're quitting me now, when there's a lot of routine stuff to do."

"Don't be an ass, Jerry, you know what ails me."

They shook hands and Hank walked out of the door.

He walked aimlessly for a long time. Part of the way he was accom-
panied by a pleasant, shaggy dog who was entertaining himself with the
notion that he was following his master on an important errand. Two
shabby urchins pleaded with him, for a block, for a nickel for their sick
mother. He passed down a street darkened by the shadow of the el-
evated tracks, through several blocks of trucks and clanging drays. Presently he found himself seated on the end of a wharf beside a toothless
old gaffer who was telling him about the wreck of the Mohawk. Hank
look at the thick, opaque water lurching against the piles below his
feet. The Mohawk, huh. He had an idea that the Norwitches had had
an interest in that boat. Come to think of it, he probably owned part of
several boats himself. He glanced out over the harbor with a flicker of
interest. For the first time in his life he became conscious of a curiosity
about his money and how it was made. Probably at the expense of such
fellows as the old man beside him, whose leg had been crushed in the
wreck and who had been reduced from an able-bodied seaman to a
garrulous old tramp, picking up a few pennies with his tales of disaster.
Well, all trades were hazardous. He thought of Terry Dolan, a cousin of
Donovan's, shot down by a drunken father whom Terry was trying to
prevent from beating a kid. He thought of himself, wounded in the line
of duty. His peal of laughter nearly sent the old man into the harbor.
He laughed and laughed, happy in his youth, the warm spring sun and
the lifting of the heavy load from his chest. "Wounded in the line of
duty," that was good; but he wasn't dead and he wasn't maimed; his
wound would heal in time and perhaps he'd learned what Emma had

tried to teach him, to stand on his own feet. At least she had stood alone, on hers. The fact that her independence had landed her in jail didn't alter the principle. What did he want to do most in the world? Why investigate crime, of course. And he'd come within an inch of throwing up a life's training and ambition just because another human being chose to go her own, instead of his, way. Very well, he'd go back to the murder, he'd go back to Donovan but not just yet. He still didn't want to see or hear of Emma until his resolution had hardened firmly in its mold. He jumped up, handed the astonished mariner a dollar, which he felt was small payment for his freedom, and walked swiftly down the wharf, whistling through his teeth.

In the meantime, Donovan was trying to vent on Pissano his bitterness against Emma and his disappointment in Hank. He got no satisfaction, however, because Pissano was a poor adversary for his venom. The ex-orderly wilted at every blast, yielded to every attack and readily told all he knew. Donovan grudgingly admitted to himself that Pissano's story of Emma's visit to the hospital and her removal of the hat somewhat lightened the cloud of suspicion around her head but he wasn't going to tell her so, not until he found out how she had learned of Jeff's whereabouts. Pissano said that Jeff had paid him two hundred and eighty-three dollars but insisted that he had no idea where Jeff had gone upon leaving the hospital. Donovan took his signed statement, warned him not to leave town and turned him loose, wishing that he could give him a bust in the nose just to clear his feelings. He avoided questioning Emma again, for he felt that her stubborn refusal to say anything really would provoke him to an outburst of violence; and he had a certain dislike, always admirable in a policeman, for striking women. He decided that he hadn't eaten for much too long; so he went to Thompson's and snapped at the waitress, just because she was of the female persuasion. There seemed to be entirely too many women on the streets and Donovan glared at them all. The sky had suddenly become overcast and rain threatened. He wondered why the weather was always cartooned as a man.

Donovan got back to his desk, resigned, but not reconciled, to a talk with Emma but there he found Tim, quivering with excitement. He had warned Donovan, he said, but Donovan had paid no attention to him and now see what had happened. Petty had done a runout. And what would the District Attorney say? Donovan felt inclined to join Tim in his lamentations. Since the publication of the Norwitch will and the revelation of the gift of the valuable collection to the museum, Norwitch had become a public benefactor whose taking off was an inestimable loss to the city. The citizens did not think that, if he hadn't been killed, the benefits of his collection would still be denied to the public; instead, they howled for the head of his murderer in letters to the newspapers which deplored the inefficiency of the police department and were signed Vox Pop or Pro Bono Publico. As a result, a certain amount of warmth was beginning to radiate from the District Attorney's office and Donovan was becoming uncomfortably aware of it. He admitted that he had let Jeff slip through his fingers. But how was he to know that a man named Oakes, who was bald and unconscious, was actually Jeff Graham, who had the remains of a head of hair and who had, it turned out, never been unconscious at all? Damn it, he wanted to find out how Emma had found him. And now, if Petty got away, his hair would be full of people. He asked for particulars.

Petty had left his hotel about quarter to seven; one of the clerks had seen him go; about seven-thirty a man had inquired for him but a ring to his room had shown that he had not returned. This had occasioned no alarm but when, in the morning, he had not responded to his customary eight o'clock call and the chambermaid had said that his bed had not been occupied, the manager had become alarmed and had notified the police. He hoped, the manager had said, that he was not being officious but he knew that Mr. Petty was concerned in the Norwitch case; and, with one man already missing, he had thought that the second disappearance should be noted.

Donovan decided that he was not going to like the hotel manager, who was probably "Pro Bono Publico" himself, or at least "Taxpayer," and sat down to think what had become of Petty. He finally set out with Connerton to interview the manager and the hotel staff, glad of an excuse to postpone his talk with Emma.

* * * *

Hank, feeling remarkably free and lightheaded, had gone home to lunch and had been lavishly regaled by Oscar with grilled sweetbreads and corn muffins. Fed and comforted, he wandered out again, spurning Oscar's suggestion that it was going to rain and that he better take a topcoat. The topcoat offered him had been a brown tweed of his uncle's; that fact might have accounted for his rejection of it. But he didn't like to wear overcoats anyhow and he suspected that Oscar's ability as a weather forecaster had no sounder basis than a twinge of rheumatism.

More from habit than from any actual desire to go there, he went down to the shop. Its deserted air oppressed him but he peeked in at the windows to see that everything was all right. He noticed the accumulation of mail inside the door and thought that he ought to get the key from Emma and look after things. Then he remembered that he didn't want to see Emma just yet and decided to let Donovan get the key. As he turned away from the door, he came face to face with a small boy leading a dachshund puppy on a leash. "I beg your pardon," said the small boy, tugging the puppy out of Hank's path.

"Not at all," said Hank, lifting his hat. "That looks like a good dog."

"It is," said the boy seriously. "I really believe his points are better than Miriam's, although Miriam . . ." His face clouded and Hank asked quickly, "Who was Miriam?"

"My other dog," said the boy, regaining his composure. "The one that was killed. I came to thank Miss Marsh for this one but I've been back twice and there's no one here."

"Miss Marsh is away," said Hank, wondering why Emma was buying dachshunds for young gentlemen who could obviously pay for their own dogs. "Perhaps," he added, "I can convey your message to her? My name is Henry Fairbanks."

"How do you do. I'm Roger Corey, III." Roger Corey shifted the leash and extended a hand that Hank noticed was normally dirty. They shook hands gravely.

"Tell her," said Roger Corey, III, "that Taxi is very well. We do not think he has worms, although Mike says he can't tell with a broken leg. And thank her very much. Although Mike says it's the least she could do, I do not feel that it was her fault."

Hank sat down on the doorstep, lit a cigarette and scratched Taxi's left ear.

"If you can spare me a few moments," he said, "tell me who Mike is, why you don't think it was Miss Marsh's fault that he broke his leg and why you call this"—Hank was about to say sausage in overshoes but decided that the comparison might be offensive—"dog," he compromised, "Taxi."

"Why, you see," Roger unbent so far as to sit on the step beside Hank, "if it hadn't been for the taxi, I wouldn't have had him. Mike is our chauffeur and he knew the taxi driver; and Miss Marsh was in it and she felt very badly about Miriam."

Hank bent to remove a match that Taxi was enthusiastically devouring. "I take it," he said, "that there was an accident."

"Oh yes," said Roger, "Miriam was quite dead and Mike had a fracture of the femur."

Hank couldn't help murmuring, "Indeed."

"There was a lot of blood; I saw it the next day and then I wished I hadn't because it was Miriam's. We had a nice funeral behind the garage, though Father says there's an ordinance against it."

At the word blood the hair began to prickle on the back of Hank's neck. He looked at Roger, who was watching Taxi's struggles to detach a wad of gum from the pavement.

"Do you," asked Hank, "know exactly when this happened?"

"Oh, definitely," said Roger. "It was the same night Mr. Norwitch was stabbed. He's your uncle, isn't he? I thought I remembered your name but I wasn't sure I should mention it. Grandfather says Mr. Norwitch was a handful when he was three sheets to the wind. That means drunk," he explained. "Perhaps you know, but I had to ask Mike. It's really more interesting than Flash Gordon. Who do you think killed him?"

Ignoring the revelations of his uncle's unsuspected past, Hank kept his nose on the scent. "Listen," he said, "I'm a sort of a detective. Oh, not very good," he added, as Roger's eyes opened wide with amazement, "but the police are letting me help on this case because Mr. Norwitch was my uncle, you see. Now I have an idea that a person connected with this case was in the accident that killed Miriam and if she was, it may give her an alibi. I'll make a bargain with you: if you'll let me talk to Mike, I'll take you down to the police station and let you see the exhibits. That is," he added, "if your grandfather thinks it's all right for you to go out with Richard Norwitch's nephew."

"Could I," asked Roger breathlessly, "see the morgue?"

"Probably not, but you could see the murder knife."

That seemed to be adequate inducement, for Roger stood up. "I believe it will be all right. Mike's in the garage, you know; he wouldn't go to the hospital because, he said if he did, Joe would steal the gasoline. Joe's driving for us till Mike's leg gets well and Grandfather won't ride with him; but his taxi is in our garage and I have a lot of fun in it."

He stopped suddenly, indignant at Hank's hoot of laughter.

"I beg your pardon," said Hank, composing his face. "I can well imagine that a tame taxi would only be outranked by a fire engine as a plaything but it just happens that a friend of mine has spent rather a lot of time looking for Joe and his cab and I bet it never occurred to him to look for them in a Back-Bay garage. Forward, Watson, where is this hideout?"

"The garage is on Hereford Street," Roger answered, a little stiffly.

Hank stood still; Hereford Street was off the route. "Where do you live?" he asked.

"Really," Roger began, "I don't believe. . ." But the thought of the knife overcame his dignity. "In the apartment house at the corner of Commonwealth and Berkeley," he conceded. "Grandfather's house used to be there and he says he was a damn fool to let my father tear it down."

"Perfect," said Hank, referring both to the location and Grandfather's sentiments. "I take it Mike was giving Miriam her evening stroll?"

"Yes, before he put the car away."

It was beginning to rain out of respect, no doubt, to Oscar's rheumatism; so Hank caught a cab and Roger had to blush for Taxi, who promptly made a puddle on the floor.

"He's very young," he said defensively.

Hank agreed that a first taxi ride might well have an unsettling effect on the kidneys; and, having reestablished himself in Roger's favor, discoursed learnedly, the rest of the ride, on methods of police investigation.

The Corey garage was one of an old row of stables not yet converted into studios or night clubs. The ramp which led up to the clumsy double doors was still paved with worn granite cobblestones and inside, a faint, homesick odor of leather and ammonia mingled with the smell of gasoline and oil. Hank had a swift picture of Roger's grandfather being driven down the new filled streets behind a pair of glossy chestnuts but it was dispelled by the sight of the Corey automobile and the missing taxicab. Roger laid a friendly hand on a scarred fender as they went toward the stairs in the rear and Hank hoped, fervently, that he would not cause the breakup of a beautiful friendship.

"Mike," called Roger, "may I bring up a friend?"

An affirmative hail came from above and they mounted the stairs. The room in which Hank presently found himself was large and cheerful. There was a masculine absence of curtains at the windows but there was a very healthy collection of plants on the sills. The chairs were shabby but they were large and comfortable; a radio offered advice from a table near one of the beds where a man was propped up on pillows. Another man sat at the table beside him. They were playing checkers.

"Mike and Joe," said Roger, "this is Henry Fairbanks. Mr. Fairbanks, Mr. Hollohran," indicating the invalid, "and Mr. Ossip."

"Grab a chair," said Mike. "H'are yuh?"

"Happier than I've been for some hours," said Hank. "But, before you'll understand that, I'll have to explain why I'm here and ask a favor of you." He looked at the two men speculatively; he had felt, from Roger's talk of them, that they were both kind but they looked very large. Mike was somewhat incapacitated but Joe seemed to be in the pink. Hank wondered whether we were a Pole or a Russian or a Finn; his hair was lightish but his cheekbones were high and broad and his shoulders were enormous. They couldn't help knowing that the police were searching for Joe and it was possible that they would resent his discovery of

Joe's hiding place. He had visions of landing at the bottom of the stairs with a loud crash. While he was wondering how to begin, Mike solved his problem for him.

"Would you be the Henry Fairbanks in the Norwitch case?" he asked quietly.

Hank admitted that he was.

"So," said Joe, "a spy, eh?" He moved ominously on his chair. "I got nothin' to say. I never seed nothin' and she warn't in there long enough to do anything."

Hank looked at Joe in amazement. "Don't tell me," he said incredulously, "that you've been doing the disappearing act just because you thought your testimony would incriminate Miss Marsh, the girl in the taxicab?"

Joe cast a sheepish glance at Mike, who answered for him: "It was something like that. She was so nice about helping Joe out of his jam and agreeing to say nothing about it, because he'd had three accidents and was afraid he'd lose his license, that, when it come out the next day in the papers about the murder, and her finding the body and all, Joe thought the least he could do was to keep still and let the police do their own work."

"Bah, the police are fools," Joe put in, and Hank decided that he was either a Russian or a Pole.

"If I told you," Hank began, "that Miss Marsh is at present in jail because she refuses to get you in bad by telling whatever it was that happened after you took her to the shop, would you tell me the whole story and help to get her out?" Hank didn't know where the hat and the blackjack came in but he did not want to confuse Joe with any side issues.

"Sure," said Mike, "tell him." He turned to Hank. "There's really nothing to it, only Joe here is scared to death of the police. Show him your back, Joe."

Joe muttered something in what Hank fancied was the original Sanskrit, but at Roger's "Please, Joe, let me see them again," began to unbutton his shirt. The back that he turned to Hank tapered beautifully from broad shoulders to a narrow waist; the faintly brown skin was marble smooth except where it was laced, from shoulder to belt, with whitish scars, smooth and broad, as though they had stretched with the growth of the flesh beneath them.

"In Ovruch, when I was seven," he said slowly.

"A year younger than me," said Roger, casting grammar to the wind.

"Christ," said Hank. "Are you Russian?"

Joe spat on the clean floor. "Polish," he said, putting on his shirt.

"They beat him," Mike explained, "for throwing rocks at a guy on a horse; so he don't like the cops; and he broke my leg and he knew Corey was rich and he was afraid he'd lose his license and go to jail and get beat again. I told him our cops wouldn't beat him but he's kinda dumb." Mike looked at Hank. "Anyhow, a rubber hose don't leave marks like that."

"I take it," said Hank, "you'd known him before the accident?"

"Oh yeah, we used to bowl for the Checkers when I was hacking," he explained. "Won the city league onct."

"Nice work," said Hank, "but tell me what happened."

"Well," said Mike, "I have Miriam out in the center grass strip, with her leash off, so's she can run around; and all of a sudden she makes a dive out into the street and I after her, because I sees this cab coming; but it ain't no good. The cab gets her with one wheel and me with the left fender and such screechin' and yellin' you never heard. Joe goes off his nut and starts babblin' in his native tongue, and this gal gets out of the cab and begins to cry about the dog, and me lyin' there with a broken leg. It's a wonder the cops didn't come a-running. I recognizes Joe and sees I gotta look out for him; so I calms 'em down and tells 'em to put Miriam in the front of the cab and me in the back, while we talk things over. We drive over to this Gilded Slipper, Joe carrying on all the time about his accidents and his license and the police, and finally I gets me an idea, and I tells 'em that if Miss Marsh'll say nothin' and get the kid another dog, I'll tell Mr. Corey that the feller that killed Miriam got away and I broke my leg on the curbing by my own damn clumsiness; because if he knew the cab broke my leg he'd have the police hunting this hit-and-run driver. And Joe can drive for me till I heal up. They say that'll be oke, and we park a ways down the street, and I sent Joe in with Miss Marsh to get me a drink, because by this time I can use one; and Joe brings me here and I phone Mr. Corey to send me a doctor. Of course, the next day, Joe goes and tells the punk, here, about how sorry he is he killed Miriam; so we tell him the whole story but he don't say nothing at home, though he musta blabbed to you."

Hank hastily explained that he had merely intercepted Roger's thanks to Miss Marsh and had put two and two together because he knew the answer. He thanked Mike for the story and told Joe that he thought he could arrange that there would be no trouble with the police. He looked at his watch. The one thing he wanted, now, was to get to Donovan with his discoveries but he remembered that he had certain obligations to Roger. He explained his bargain to Mike, who looked at the clock.

"Go ahead and take him," he said. "He's got three quarters of an hour yet but be sure he's home at quarter of six, or Gramp will raise hell with me. Beat it," he said to Roger, "and behave yourself. I'll take care of Taxi but, if he makes a puddle on this floor, I'll break his neck."

Not at all disturbed by this threat of violence, Roger hopped excitedly on one foot while Hank telephoned for a cab.

When they arrived at the station, Donovan was not there; he was reported to be at Petty's hotel. Hank had not thought of Petty for several hours; he wondered what that gentleman had been up to, but no one seemed to know. Hank wanted very much to find out but, instead, he took Roger on a thorough tour of inspection. The murder knife was a huge success with Roger but the laboratory was an even greater one. He viewed every piece of apparatus carefully but kept his hands, Hank was gratified to note, firmly in his pockets. While Hank was explaining the calipers, Liebowitz, one of the technicians, came up to them and asked if Hank had seen Donovan. Hank had not. Liebowitz wanted to know if Hank had seen the report on the stains on the slipper. Hank winked at Roger.

"No," he said, "I haven't seen the report but I can tell you that the blood was dog blood and, furthermore, that it was from a female of the dachshund breed."

Roger snickered with excitement.

"Go on," said Liebowitz, "how'd you guess it?"

"This," said Hank, introducing Roger, "is the owner of the dog."

Entranced at his new importance, Roger had to be shown the slipper and the process of testing for bloodstains, and had to explain about Miriam. The explanations lasted until it was time for him to go. Hank had intended to go with him as far as Petty's hotel, on the chance of finding Donovan still there, but a call from Oscar interfered with his plan and he sent Roger off, with explicit instruction to the cab driver and to Roger as to safe driving and what was to be told to Grandfather. Their parting was very formal, with mutual hopes of future meetings; but Roger's eyes shown with pleasure and Hank would have agreed with Emma that some of the days which seem hopeless turn out very well.

But Hank's day was not over. The call from Oscar had indicated that Mrs. Graham was trying to reach him. What for, he couldn't imagine, unless to find out where Emma was in order to get some money. He wished that he could get to Donovan so that Emma would be free to handle her own problems, but he reluctantly dialed Mrs. Graham's number.

As soon as he made himself known, the languid hello changed to a violent storm of abuse that made Hank flinch when it hit his ear. What did Emma Marsh mean by shutting up the shop and leaving Mrs. Graham without a cent? Just because Jeff was gone was no reason for her to neglect the business. Who did Emma think she was anyway? And why was she, Jeff's wife, being followed everywhere she went? It was most embarrassing to have a third party along—especially one that looked and acted like an ape—every time she went out with her gentleman friend.

Hank didn't recognize Tim from the description but he thought that the shadowing was doubtless some of his doing. He told Mrs. Graham that it was just a habit of the police in murder cases and that she mustn't mind.

Mrs. Graham did mind and she expected him to do something about it, in return for having been taken home by her on an evening of recent date. Hank groaned and promised to do what he could. He tried to be very noncommittal about Emma's whereabouts; but, by inventing a mythical errand on which she was engaged, only succeeded in provoking another storm. Mrs. Graham was sure that Emma's errand concerned Jeff, which meant that there had been news of him and that she hadn't been told. Where, she wanted to know, was he? Hank assured her that he hadn't the foggiest notion but she made it quite plain that she didn't believe him. Of course, she was only his wife and not entitled to any consideration. Hank decided that, if he were Jeff, he'd never go home and that the boy friend probably wasn't hearing these vigorous expressions of opinion. Hank knew that Donovan had wanted the finding of Jeff's car kept quiet and he did not see that it would do any good to tell her of Jeff's stay in the hospital, since he was lost again; but he blandly assured her that she would be informed the moment there was any trace of him and that Miss Marsh would be back in the shop on the next day. Mrs. Graham hung up, somewhat mollified, leaving Hank free, at last, to try to catch up with Donovan.

He was still several laps behind, for Donovan had already left the hotel when Hank arrived there. The doorman said that he had seen Donovan and the sergeant going across the street in the direction of the shop and Hank went after them, wondering what they were up to. They were neither inside nor outside the shop, and Hank was trying to decide what to do next, when a yellow envelope in the pile of mail just inside the door caught his eye. The glass panels in the door were long and low and the letters, though quite out of reach, were plainly visible. The yellow envelope was clearly a telegram and, by peering closely in the fading light, Hank could make out that it was addressed to Emma. Acting on a sudden impulse, he went across the street again and called the telegraph company. Yes, they had a wire for Miss Emma Marsh but the message had been delivered; and, as he was obviously not Miss Marsh, they were obstinately stubborn in their refusal to read it to him. Hank did not feel that he could invoke the majesty of the law without Donovan and hung up, baffled again.

It was raining harder now and Hank stood looking disgustedly out of the door of the drugstore. If he hadn't been so upset at the evidence of Emma's perfidy, he wouldn't be standing here without any overcoat or anyone to eat dinner with and minus a lot of information that he wanted especially to know about. It was becoming clear that Emma was not as black as she had let herself be painted, but there was still the hat and the blackjack to explain. If she chose to protect strange cab drivers at the risk of her own neck, rather than to tell him the story and let him handle it as he thought best, he supposed that it was her own business but it certainly indicated a lack of confidence in his abilities and discretion. Hank knew that all the bitterness had gone out of his feelings about Emma but he thought that something else had gone too. He wanted to get to Donovan and get her out of jail because, obviously, jail was not the most comfortable place to be and he could explain away part of the situation that held her there; but both her discomfort and her well-being had ceased to be a matter of deep personal concern to him. He wondered if this was the first step in becoming Indifferent to Women. The long, comfortable bachelorhood of his uncle suddenly appeared to him in a new light and he made up his mind that his future relations with Emma, while they would certainly be friendly, would be decidedly impersonal. He pulled his eyes away from the streaming street; this kind of thinking was all very fine and quite in the best disillusioned tradition but what he wanted was action. Or was it something to eat? The thought of food was distinctly not unpleasant but acquiring it seemed to involve considerable difficulty and the certainty of a wetting. Unfortunately the drugstore, in which he was, took its business seriously and did not pretend to be a restaurant or a hardware store. Horehound candy or a chocolate bar seemed to be about all there was in the way of nourishment, unless he felt that he could grapple with a pound of hard and chewy centers. Hank concluded that, if he had to eat alone, he might as well make the best of the Greek's up the street and turned up his coat collar for the dash through the rain.

When he had chosen fried scallops, in preference to ham hocks and sauerkraut, and collected the various oddments of a meal on his tray, he looked around for a place to sit. The tables were well filled, for it was only a quarter to seven, but he would probably have sat with Stephana Mathews anyway, as soon as he caught her wave and pleasant smile. She looked very calm and peaceful and Hank felt that such a person would put no strain on his newly acquired position as an eligible, but indifferent, bachelor.

Stephana inquired for Emma, saying that she had gone to the shop intending to repay the invitation which she had been unable to accept the night before but had found no one there.

Hank stuck firmly to his story that Emma was away on business and then excused himself to telephone Donovan. He left word that he would be at the station as soon as he had eaten, gave the number of the restaurant should Donovan return and wish to call him, and went back to a meal that was turning out better than he had expected. He asked Stephana if she had succeeded in finding a job and rejoiced with her that she had, although agreeing that a real estate office gave little scope for the talents of a costume designer. He noted down the address and inquired for her own telephone number. She gave it to him readily, explaining that it was not really a private phone but rather that of the apartment house on Newbury Street in which she lived. She wanted to know if Emma would be back the next day. Hank thought it almost certain.

Stephana looked at him quizzically. She leaned forward and said in a low tone, "She's not in trouble, is she? I mean with the police?"

Hank wanted to know why she should think that possible.

"Because," she explained, "I was there when that policeman—Donovan, is that his name?—came to the shop for her. I'd hate for her to be involved in this."

Just how involved Emma was, Hank didn't think it necessary to tell her. He said that Donovan wanted to ask her about a telephone call that had given them a clue to the place where Jeff had been.

Where was that, Stephana wanted to know?

Hank told her, briefly.

Had he been hurt, then?

Hank bathed a scallop with the tartar sauce before he told her that Jeff had met with a little accident. If the police ever got hold of Jeff it would all be in the papers but he didn't feel that it was his business to reveal the nature of Jeff's injury.

"How would you like," he said, thinking that a change of subject was indicated, "to go to the theater with me some night?"

Stephana's brown eyes widened with pleasure. "I'd love it," she said. "There are two shows I want to see; I know some of the people in them but I haven't had a job and I didn't dare spend the money."

"And now," said Hank lightly, "that you have a job, I come to, and ask you to go with me. They tell me that the Bible has some words for that situation."

They fell to discussing plays and possible evenings. Stephana wondered what Emma would think when she learned that Hank had invited her out. Possibly things weren't as serious between those two as she had imagined. She certainly wasn't going to ask if it were all right with Emma for Hank to take her. After all, she would enjoy the Norwitch money just as much as Emma; she wiped her hands surreptitiously on the napkin because a cold sweat had broken out on them at the thought of the chance that she might marry Hank right out from under Emma's nose. The idea certainly was worth considering but she mustn't go too fast; and, especially, she mustn't make an enemy of Emma. Her best chance of seeing Hank, for a while, until she was surer of him, was to continue her friendship with Emma. She smiled at Hank and said that Thursday night would be fine.

Would she also have dinner with him? Stephana wasn't sure but she thought it could be arranged. Life, for Stephana, was decidedly looking up. She had a job and, God willing, in a little while she'd have a man. Hank had made the theater suggestion in the first place to change the subject of conversation, for he knew, or at least Emma had told him, that the surest way to set a girl thinking about clothes was to ask her to go somewhere. The dinner invitation had been added partly as a result of Stephana's obvious pleasure at the thought of an outing and partly because he decided that he really would enjoy more of her company. It had occurred to him that his day was getting pretty full of good deeds and that he might as well do one for himself.

The telephone rang. The proprietor, catching Hank's eye, motioned that the call was for him. Excusing himself, Hank walked to the phone and picked up the receiver. Donovan beat him to the punch.

"Where the devil have you been? I've been hunting you for hours."

"I guess," said Hank, "that I've been following you. First of all, can I take back what I said this morning?"

"Oh sure. I never believed you anyway. Say, do you know anything about Petty?"

"I had an appointment with him last night but he ran out on me."

"You what?"

"About that blood, you know it's dog blood. . . ."

"Sure, I know it's dog blood. Do you realize that Petty is gone?"

"Oh really? Well, he didn't keep the appointment. And the dog was killed in the accident—that's what took so much time—and Mike broke his leg; so they didn't want the police . . ."

"Listen," said Donovan, "if you've gone crazy, I'll send the wagon for you; if not, get down here as fast as you can."

"I'm not crazy. Emma didn't do it. . . ."

But Donovan had hung up on him; so Hank called a cab and went back to get his hat and check. He had almost forgotten Stephana.

"Business," he said. "I have to go. I'll be seeing you," he added in the casual slang of his college days.

To Stephana, however, the words were a promise.

Chapter

11

"YOU," SAID DONOVAN, as Hank came in, "had me worried. If anybody else disappears in this case, I'm going to resign. I'll have to or I'll be fired."

"Listen to me," said Hank, "I can explain everything about Emma."

"Why," asked Donovan, "did you make an appointment with Petty?"

"To take him to dinner. You see the taxi ran over this dog and the driver . . ."

"O.K.," said Donovan, "I give up. Maybe I can ask a few questions if I let you tell me all about Emma and the dog and the taxi driver. Say," he said, interest growing in his voice, "you haven't found that missing driver, have you?"

"That's what I've been trying to tell you," said Hank, somewhat nettled. "Lost cabby, explanation, everything all sewed up; and you sit there and heckle me about Petty."

"Petty," Donovan interpolated dryly, "may have some slight importance in this case; but go on, he can wait."

All brakes released, Hank told his story fully and with gusto. He wanted to rag Donovan about his inability to find Joe in the disguise of a respectable chauffeur but he remembered that he had promised that the police would not take up the matter of the accident, and stressed Joe's simple kindness in helping the friend he had hurt. Mike, he pointed out, was not primarily deceiving the police as to Joe's whereabouts but rather protecting him because of his understanding of Joe's childhood horrors, just as he watched over Roger. He painted a lovely picture of mutual sorrow and devotion between Mike and Joe and touched it up with a description of the grief-stricken Roger that would have made that dignified young gentleman blush with shame. When he had finished, Donovan stared at him in wonder.

"And this," he said, "is what she wouldn't tell anybody?"

Hank knew to whom Donovan was referring. "You see," he explained, "she's pretty much of a sap about anyone who's in trouble. She promised she wouldn't tell and then Joe disappeared and she couldn't produce him for an alibi, not knowing that he was practically just around the corner. And when the news of the murder came out, Mike and Joe kept quiet, not wanting to get her in bad. Oh, everyone was being very loyal and helpful in a nice muddle-headed sort of way; and, if Roger hadn't had the manners to come around to thank Emma for the dog, she'd probably have gone on being heroic about the whole thing until hell froze over, being, by nature, somewhat stubborn. Are you going to let her out or does the hat and the blackjack still keep her here?"

Donovan explained that Pissano had cleared up the mystery of the hat.

"There, you see," said Hank, determined to make Emma a noble, if somewhat misguided, character, "she can't let people take care of their own troubles; she has to bustle around helping them out. She sees the initials in Uncle's hat and decides that, guilty or not, Jeff has to be protected. She puts the hat in the car and, I bet a nickel, forgets all about it. I sometimes wonder what I see in her."

"There is still," said Donovan, "the matter of the blackjack."

"Oh sakes, she probably thought it had my fingerprints or Jeff's on it and just hid it on the off-chance. I don't know when she took it, though, because Joe agrees that she wasn't in the shop but a few seconds and I'm positive it wasn't there the next morning."

"Well, you can be sure," said Donovan, "that she won't tell you."

"Don't be bitter," said Hank. "There's some explanation for it. Go on, let her out."

"Don't get excited." Donovan had certain things he wanted to know and he was not going to have his questioning interrupted by any lovers' reconciliation scene. "Keep perfectly calm. Emma better stay where she is for a while, so she won't feel obliged to answer your questions for you. Petty has taken himself off. The only clues we have are the man who waited an hour or so for him at the hotel—you answer the description, so I guess that was you—and a telephone call that he received at quarter of seven. The hotel does enough business so the operator don't listen to the phone conversations but she thinks a woman called him. Now, if you know anything, spill it. You don't have to protect anybody that I can think of because Emma was safe down here when that call went through. Did you call him?"

"In my best falsetto, you mean?" asked Hank, grinning. "No, I didn't. At quarter of seven I was coming back from Watertown, where I had delivered a bundle for J. Graham, Antiques. I knew I was going to be late for the appointment but I didn't stop to phone because I thought that would only make me later and it didn't occur to me that Mr. Petty was so popular that he wouldn't wait for me."

"Why did you want to see Petty?"

"No particular reason." Hank wriggled a little with embarrassment. "I didn't want him to think that I resented his being a Norwitch and getting some of the money; so I asked him out to dinner. Sort of gesture of good will, hands-across-the-sea business. That's all, absolutely."

"What time did you get to the hotel?"

"About seven-fifteen; I was supposed to be there at seven."

"But it was seven-thirty when you inquired at the desk?"

"I was to meet him in the bar. When I first got there, I was just relieved that he was later than I; so I had a drink and waited. When he didn't appear, I had another drink and then sent up word that I was there. When the clerk said he had gone out, I had another drink while I thought things over. Then I got mad and had several more and tried to call you and Emma and couldn't get anybody and got feeling sorry for myself and got plastered. And, by the way, I ran into Mrs. Graham and the boy friend and she wants you to quit shadowing her."

Hank stopped his headlong chronicle because he was trying to think of what it was that Mrs. Graham had said to him that had seemed so important.

"She's just got a guilty conscience," said Donovan. "We haven't had a man on her since the inquest."

"Well, someone is following her and she's all steamed up about it."

"Tim," said Donovan, "are you pulling another private investigation on me?"

"No sir," said the sergeant hastily, "I haven't been near her."

"Well, get near her and find out what's up. Do I have to do all the work?"

"Yes sir; no sir," said the sergeant, feeling as though he had been bitten by the hand that fed him.

Donovan drew squares and curlicues on the pad before him. "It's not going to look so good," he said morosely. "You and Petty get the money and then Petty does a fade-out after talking to you. We were after him; so you help him get away. Oh me, why do I ever let you out of my sight? Half the force thinks we had a fight this morning when you walked out and some old Aunt Berthas are sure to think you came back just because we found out about Petty."

"Don't feel so bad," said Hank soothingly, "I'll get out again if it will make you any happier."

"Oh, be your age," Donovan snapped. "You're no use but I like to have you around. Now where the devil do you suppose Petty is at?"

"Who," asked Hank sociably, "can tell? Maybe he just stepped out to get a package of cigarettes and vanished, like Charlie Ross. Or was it

Judge Crater? He'll turn up."

Donovan threw his pencil across the room. "He'll turn up," he mimicked. "I'm good and sick of hunting for people. Is this a murder investigation or the Bureau of Missing Persons? He'll turn up! Yeah, why doesn't Jeff turn up? They'll both turn up in South America and live off that damn secretary and Petty's money."

He stopped, enchanted with the idea his imagination had presented to him. "You don't suppose they were in this together, do you? They're both in the same business and they knew each other and Petty told Jeff he was coming on that particular night and they planned to do the murder and beat it together."

"That's just dandy," said Hank, "except that I can't see Jeff Graham killing a man as a favor to someone else. You're not going to get much forrader until you find Petty and Jeff. I suppose you've called New York?"

Donovan restrained the obvious remark. "He wrote his shop that he would be here indefinitely but he'd write the same whether he meant to go or stay. He's thirty-nine years old, his wife died five years ago and the only relative that his secretary ever heard of was some kind of a cousin who runs a grocery store over in Jersey. No one answering his description took a train or a boat out of here. But why did he go just now? If he were scared, I'd think he'd have gone sooner; we weren't bothering him much."

"I was about to ask," put in Hank, "where his watchdog was."

"The big lug," said Donovan, "sees Petty come in and go to his room; so he goes out for his supper. It was O.K. There was only one man on the job and he had to eat sometime but it's just an example of how the breaks are going in this case."

"It looks," Hank was thinking out loud, "as though the telephone call tipped him off to something. Have you traced the call?"

"New, it was from one of those private dial phones."

"Say," said Hank suddenly, "there is somebody in on this that we don't know about. There's the call that sends you to the hospital and this one that takes Petty into the blue; and both times it seems to have been a woman."

"Don't make it any harder than it is. I think the first call was from a nurse that had got wise to Jeff but didn't want to get mixed up in this mess. On the one to Petty I haven't an idea, but Petty's been in town before and it stands to reason that he might know a woman or two who would call him up. It might even have been a customer."

"Always the optimist," said Hank approvingly. "But knowing a lot of women wasn't Petty's reason for killing Uncle, unless they were fighting over one, which slander I do not entertain for a minute; and, unless he killed Uncle, why would Petty vanish? Unless he turns up tomorrow with a bad headache, I move we elect him the murderer and adjourn the meeting."

"And all we have left over," began Donovan sarcastically, "is Jeff, your uncle's hat, the missing key, and the blackjack. What do we do with those? Bury them in the backyard?"

"Jeff may be already buried," said Hank. "And I'd forgotten, for the moment, about the key. Look here," Hank straightened out his spine in an excess of enthusiasm, "the murderer may still have that key and, if he has, he can get into the shop anytime he pleases; so he takes the blackjack and plants it on Emma. Now will you let her out?"

"A more unlikely notion," said Donovan, "I never heard. Why would the criminal load himself up with a blackjack that would be certain evidence against him?"

"Just for that reason: to have something with which to incriminate Emma."

"Who would want to incriminate Emma and why?"

"Well, there you have me," said Hank.

Donovan favored Hank with a look and pressed a buzzer. "Tell the matron," he said to the head that appeared in the door, "to bring Miss Marsh. And all her things," he added. "She's going out."

Chapter

24

HANK WONDERED, afterward, how he had expected Emma to look. Disheveled, probably, and haggard, after sleepless nights of worry. Not tear-stained, no not quite, but with a hint of suffering in her eyes. And he had planned to be very magnanimous and fatherly and forgiving for, while Mike and Joe had explained away her apparent falsehoods, there still remained the fact that she had not chosen to take him into her confidence. Things, he was sure, would not be the same.

But when Emma marched in the door of Donovan's office, trim and spruce, her hat cocked on the back of her head and actually giggling at some quip of the matron's, another, stronger emotion overlaid his surprise. Here was his peace, his home, his native land; she was his rooftree, his hearthstone, the Statue of Liberty and the Sacred Cod all rolled into one. As Donovan would have put it, she was his girl and he wanted to take her in his arms and kiss the face half off her. He started to suit the action to the thought. "Darling," he said as he went toward her.

"Well," said Emma, "it's about time you showed up."

She walked past him to Donovan. "Have you found Jeff and has he confessed; or to what change of heart shall I attribute this sudden freedom?"

"No," said Donovan, "no Jeff. I let you out because, if you have him hidden in your basement, he might starve without you. And the next time you run over a dog, try to be sensible."

Emma did not so much as flicker an eyelid in Hank's direction. "So you found out about that, did you?"

"Yes," said Donovan, "and I know about the hat but I don't want to pry too much into your private affairs; so I'll stay in the dark about the billy. With you on the loose again, something is bound to turn up."

"Jerry," said Emma, "you're being sarcastic."

"Go on home and take that one with you. And," Donovan added in a muttered undertone, "give him hell."

"Don't worry," said Emma. "And besides, I need the change."

They surveyed each other for a moment with respectful understanding.

"I'm glad you enjoyed your stay with us, good-by."

"Good-by," said Emma, "the meals were fine but the bed could be improved."

Drawing Hank in her wake with a glance, Emma went quickly out. Her exit would have been more impressive if she had remembered where the front door was but she suffered Hank's guidance to the steps in silence.

Hank motioned to a loitering cab but Emma waved it away, saying, "I want to walk."

"But it's raining," said Hank.

"My exercise in the last thirty-six hours," said Emma pointedly, "has been somewhat restricted. I'm going to walk."

She set off briskly down the street and Hank followed her, grimacing in disgust as the rain lashed at his face.

A cold wind had set in at sundown, had risen with the dark and now drove the rain viciously before it, ruffling the puddles in the street, creaking the hanging signs and slatting even the fast-lashed awnings. The narrow street was gloomy and deserted. Latches, bolts and wires, unobtrusive and unnoticed in the daylight, took on life as the street lights struck their wetness, and glittered unexpectedly from dark corners. Eerie whistles arose from gratings and screaming gusts reached out from doorways. The wind had taken over man-made objects and was using them for some dark purpose of its own.

Her hat pulled firmly down, Emma strode stoutly ahead for a few blocks, glad that the out of doors was tangible on the night of her release, rejoicing that her body was free again to try itself against a force from which sought shelter would be voluntary. On a windswept corner she paused for breath and felt Hank's hand upon her arm. She turned an exultant face to him. Then her expression changed and she moved away.

"Haven't you had enough?" Hank asked. "I want to talk to you."

"That's too bad; I've become rather accustomed to your silence."

"Oh please, Emma, try to see it my way. When Donovan showed me all those things, I thought you'd known about Jeff all along and had just been putting me off so that he could make a getaway."

"And why," Emma asked scornfully, "wouldn't I? I've known Jeff longer than I have you. He took care of me when he'd known me two weeks; he kept me from buying stock on a margin; and if I make a mistake with the customers, he takes the blame."

"But, Emma, this is murder; there was the blood on your shoes and the billy in the sofa, and all the time you were gone "

"And the hat in the car," Emma added for him.

"And I thought you'd been there and seen it. . . ."

"I don't give a damn if you thought I killed him myself but I do care that you walked out on me when I was in a jam. What are friends for, if not to think the worst, and yet do their best for you?"

"But I did!" Hank's voice was rising against the wind. "Holy cats, I spent the whole afternoon finding out that all your dither was over a dead dog and a mug with a broken leg. You can thank me that you're out of jail now."

"Oh, that," said Emma, "would have come out eventually. I'd have appreciated some cigarettes and a potted plant much more. You've no idea how dull a jail can be."

"Well, damn me," said Hank furiously, "the next time you get in jail you can just stay there. You don't know the meaning of the word gratitude."

"Just how," asked Emma curiously, "did you find out about the accident?"

"I was standing in front of the store," Hank said shortly, "and a kid came along with a dog and asked for you and we got talking...."

"So," Emma interrupted him, "you weren't out working your fingers to the bone to free me from my horrid shackles. You were standing around and, if Roger Corey hadn't happened along and explained my suspicious actions, you never would have showed up at all; and Donovan would have let me out anyway when he got the lab's report on the bloodstains; and what gratitude would I owe you then?"

"That isn't the point at all," said Hank wearily. "I may not have put it in writing but I'm really very fond of you. We usually get on together. This is the first big case I've ever had a hand in and, aside from personal reasons of which I choose to make light, it means a lot to me. I've tried to be fair about Jeff, when God knows I have every reason to think he killed Uncle. I've gone over Uncle's papers inch by inch, trying to find some clue that would point to someone else and I've talked Donovan out of issuing a warrant for his arrest. I've done this because Jeff is your friend and my friend, but mostly because I know how his guilt would hurt you and I don't want to have you hurt. Bearing this in mind, please consider how I must have felt when I find that not only have you known where Jeff has been, have helped him get away and have attempted to destroy evidence, but that there are actual clues to your presence at the scene of the crime. You weren't playing fair with me; all my notions of your loyalty vanished and our partnership dissolved with a loud bang."

This time Emma put her hand on Hank's arm. "Darling," she said, "you're undoubtedly right from your point of view. And believe me, I have given you credit all along. You talk of loyalty and partnership; our conception of those things is miles apart; and, unless you can understand mine, I don't ask that you agree with it, there can be no partnership for us."

"Tell me," said Hank.

"It's like 'truth' and 'beauty' and the other things people argue about. You form an opinion, to the best of your ability, about a person or a thing; even if it's a favorable opinion, there are almost always certain reservations. You see a chair, one arm may be mended but the rest is beautiful. It serves you well, spiritually and physically, but you don't claim that it is a perfect chair. You make a friend, acting on your own judgment, and then see him beating a horse. Well, you ought to wait before crossing him off the list till you know whether the horse is a man-killer, or whether the friend has a bad temper and ought to stay away from horses, or whether he's just naturally mean. In the last instance your judgment was at fault; the man had the meanness when you decided you liked him, and there is no sense or justice in making an enemy just because you made a mistake. Ease him out gently and, in the process, you may find qualities that make you want to ease him back again.

"I'm getting off the point and I sound like a Sunday School lecture; what I'm trying to say is that people ought to be let make their own errors or hits; and if you have given your friendship, you shouldn't take it back when you don't understand why the success turned into a failure."

"My dear," said Hank, "if you want to rob a bank, I'll not try to stop you. May I kiss you now?"

"Please do," said Emma.

The wind and the rain could not tear them apart.

"Here now, here now! What's this?" A figure that glinted and gleamed in wet rubber encasements loomed beside them. Hank took off his hat with a low bow.

"Sir," said he, "you may congratulate us. We have made up."

"Git along," said the cop. "You're sopping wet."

"'My eyes are wet, but not with tears,' Longfellow," said Emma idiotically.

"Byron," said Hank sternly, "and badly paraphrased."

"If you're drunk," began the cop, "I'll have to—"

"I've checked out," cried Emma, "and paid my bill."

She grabbed Hank's arm and they sprinted around the corner into the comparative brightness of Boylston Street. They stopped, breath-less, behind the subway entrance and Hank peeked around the corner to see if they were pursued. The sight was too much for Emma. Hank was teetering on one leg like an anxious crane. A lock of hair was plas-tered to his forehead. His hat was a shapeless mass and his sodden tweeds had assumed the outlines of a disheartened burlap bag. Emma leaned against the rain-darkened granite and gave vent to shouts of laughter.

"Hush up," admonished Hank, "or you'll have the riot squad here."

"But you look so funny!" Emma went off in another spasm of mirth.

"You don't look so good yourself." Hank took in the soggy details. "In fact you look like something a sailor wouldn't pick up. Let's move on, before we're pushed."

Giggling amiably, they started down the street, arm in arm.

"Tell me," Emma began. "What were you doing down at the shop when Roger appeared? Thinking of me?"

"No," said Hank, "I was reading the paper."

"Such devotion!" Emma put in.

"That reminds me," Hank went on, ignoring the sarcasm, "there is a telegram for you at the shop, I saw it through the door."

"Snooping, eh?" said Emma. "Maybe someone has left me some money; we better go see."

They changed their course, met the full force of the wind crossing the Garden, and struggled silently along, making headway together against the elements that sought to dissuade them. When they reached the Beacon Street corner, the sheltering buildings gave them a moment's respite.

"Whew," said Emma when she could get her breath, "it will take a lot of money to make up for that."

"What?" asked Hank, who had been thinking of other things. "Oh that. I was wondering if it might be from Jeff."

The dark night, the rain and the wind closed down on Emma. She was conscious that she was wet and very cold. All her troubles, seem-ingly picked up by the eddying gusts, rushed at her with the force of a gale. She pressed closer against Hank, who patted her arm, sensing her worry and discomfort.

Ordinarily, Emma was very fond of Charles Street. Physically, it was as familiar to her as her own room. She knew all the shops and the spiritual plusses and minuses of the people who ran them. Tonight, at least, the street might have greeted her with a welcoming affection; instead, it was dark and hostile, as though it warned her to stay away. The shop windows were like black mirrors and gave back only the re-flection of her troubled face. A ship's figurehead loomed like a ghost in a doorway; and, as they passed the florist shop, a string of gourds clattered suddenly, like dancing bones. Before the store Emma fumbled with stiff fingers for the key. The leather of her purse was slippery and seemed to evade her control but finally she conquered it, found the key, turned it in the lock and opened the door. As Emma turned on the light, Hank, stooping, picked up the mail and handed the telegram to her. She tore it open clumsily, read the message and, after a moment, handed it to Hank. It was sent from Old Lyme, Connecticut, and read, "Secretary found arriving six-ten Thursday A.M. meet me Back Bay."

"What do you know," said Hank, "he's found the secretary."

"Isn't that swell," said Emma.

Neither of them was thinking of the secretary.

The sound of the rain on the glass was very loud in the stillness; the wind tore away minutes of time.

"I'll tell Donovan myself," said Emma, starting for the office. Hank, turning slowly to follow her, heard her gasp but was not in time to catch her as she sank to the floor.

Had time turned back, Hank wondered, or was this a recurring nightmare that would vanish with the morning? Surely there could not be another body lying where his uncle's blood had made the dark pool. The very boards would resent such a heaped-up horror. But Hank knew that he was not asleep. It was night, not morning; the body there was not that of Richard Norwitch but that of Petty, Richard Petty, who had no business there at all and no reason for being dead. Hank put his arm under Emma's shoulders, letting her head fall forward but there was no sign of returning consciousness. He wondered if there was any whisky in the washroom. He had to get whisky, he had to call Donovan and he ought to lock the door. Only if he had arms like an octopus could he do all these things at once. He laid Emma gently on the floor and straightened up just in time to see Nels Peterson, the night cop, open the door.

"Thank God," said Hank without explanation. "Get some whisky out of the washroom, there, while I get the police station."

The body in the aisle was hidden from Peterson until he was nearly upon it and his startled ejaculation reached Hank, already at the phone.

"Never mind the body, get the whisky," he shouted, somewhat to the surprise of the officer who was trying to answer his call. Donovan had left, but he could be reached and his prompt appearance was promised.

Hank hung up and went to the assistance of Peterson, who was standing, holding the whisky, and looking from one recumbent form to the other as though doubtful where he could do the most good.

Hank snatched the bottle from his hand and, bending over, tilted it to Emma's mouth.

"Accident?" asked Peterson.

"Murder," said Hank. He was frantic that he could not examine the body; he was not even sure how Petty had died; he was beginning to be a little annoyed with Emma for so obstinately refusing to come out of her faint. Most of the whisky seemed to be running around into her ear but he thought she was swallowing some of it. He gave her a little shake, experimentally, but nothing happened.

Peterson, who had been looking at the body, stood up and scratched his head.

"It's no use," he said, "he's been dead quite awhile. She must have shot him yesterday. Did he shoot her?"

Hank was about to concur with the general opinion of the intelligence of Peterson's ancestry when he realized that the supposition that Emma had shot Petty was not completely illogical.

"She didn't kill him," he explained patiently. "She just came in with me and saw him first and fainted."

"Oh," said Peterson, "then who did shoot him?"

"I don't know. How do you bring people to?"

"Slap 'em; throw cold water on 'em."

Hank decided for the water cure since Emma was already so wet that there could be no further damage to her clothes.

"Get some water, then; there's probably a glass where you got the whisky."

Hank took the water that Peterson offered and flung it full in Emma's face. She blinked her eyes, opened them and said, rather thickly, "Gee, it's sure raining."

She struggled to sit up but Hank, bending to help her, gave her a clear view of Petty's crumpled body. She shut her eyes. Hank, fearful lest she faint again, picked her up and put her in the pink brocade wing chair. She did not present the picture that Stephana Mathews had made there but the comparison did not occur to Hank. He rubbed her hands and said, "Don't look, sweet, and please don't faint again."

"Is he dead?" asked Emma.

"I'm afraid so."

"Thank God that Jeff is out of town."

Hank said nothing about Peterson's remark that Petty had been dead for some time and did his own thanking, privately, that Emma had been safely in jail since the moment she left the shop. He handed her the scotch and the glass.

"Drink this," he said.

Emma did as she was told and felt better. She achieved a sort of smile, feeling that Jeff was out of it.

"Go on, bloodhound," she said, "before the scent gets cold. I'm all right."

"Good girl," said Hank appreciatively.

He turned to Peterson. "Have you found the gun?"

"No gun."

"Then we don't have to argue about suicide. Anything else?"

"He has something in his hand."

That something looked like a handkerchief. "Probably," said Hank, "he was blowing his nose and didn't know who shot him."

"We can't ask him," said Peterson.

Hank looked up quickly but there was no sign of mirth on the broad pink face. Just a realist, thought Hank, and went on examining the body. Petty had been plugged very neatly, right smack dab through the heart, Hank guessed, and from very close range. There were powder burns on the blue suit. That might mean either an ambush or someone that Petty knew. Hank glanced at the face. In stories the features were usually contorted in a grimace of terror or rage but Petty's face was much as Hank remembered it, except for a slight relaxation of the jaw.

The door opened noisily, pushed by a long baffled gust of wind. Donovan came in, and Tim, and Saunders, the fingerprint man, and the medical examiner, looking rather hastily thrown together. Again Hank had the sensation of experiencing a recurrent nightmare. He looked at Donovan blankly for a moment, as though waiting for him to grow larger and larger and finally explode.

Donovan came closer and said, "Well, you prophesied this, didn't you?"

Why, so he had. For the first time since Emma fainted, Hank felt normal. His mind ceased to be the prey of the emotions which had been dragging at it ever since he had faced Donovan over the hat and the bloodstained shoe. He glanced at Emma. She smiled back at him but she looked as though she were going to cry. He motioned for her to finish her drink and stepped aside to let Donovan through the narrow space to the body. Telephone calls, keys and motives began to marshal themselves orderly in his mind.

"We haven't touched him," he said. "In fact I've hardly looked at him. Emma saw him first and fainted and I had considerable difficulty bringing her to. It's been quite a day."

"It's going to be a worse night," Peterson put in. "Storm warnings are out all along. The radio says that the sea wall at Winthrop is full of holes right now. It's the equinox."

"The what?', asked Donovan.

"The vernal equinox," Peterson explained.

As though overcome by this pronouncement, the lights began to dim slowly.

"He means the line storm," said Emma, beginning to cry.

Hank looked at Emma as the lights came back to brightness again and saw, with consternation, that the bottle of scotch in her hand was nearly empty.

"Sacred cats," he exclaimed, "she's drunk it all."

"You told me to finish it," Emma said defensively, the tears trickling down her cheeks. "I'm all right. Really I am, only I can't stop crying."

This time the lights went off suddenly.

"A crying jag," said Peterson, his flashlight picking out Emma's face from the darkness.

"Bullet wound," came the voice of the medical examiner, "to the left of the sternum, probably nicked the fourth rib. Death was instantaneous, as the bullet pierced the heart, and probably occurred at least thirty-six hours ago. The body has been in a warm place and the reactions would be normal. Thirty-two caliber gun, fired at close range. Is there any kind of a lamp in this place?"

Emma felt them all turn to her and got to her feet. "There ought to be some c-candles, somewhere," she sobbed.

In the street, the driver was turning the ambulance so that its headlights would illuminate the shop. The candles, thought Emma, should be in the bottom drawer of the tall chest, under the old beaver hat. She went unerringly to the chest, opened the drawer and put in her hand. She was glad she had remembered the hat, because it felt warm and soft and strangely alive as she touched it. She wondered if she would always be abnormally hat conscious. And how the devil had that billy got under her cushions? She fumbled in her pockets for matches but they were wet when she found them, and she went back to her desk where there were sure to be some. It was characteristic of her that she did not ask one of the men for a match. She had been told to produce a light and her experience with Jeff had taught her that that meant not only finding a candle but also lighting it and finding a holder. The illumination from the ambulance did not penetrate to the office but Emma put her hand to the spot where she kept a useful box of kitchen matches. She groped around, finally found them and lit three candles, saying, as she did so, "The things on my desk have been moved. Somebody has been in here."

"It seems likely," said Peterson.

"Listen here," said Donovan, "it's a bad night but you have a beat that may be full of drunks and robbers; you better go take a look at it. Report to me in the morning."

Peterson took a reluctant departure.

"Just a minute," said Donovan to Emma, who was hunting for candlesticks. "Give us those searchlights and don't touch anything else on the desk."

"It would seem," Emma was muttering, "that a good antique shop would have some decent candlesticks."

All she could find were a pair of delicate Dresden ones and these she entrusted tearfully to Donovan and Hank. To Tim, with whom her Dresden would have been safest, she gave a dripping candle.

As they ranged themselves beside the body, the scene took on the semblance of some strange funeral. For a moment they stood silent, gazing down at Petty in the wavering light; Emma, sobbing quietly in the background, became the chief mourner. Tim crossed himself. Then the medical examiner cleared his throat and the spell was broken.

Donovan got out his tape line, measured the position of the body and sketched its outline with chalk. As the body was being removed, he took the handkerchief from the relaxed fingers and looked at it carefully. It was a man's linen handkerchief, of good quality, clean but crumpled. There were no initials but there was a laundry mark on the hem. Donovan put it in his pocket.

"We can't do any work in this light," he said, "so we might as well lock up and go home. But," he added, thinking of the missing key, "Tim had better stay here for the rest of the night."

Emma stopped crying long enough to sneeze, three times.

"Are you catching cold?" asked Hank anxiously.

"Probably," said Emma, gloomily, "I've cried so much I haven't had a chance to dry off."

"You'll come home with me," said Hank. "Oscar will fix you up."

"That'll be fine," said Donovan. "Mr. LeBotien won't worry; he'll think you're still in jail."

"Why, the sweet thing," said Emma, "I suppose he did worry."

"Hank got him all upset, and then forgot him," Donovan explained. "So he called the station and I told him we were keeping you there to protect you."

"Thanks," said Emma, "for being so careful of my reputation."

"Don't mention it," said Donovan, "you'll need all you've got left."

They settled the sergeant in the pink brocade chair. He became it least of all its recent occupants. They left him one lighted candle for company and were about to leave when Emma saw the unopened mail, which some careful soul had piled neatly on a table.

"Oh," she said suddenly, "where's the telegram?"

Hank produced it from his pocket, where it had been forgotten and gave it to Donovan.

Donovan read it through. "Thank you," he said to Emma. "I'll meet him."

There was no threat in his voice.

"I'll meet him too," said Emma quietly. "He asked me to."

They were too tired to talk on the short ride to Hank's house. As though from a great distance, Emma heard Donovan arrange to meet Hank at the shop in the morning but what they might do or find had ceased to interest her. She had given Jeff up. What happened to him now was in more competent hands than hers. She had stopped crying, but she was very cold; her teeth chattered convulsively. Her mind seemed to be hanging in midair, about two feet above her head, waiting, wondering, but with no great enthusiasm, to see if the body it once inhabited would ever get warm.

Hank rang the bell to warn Oscar of their arrival and then led Emma into the hall. Oscar was not slow in coming. He might almost have been expecting them for, in a very short time, Emma was feeling the warmth of hot blankets and hotter tea. She wiggled down comfortably and fell fast asleep, without remembering to say thank you.

Hank started to bed because he was tired but he was not sleepy. By the light of a fugitive gas bracket which had found shelter in a corner of his bedroom, he discussed, with Oscar, the new crime and the advisability of having a female permanently under their roof. Oscar seemed to feel that he would be better able to make an estimate of Emma on the following day. As to Petty's murderer, Oscar felt that, in spite of Petty's semi-respectable background, he might have innumerable unknown enemies. Hank pointed out that Petty's unknown enemies could hardly be expected to come up from New York to murder him in Jeff Graham's shop. The opportunity for this crime depended, Hank was sure, on the possession of the key—unless Emma had forgotten to lock the door again. He'd have to ask her about that. And he wondered when Jeff had left the hospital. Hank hoped that Jeff had been well on his way to wherever he was going at the probable time of the killing but he was curious to find out. It was a little strange that two antique dealers and a valuable secretary should be involved in a murder and that one of the dealers should be subsequently killed. But Jeff had found the secretary, so his wire said. And someone had tried to kill Jeff. There might be more to this desk business than any one of them had thought. There had been, Hank realized, a certain deception practiced in its purchase but the vision of the Natick lady, brandishing knife and pistol and destroying the commercializers of her treasure, seemed slightly fantastic. Furthermore, she would go for Emma first; and Emma, unless one accepted the fact that the blackjack had been planted, had been left unmolested. Perhaps, though, the old lady deserved at least a look.

Oscar was wanting to know what kind of woman Mrs. Graham was.

Hank pointed out, not without a certain reluctance, that Oscar had seen her on the night of Hank's glorious homecoming.

Oscar said, "Oh indeed."

Hank buttoned his pajamas; he had been punctuating his sentences with the removal of his various articles of clothing. He climbed into bed and sat, hugging his knees. Well, what kind of a person was Mrs. Graham? She was good looking, in a dark, languid sort of way; but, until the night of his carouse, he had always accepted her at Emma's valuation, which was pretty low but hardly menacing. Emma didn't like her because she made Jeff unhappy but the point of view might be biased. From what he knew of Jeff, Hank thought that it was highly probable that he made Mrs. Graham unhappy too. Jeff was decidedly not a homebody. How come, Hank wondered, Jeff had married her in the first place? He'd have to ask Emma about that too. There were a lot of things he wanted to ask Emma. Had Jeff, for example, given her any hint as to the identity of the person who shot at him? There was so much that he might have told her at the hospital and she had never breathed a word of it, the little wretch. Hank had half a mind to wake her up and ask her questions but he didn't. He fixed Oscar with an absent stare and tried to remember what Mrs. Graham had said to him at the Royal Palms.

Oscar looked at his watch and said that it was two o'clock and that they better get some sleep.

In four hours, thought Hank, Jeff would get off the train and be met by Donovan. Emma had wanted to meet him. Heaving a deep sigh, Hank instructed Oscar to let Miss Marsh sleep but to see that he, Hank, was at the Back Bay station at six o'clock. Perhaps, Hank thought, doing that would square him a little with Emma. He pulled the covers into a comfortable wad and was asleep before Oscar turned out the light.

Chapter
13

WHEN EMMA AWOKE, the sun was shining on the polished top of a six-legged lowboy. Emma decided that it was one of the nicest lowboys she had ever seen. The trumpet turned legs were small and the turnip feet, although worn, showed no signs of cutting or mending. She wondered how much they would have to pay for it. It was just the kind of thing they could sell Mr. Norwitch. Emma sat up in bed and took in the delicate four-poster, carved and fluted; the highboy that, unless her eyes deceived her, matched the lowboy; the Sheraton washstand, whose bowl and basin were probably Royal Worcester, although Emma wasn't always sure about china; and the pair of Flemish chairs, incredibly carved, their cane thin and brittle but intact.

The periods were badly mixed, Emma thought to herself but at least she knew where she was. Jeff had sold Richard Norwitch the Flemish chairs. It seemed a shame to send the bed to a museum; it was so very comfortable. She looked around for her clothes, wondering whether Oscar's or Hank's modesty accounted for the fact that she was sleeping in her underwear. Her suit had disappeared but there was a dressing gown on a chair beside the bed. Emma pulled it over her shoulders and tweaked the opalescent glass handle of the bellpull that hung by her pillow. In a few moments there was a discreet tap on the door.

"Come in," said Emma.

Oscar entered, looking very businesslike in a striped apron and exuding the combined aromas of linseed oil and brass polish.

"Good morning," he said, drawing a candlestand to the bedside and depositing a smoking cup of coffee. "How are you feeling?"

"All right," said Emma. "What time is it?"

"Mr. Fairbanks told me," Oscar explained, "to say that he met the train. It is nearly eleven o'clock. We felt that you needed to sleep."

That made it, Emma thought, almost all right. Jeff wouldn't think she had turned him in and abandoned him. She smiled reassuringly at Oscar.

"This is elegant coffee. Can I have a bath?"

Oscar relaxed. He had half expected a storm to break about his head. Hank had warned him that Emma might be upset if she overslept.

"Thank you," he said, "we grind it ourselves. The bathroom is across the hall. I'll fill your tub and bring up your suit, which I have succeeded in reshaping somewhat."

"A victory," said Emma.

"Thank you," said Oscar and went out.

When he returned with the suit, he brought more coffee, chops, fried apples and rolls; and Emma wondered why Hank ever ate out. As she was finishing the last of the three chops, she heard the telephone ringing below stairs. Oscar appeared directly with the message that Hank was waiting for her at the shop. Emma finished her coffee reluctantly. The Norwitch house was a very comfortable place. She felt that she would like to stay in the quiet room, filled with the fragile reminders of the past, thinking of nothing and depending on Oscar to provide her with the necessities of life. If Richard Norwitch had stayed there, he might still be alive. Instead he had gone to the shop; first Norwitch and then Petty. She did not want to leave. And the one place she did not want to go was to the shop. She lifted rebellious eyes to Oscar. There was sympathy in his face.

"It's like getting back on a horse after he's thrown you, isn't it, Miss Marsh?"

Emma's backbone stiffened. Of all people, she could not let Oscar think she was weak-kneed; she might have to live with him. She got up.

"It will probably be," she said, "a busy day—what there is left of it. Thank you, Oscar, for everything."

* * * *

Hank and Donovan and a strange policeman were at the shop when she arrived.

"Hi," said Hank, looking at her anxiously.

"Hi," said Donovan, "you look better."

"Hi," said Emma, "I'm swell, thank you."

"Atta girl," said Hank.

"This is Officer McKinnon," Donovan put in. "You can keep shop but there is going to be a little supervision. There'll be another man on at night. It may be a case of after the horse is stolen but Jeff says he does not have the missing key."

"I knew that," said Emma absentmindedly.

There was a little pause. Emma took off her hat and gloves and sat down calmly in her own desk chair.

"Tell me," she said, "about Jeff."

"Jeff," Donovan answered her, "is a fool."

Emma bristled but Hank laughed. "Jerry's just mad," he explained, "because Jeff told him everything and he didn't have a chance to third-degree him. Jeff wouldn't even wait for his lawyer to get there before he talked. Jerry's so sore he won't charge him with the murder; he's just holding him for investigation. But Jeff arrested the easiest of anyone I ever saw."

"You'd think," said Donovan plaintively, "that he wanted to go to jail!"

"I think," said Hank, "that he does."

"You're nuts," said Donovan wearily.

"Boys, boys," Emma interrupted soothingly, "draw lots and one of you tell me what Jeff says. And lock the door," she said to McKinnon, "I'm in no condition to talk softly to customers or reporters."

"All right." Donovan settled himself and undid the offending button of his tunic. "You needn't have been so worried for fear we'd find out something about Jeff. Apparently he was just waiting till he got hold of this desk before he gave himself up."

"Uh-huh," said Emma.

"In the first place," Donovan went on, "he admits he was in here the night of Norwitch's murder; he says he came in the unbolted corner door—"

"But it was bolted." Emma was positive. "Hank bolted it."

"I don't suppose," Donovan's tone was sarcastic, "that you could have unbolted it, either for Jeff or just out of dumbness?"

"I didn't," said Emma. "Go on."

Donovan took a deep breath. "But he claims he wasn't in here until about eleven-twenty—"

"Eleven-twenty," Emma broke in, "that's too late. I mean," she looked at Hank, "I thought you'd decided that Norwitch was killed earlier, before Petty came."

"He didn't have to be." Donovan refused to admit that the time of Jeff's visit would exonerate him. "Maybe Norwitch was later than we thought or maybe he just didn't let Petty in as, I believe, you suggested; then he could let Jeff in at eleven-twenty."

"That's not," Hank put in, "the way Jeff tells it."

"Then let me tell it without you butting in. Jeff says," Donovan went on, "that he walked in, turned on the light and bolted the door. He was headed for the washroom and says he almost stepped on the body. He was drunk and he got scared and tried to call Sullivan. Then he took a drink and then he decided to go find Sullivan. He says he didn't touch

Norwitch, so he wasn't the one who pulled the body back out of sight, but he took the wrong hat. He locked the door and went around the corner where he'd parked his car. Then somebody took this shot at him, the shot Blanchard thought he heard, and he says all he can think of is to get to the hospital. He says he was scared it was some of the boys from the game—it seems a pretty profitable royal straight flush was the reason he was late—so he gets the idea he has to hide and bribes the orderly to fix him up."

"That last," said Hank, "is the part of the story I don't believe."

"It's just what he told me," Emma said hotly. "Except," she added, "he didn't tell me who shot at him or about the corner door."

"Never mind," said Donovan, "I'm tellin' you what he says. Do I go on?"

"Go on," said Emma.

"O.K. He's shot and he's drunk; the docs put him to sleep; and the next day, when he gets the news, here's the story all over the papers: he's wanted and the secretary's gone. He thinks that if he gives himself up he'll never get the secretary back and three thousand dollars is more money than he's seen in some years. He admits he's scared, on account he was there—here, I mean—and he knows about the notes; so he gets to you, after he's seen Sullivan and made a signed statement, and arranges to get out of town."

"So that was what he wanted Sullivan for," said Emma.

"Partly," added Hank; "he made a will too."

"A will?" queried Emma. "But he was getting well, he wasn't going to die."

"That's just the point," Hank almost shouted.

"I tell you you're crazy," Donovan shouted back. "If he thought he was going to die, he knew damn well it would be on the hot-squat."

"Why don't you charge him with the murders then?"

"Murders?" asked Emma excitedly. "Why, he was out of town when Petty was shot."

"No," said Donovan, lowering his voice. "He says himself that he wasn't. He came to the shop right after you left. Your leaving the door unbolted for him and saying nothing to me was certainly a help."

Emma returned Donovan's gaze squarely and said nothing.

"That must have been around six. He got the money and had a drink. Unfortunately, after you got through nursing that bottle, there weren't any other fingerprints on it. At six-thirty he took a taxi to the South Station—that's been checked—but he didn't leave until the eight o'clock train for Providence pulled out. He says he got a sandwich and read a magazine, but he could have come back on the subway."

"But," Emma wanted to know, "if he bolted the door and didn't have the key, how did he get in?"

"How," asked Donovan grimly, "did he get in the shop without a key the night Norwitch was killed if, as you say, the door was bolted? There's nothing to prove, except his word, that he didn't have the key all along and throw it away afterwards. I'm not arguing with you; I'm just tellin' you what Jeff says. You can see for yourself that his tale of sitting in the station for an hour, while Petty was getting killed, ain't going to do him no good."

"Jeff would have no possible reason for murdering Petty."

"How do you know? Maybe Petty knew more than he was telling about what happened the night Norwitch was killed. He wouldn't be the first one to hold out on us."

"It occurs to me," said Emma mildly, "that that's about the second crack you've taken at me."

"Pay no attention," Hank put in, "he's just nervous and upset."

"I ask you," Donovan addressed himself to Emma, "a guy— forget it's Jeff for a minute—tells you he was around while two murders was committed, has no alibis, in fact does everything but confess the killings; and this dope here," he was referring to Hank, "asks me to believe that it's just because he wants to go to jail, because he's afraid he'll be shot if he isn't in some safe place."

Emma turned a surprised gaze on Hank. "Why—" she began.

"Sure it's crazy," Donovan interrupted her. "And look at this."

He held out to Emma a crumpled bit of paper. Roughly, but unmistakably, sketched thereon was a swell-front tambour secretary; below it was written, "R. V. Scott, Old Lyme, Connecticut."

"That," said Donovan, "was found in Petty's pocket. It was at R. V. Scott's that Jeff found his secretary. How," Donovan stressed the words, "did he know exactly where to look for it?"

Emma looked at the sketch. "Maybe he talked to Petty on the phone; he talked to me. How does he account for it?"

"He says that he got hold of a pal of this Dunn, who told him that Dunn had been in Connecticut; Jeff says this Scott is the only collector in the state with enough money to buy the thing; so he beats it down there, stopping off in Providence to talk to another feller who once inquired for a swellfront what-do-you-call-it."

Emma stopped her study of the sketch. "He's probably right. If Scott wanted a secretary like this, he very likely told Petty to look for one on this trip and drew him a picture of it. This isn't a picture of our secretary; it's any swell-front one. Ours had a broad strip of inlay where the doors pulled together that matched the inlay on the corners. It makes quite a striking effect and would be the thing one would mark that particular desk by. Here the inlay is only indicated on the legs and on the top. And I remember the gent in Providence. We were going to try him next if Norwitch didn't buy. Dunn would sell in Connecticut because it's farther away."

"I don't believe it," said Donovan flatly. "A third-rate hanger-on like Dunn wouldn't know the one man who, you say yourself, would buy a thing like that. Petty got him to steal the secretary and told him where to sell it. That's what Jeff found out from this pal of Dunn's; so he calls Petty to the shop, accuses him and kills him in the quarrel. And I'm going to prove it."

"Jeff," Hank put in, "ought to see a psychiatrist; he's getting so that he can't have an argument with anyone without killing him."

"Bein' smart, eh?" Donovan was a little nettled. "Well, let me tell you that's not so dumb. Let him be bats; let him plead insanity; but for God's sake don't let him sit around and tell me he was here, there and everywhere, whenever there was any killing, and expect me to hunt for some other guy to pin it on."

"Go on," said Hank, who was apparently enjoying himself, "charge him and I'll arrange for his defense."

"Frankly," said Emma, "from your point of view, I don't see why you don't."

"Yah." Donovan got up and reset his buttons. "Go on and tell her and, if she listens to you, she can go with me and have her head examined. I'm going back to see Jeff and to see what they found in Petty's room."

He paused by the door for one more protest. "Where," he asked sarcastically, "do you put Petty in this picture of yours?"

"It's an old master," Hank explained. "You clean off the top layer and there's your Pieter van der Vogel plain as day."

"Why don't you go to bed to have nightmares?" asked Donovan as he slammed the door.

"What on earth are you two bickering about?" Emma wanted to know.

Hank sat down in Jeff's chair, braced his feet in the customary way and lit a cigarette. It seemed to Emma that he should be badly in need of sleep but, instead, his eyes sparkled with unusual animation.

"Listen, duckie," he said. "I met the train this morning and I saw Jeff get off and I have an idea that Donovan thinks is crazy but it's enough to make him lay off Jeff and postpone the inquest until I see if I can back myself up. Now who, I want to know, would want to kill Jeff?"

"Aside from me, on most days, that is," Emma began, "the New

England countryside is filled with people from whom he has painlessly extracted valuables at, well—say a fraction of their value, and who would be very glad to wring his neck."

"That reminds me of something," Hank interrupted, "but for the moment we'll skip it. Be serious. I really mean, do you know of anyone who dislikes Jeff enough to kill him?"

"I can't," said Emma, "fancy anyone wanting to kill anybody but apparently I underestimate a lot of people. No, seriously, I don't. There's Blanchard, who hates him like a relative, but I don't think he'd kill him. He has a lot of tough friends, bookies and such, but I have only a bowing acquaintance with them and I wouldn't know their motives."

"It's a possibility," said Hank absently, "but Donovan has checked all the boys in the game that night and they all alibi each other; they even admit Jeff didn't leave the game until after eleven. No, it's something else. Look, you tell me everything you know about Jeff; don't try to tell it in the light of picking out a potential murderer, just tell me what you know about him."

"Good lord," said Emma, "don't you want any lunch?"

"No," said Hank, "and, strangely enough, I don't want a drink. It's funny, isn't it? We could hardly wait for them to get Uncle out of here before we had our noses in a bottle. We must be growing up."

"Growing up?" repeated Emma bitterly. "I'm a hundred and four right now but I never could get my nose in a bottle."

"All right, Grandma, get on with your reminiscences."

"Well, Jeff was born of poor Scottish weavers who came to Lowell in eighteen something; he was born there, but barely."

"Less wit, please," said Hank severely.

Emma looked hurt but went on: "I guess he went to school some but his chief crony, aside from the boys at the pool hall, seems to have been a duck who made ship models. Jeff is clever with his hands and used to help him. I think he got his start in the antique business from listening to the men who brought models in to be repaired and maybe that was why he was in the Navy during the war. At least I have the impression he was in the Navy; I've heard him say some very bitter things about cockroaches."

"Your assumptions," said Hank, "are farfetched and probably valueless. Stick to the facts."

Emma sighed and cast back in her memory for the bits of facts that came bobbing to the surface of Jeff's conversation from time to time.

"He was a pretty good wrestler," she went on, "and he ran away with a carnival once. You know: taking on the village lads. Five dollars for them if they threw him. And then he graduated to running one of those wheels that give you a woolly white dog or a nice cotton Indian blanket if you hit the lucky number, only you never do. Jeff explained it to me, they do it with bits of matches."

"I thought it was mirrors," put in Hank, "but never mind. Go on."

"And sometime or other," Emma continued patiently, "he went to business school, I can't imagine what for. And one summer he worked on a farm in Connecticut and sort of got back into the antique business. A runner came around and offered the woman on the farm ten dollars for an old chest. Jeff got a hunch, persuaded her not to sell it and then bought it for twenty-five. It turned out to be a Hadley chest and he sold it for five hundred to a fellow who sold it for a thousand. That made Jeff so mad he decided to find out about old furniture."

"It must be the runner who's after him," said Hank.

"Oh, and listen to this. A funny thing happened that summer. There were some Bohemians who had the next farm to the one where Jeff worked. They had a lot of kids and Jeff used to go to dances with them Saturday nights. There was one of the girls that he liked a lot and she liked him; but she was supposed to marry a cousin who had some money, or the next farm, or something and when her family found out about Jeff, they locked her up. Apparently Jeff didn't look like a good matrimonial bet. But the night before she was to be married, while the family were good and drunk celebrating, she got word to Jeff and he got her out of a window and they ran off."

"Well," said Hank impatiently, "what happened then? I hope he married the girl."

"I think he did," said Emma seriously. "And I think he's been sorry ever since. He wouldn't ever tell me the girl's name and I've never been clubby enough with Mrs. Graham to ask her about it but I suppose there are ways of finding out. Her name's Martha, Mrs. Graham's. It could be Bohemian, I suppose, and the rest of it would be on a marriage register somewhere."

"Mmmm," said Hank without much enthusiasm. "It's a little late for the good family to start shooting, isn't it? After all, he married her."

"Maybe it's the deprived cousin," Emma helped out.

"Not if he's seen our Martha lately. She's forgotten that hay grows or that milk comes from cows. She'd be no use on a farm." Hank drummed on Jeff's desk with his fingers and then looked at them with disgust. "My aunt, don't you ever clean around here ?"

"My daily dusting," said Emma sadly, "has been lately interrupted, through no fault of my own."

"This isn't dust," said Hank bluntly, "it's dirt, grit: loam, as we farmers would say or, in city parlance, dried mud."

"Keep your feet off the desk," said Emma, "and there won't be any mud there." .

"My feet," Hank said with dignity, "haven't been on the desk."

He peered closely at the green blotter. "But, by gum, some feet have. Look here."

Together they studied the blotter. Beneath the small flecks of compressed dirt, there were groups of little indentations, five in a group.

"Gimme your shoe," said Hank.

Emma undid the strap of her not too sturdy walking shoes and together they examined the heel. Three nails and a brass screw formed the pattern there, but the heel was approximately the same size as the pattern on the blotter.

Hank gazed inquiringly up at the shelf of books and checked Emma, who was about to climb onto the desk.

"Gently, my friend." He removed the blotter and placed it carefully on Emma's desk. "Now, pay no attention to the mahogany; go right ahead."

Emma climbed up, narrowly missing the row of ship models which lined the partition at the end of the desk. On top of the books in front of her was a roll of adhesive tape.

"Oh," said Emma, flatly, holding out the roll for Hank to see. "That's what I did with it."

"All right." Hank took the tape from her and put it on the desk. "Now that you know where that is, see if you can see anything else."

"Not the tape, silly, the paper cutter."

"Good grief, what are you talking about?"

"The paper cutter," said Emma patiently. "I remember now. I was cutting the adhesive tape with it when Mrs. Graham came in wanting some money and I got down and left them both up there."

"This may be very important," said Hank seriously. "Are you sure?"

"Of course I'm sure. Jeff decided to put the ship models up here." She pointed to the partition. "Two were new but he got them up before I had a chance to mark them; so I had to get up here to do it. I put tape on these two; you can look up the numbers in the stock book for the date. Damnation. Look."

She stopped abruptly, pointing to one of the models, a barque, delicate and well-made.

Hank looked. The end of one of the yards on the mizzenmast was broken off and hung down, supported by the rigging.

"That was a perfect model and a good one," said Emma sadly. "I suppose I did that climbing up here."

"You didn't," said Hank. "I was watching you and you didn't touch it; but someone has been up there who didn't realize or who couldn't see how far those spars stuck out. Come down here."

Emma came, still bemoaning the breakage, but Hank was thinking of other things.

From the stock book it was determined that the models which Emma had been marking had been purchased on March ninth, a week and three days before the murder—the same general amount of time that Emma had declared the paper cutter to have been missing.

Hank next wanted to know on what day the shop had last been cleaned.

Mary, the charwoman, came on Wednesdays; and, with recourse to the calendar, Emma decided that her last visit had been on Wednesday, the seventeenth, the day before Norwitch's murder.

"If she came yesterday," Emma remarked, "she couldn't get in. I was in jail."

"Thank God for that," said Hank earnestly. "I shudder to think of the time this blotter has been here, at the mercy of anyone with a taste for cleaning up. That dirt is going down to the laboratory and those heel prints are going to be traced."

"What are you going to do?" Emma was interested. "Carpet the place with blotting paper and compare tracks?"

"I have a place to start," Hank said grimly. "If you recall, you said that Mrs. Graham came in while you were putting on the price tags. That makes her about the only other person on earth who would know that the paper cutter was on top of those books and don't forget that you told her about Jeff's appointment with Uncle."

Emma began to hedge. "I know she came in because I made her wait while I finished putting the price on the tags, but I don't know that she saw the paper cutter. I couldn't swear to it—not if it meant hanging her."

"People don't hang in the Commonwealth of Massachusetts," Hank corrected her. "They fry. And why would anyone climb up on the desk except to get a knife that she knew was on top of those books?"

Thinking hard, Emma looked around the tiny office. "She, or he, might get up there to hide," she suggested. "If someone was here when I came," she went on somewhat aghast at the thought, "they would hear me coming and hide somewhere. They couldn't hide in the office without getting up there because you can see both of the chairs from the door. And perhaps," Emma was trying hard to untie the knot she seemed to have fastened around Mrs. Graham, "perhaps those are my heel prints after all. I may have had on a different pair of shoes when I was up there."

"You were up there," Hank reminded her, "almost a month ago. The place has been cleaned three times since then."

"That would remove the dirt but not the prints. Maybe Mary made the marks, although," Emma added honestly, "she usually runs on a somewhat broader track."

"Please," said Hank, "don't pick holes in the first good idea I've had. Just be thankful that those aren't Jeff's heel prints."

The telephone rang and Emma picked it up.

"Hello," she said. "No, Donovan's not here. Do you want to talk to Hank?"

While Hank was answering the telephone, Emma started opening the piled-up mail on her desk.

"Hello," said Hank. "Oh hello, Tim. Why will I be disappointed? Oh—oh, you have? It is? Well I'll be switched. Yes, I'll tell him if he comes back."

Emma was waiting impatiently for him to hang up.

"Look at this." She held a sheet of common tablet writing paper under Hank's nose. On it was written in a precise, neat hand: "The Lord is punishing you."

"Who," asked Hank, "you?"

"No, Jeff."

"Where from?"

Emma produced the envelope, which did not match the paper it had enclosed. It was addressed in the same handwriting and postmarked Boston, on the date of the preceding day.

"That's no help," said Hank, continuing to study the message.

"You know," he went on, "I've a notion I've seen this writing before—you don't often see such flourishing L's—but I can't think where."

Emma considered the looping capitals but shook her head.

"Providence certainly moves to strange coincidences," Hank misquoted. "Tim just called to tell Donovan that the laundry mark on the handkerchief that was in Petty's hand has been traced to Jeff; and practically in the same breath you get a note saying that the Lord has taken hold and is going to make things hot for him. That may be just a crank letter that we can overlook temporarily. But how am I going to explain away this handkerchief business?"

Emma chewed at the corner of an unopened envelope. "It was a clean handkerchief, wasn't it?" she ventured. "I haven't seen it around here; so it came in with Jeff. His clothes must have been washed at the hospital and, incidentally, he was lucky to get his own back. He came in here, got his money, had a drink and called a cab. He may have shifted the contents of his pockets around and neglected to put the handkerchief back. After he went, Petty came in, wanted to blow his nose, picked up the thing and got shot. How's that? "

"Of course, Petty did have the flu," said Hank dubiously, "but, just the same, that explanation strikes me as a little weak."

"Check it," said Emma. "I've got a better one. Petty was fussy as a cat about dirt. If he went to the washroom to get a drink, he'd wash the glass and he'd want to wipe it. A clean handkerchief would appeal to him more than our slightly soiled towels."

"Assuming," Hank threw in, "that he did go to the washroom for a drink."

"He'd be the first one in here who didn't, in my years of experience," said Emma.

The telephone interrupted their theorizing. This time the call was for Hank.

"It's a woman," Emma said in a loud whisper as she handed over the set.

"Yes?" said Hank. "Oh, hello. No, I hadn't forgotten."

Wondering why Hank was blushing, Emma went back to her letter opening. There were a few welcome checks; she credited them on the books, her very normal curiosity keeping her conscious of the conversation going on beside her. She heard him say, "Yes, I'll be there at six o'clock," and hang up.

"What," she inquired, looking up from the ledger, "are you up to now?"

"I—er—ah." Hank stopped, cleared his throat and lit a cigarette.

"Why, Hank Fairbanks, what on earth's the matter?" Emma wanted to know. "You're bright red."

Hank put the cigarette in his mouth, took it out and tried his hands in various, apparently uncomfortable, positions.

"Emma," he began, "I don't know what got into me yesterday; I made a date."

"With whom?" Emma was still mystified. "Mrs. Graham? What will the boy friend think?"

"No," said Hank glumly. "You don't understand. Yesterday I thought I was through with you. I was through with women. Then I met Stephana Mathews eating dinner. She seemed sort of sweet and restful and I asked her out to the theater. Honestly, darling . . ."

He broke off, surprised, at Emma's shout of laughter.

"You simply slay me," said that young lady, controlling her mirth. "You're through with women; so the first thing you do is to ask the first one you see to go out with you."

Hank was somewhat annoyed that his penitence should go unnoticed. "You don't understand. I was through with caring for anyone; Stephana happened to be the one I ran into; so I invited her but she was meant to be the beginning of a long line."

"The Rake's Progress," giggled Emma, "picture number one. Go right ahead. Don't mind me."

"Go on, rub it in; I suppose I deserve it," said Hank abjectly. "Only you know I don't feel that way any more."

"You're forgiven." Emma gave him a consoling pat. "But I still think it's pretty funny."

Hank groaned. "It may be a joke to you but here I am with cocktails, dinner and the theater on my hands . . ."

"My," Emma broke in, "you were certainly starting out for a large evening; you never treated me that elegantly."

"Shut up," said Hank crossly. "And here I am with no sleep and a thousand things I want to do. I'll either go to sleep or be so absent-minded she'll think I'm sitting in the next row."

"Can't you call it off?"

"Not now. She took me so by surprise over the phone that all I could do was say yes. And she seemed so pleased when I asked her that I wouldn't have the heart to, anyway. She's sort of alone and pathetic."

"Uh-huh," said Emma. "The lady obviously appeals."

"Sure she does," Hank admitted. "And, if you're not very, very kind to me from now on, I'll take her out again when I'm in full possession of my faculties."

"Don't threaten me, mister," said Emma. "You better run along and get yourself prettied up. I'll tell Donovan about the tracks and the paper cutter."

"And take all the credit for finding them, I suppose." Hank rose reluctantly to his feet. "I hate to leave you; I want to talk to Donovan, and there's your car to get back and I'd really much rather be with you than Stephana."

Emma smiled up at him. "Strangely enough," she said, "I believe you. But don't worry about me. I'll get hold of the car or take a taxi and I've enough work to do here to kill a horse."

"You're sweet," said Hank, "and I adore you."

The policeman coughed warningly from his corner and Hank left hurriedly.

Hank would, Emma hoped, dodge the reporters. The title of "Playboy Detective" did not fit him but it would certainly be applied if he were caught squiring an attractive woman on the night after the murder, when he might reasonably be supposed to be deep in fingerprints and clues. With a sigh for Hank's quixotic notions, Emma went back to work. She was grateful for McKinnon's presence for, in spite of her remarks to the contrary, she had rather counted on Hank's company for the evening. She called M. LeBotien, told him that she would be home later in the evening and asked if he minded very much waiting up for her. His pleasure at hearing her voice and his assurance that he would gladly await her return made Emma feel good. At least there was a little friendliness in the world. She listed checks industriously for a few minutes, preparing for the next day's deposits. As she neared the bottom of the stack of mail, she came upon an envelope addressed to her. She slit it open. (A silver meat skewer, safely blunt as to edge, was now serving as a letter cutter.) The message was the same as in the note to Jeff. The Lord, it seemed, was punishing Emma also. She glanced again at the envelope—it had also been posted in Boston—but the date on it was earlier; it was postmarked Wednesday, the day of her involuntary retirement. Emma considered that fact for a moment. The punishment, then, did not refer to her being jailed, for the letter had been written before that incident occurred. It was odd, though, that both she and Jeff should be warned of the Almighty's wrath so near to the time when the bars clanged on them. Who knew so much? Involuntarily, Emma cast a glance around the shop but the sight of the solid blue figure reassured her. She clipped the two letters together and put them in the drawer of her desk. A penciled note in Hank's writing caught her eye. She was to send Mrs. Graham a check. The old leech, thought Emma, as she viciously dug pen into paper, complying with the request. Did she know, Emma wondered, that Jeff was in jail? It occurred to Emma that the cause of the dissension between Hank and Jerry had not been explained. It obviously had something to do with Jeff and the importance that Hank attached to the shot taken at him. Petty had been shot, too, but Mr. Norwitch had been stabbed. Poor Petty, Emma thought, no one seemed to be paying much attention to his murder. Hank was going back to the attack on Jeff. Why had all the killings centered around the shop? Apparently no one who came near there was safe. Again Emma looked around.

"Officer," she said suddenly, "would you mind going down cellar, just to look? I seem to be getting the jitters."

McKinnon went down obligingly and came back, peacefully shaking his head.

"All serene," he said.

Emma thanked him, feeling a little silly and answered a couple of letters that seemed to demand immediate attention. One, from the purchaser of the chandelier, was couched in biting terms. A dining room and an important dinner party in Schenectady were being kept waiting.

Emma supposed that the people in Schenectady didn't read the Boston papers and wondered if Donovan would let Jeff wire the chandelier in jail. She wrote a soothing letter, saying that Mr. Graham had been ill, that he was recovering and that the chandelier would be attended to as soon as possible. That, she thought, was approximately true.

A rap on the door caused her to look up. There was Donovan, trailing a cloud of reporters. Emma opened the door apprehensively but Donovan banked the cloud with a gesture and came in alone.

In answer to his inquiry, Emma explained about Hank's date.

"Serve him right," Donovan muttered, "if I never showed him this."

Pulling a piece of paper from his pocket, he slumped wearily into an office chair, studying the paper. Finally he handed it to Emma. "Mean anything to you?" he asked.

There was a long list of typewritten notations:

Feb. 3, Mrs. Graham and Mr. Remington seen leaving the hotel New Yorker.
Feb. 3, Mrs. Graham and Mr. Remington at the Versailles...took a taxi. Lost track.
Feb. 4, Mrs. Graham and Mr. Remington lunched at the New Yorker.
Feb. 4, Mr. and Mrs. Remington checked out of hotel New Yorker.

The document was signed R. N. Petty and attested a true copy before a notary.

"For heaven's sake," said Emma and added, "Who is Mr. Remington?"

"I thought you might know; the current boy friend is named Swartz."

"I'm sure," Emma pondered, "that Swartz was the one even before February. Perhaps Remington is just their *nom de nuit*. I'd prefer it to Swartz myself."

"*Nom de nuit*," Donovan repeated slowly. "I get it. I suppose it was too much to hope for, that this would be the one murder without a sex angle. How well does Mrs. Graham know Petty?"

"I didn't think that she knew him at all. She came in while Petty was here, the evening before Mr. Norwitch was killed, and didn't speak to him. And I didn't think Petty knew her from the way he acted. Do you think he was following her then?"

"I don't think; Hank is supposed to do the brainwork for this team. But I know that this paper," Donovan flicked it with his finger, "is a real, grass-green motive why somebody would want to kill Petty. I wonder what Jeff's going to say when he sees it."

"Oh," said Emma, "do you have to show it to him? Tonight, I mean?"

"And why not?"

"Isn't it almost enough for one day, to be put in jail and practically accused of murder, without being told that your wife is parking around in hotels with strange men? And besides, consider what a dandy ace-in-the-hole this will be against Mrs. Graham. She'd probably do anything for you rather than have you show this to Jeff."

"You just thought that up," Donovan accused her, "to keep me from telling Jeff but you may be right. I'll consult the boy detective, if he ever gets his mind back on his work."

"That reminds me," said Emma.

Donovan raised an eyebrow.

"Of several little items," Emma continued blandly, "on which Hank will want your best opinion."

She began with the identification of the laundry mark on the handkerchief, stressing the harmless way in which the handkerchief might have come into Petty's possession. Donovan was noncommittal. Then Emma produced the letters, calculating that they would distract Donovan from the laundry mark. They puzzled over them together. The capital L's, which had been familiar to Hank, meant nothing to Donovan. He was inclined to dismiss the notes as the work of a crank. He was all attention, however, over the location of the hiding place of the paper cutter, the heel prints and Mrs. Graham's further implication.

"It begins to look," he said jubilantly, "as though the kid might be right."

"Right about what?" asked Emma. "I still don't know what it is that Hank thinks he has up his sleeve."

"Didn't he tell you? Well, I'd be ashamed to tell it too if I had thought it up. He just claims that Jeff didn't kill old Norwitch because Jeff is scared someone is trying to kill him. I can't see that that's any proof. But this New York business and Mrs. Graham's being here when you had the paper cutter, besides knowing about the appointment, certainly makes me want to say a few words to that lady."

"Petty," Emma mused, "knew what Mrs. Graham was up to. Petty certainly knew Norwitch—you don't suppose that they did get together the night Norwitch was murdered, do you? Petty testified that his appointment with Norwitch was for ten-thirty and that Norwitch didn't show up but maybe he saw him earlier. What I mean is this, if you could prove that Petty talked to Norwitch, you might suppose that he told him about Mrs. Graham; then there would be a motive for murdering them both."

"No soap," said Donovan glumly. "We checked Petty's movements pretty well when we thought maybe he killed Norwitch. He could have done it; so he could have talked to him; but we couldn't get any proof.

He said Norwitch made his appointment by phone."

"Petty could have told him then."

"Imagine him doing such a thing."

"A woman would," Emma persisted. "She'd start right in, 'Guess what I saw your friend Graham's wife doing in New York?' and blab the whole story. But I guess men aren't like that."

"Not," said Donovan, "if they're normal and expect to inherit a quarter of a million from the guy they're talking to."

"All right," said Emma. "You figure it out."

"I'm trying to. Gimme an envelope."

While Emma held the envelope, Donovan carefully tapped the dirt from the blotter into it. He folded the blotter, carefully avoiding the tracks, put it in his pocket and picked up his cap.

"If you don't mind," he said, "there's going to be an officer over at your house tonight. You can entertain each other making prints of your shoe heels. You don't mind doing that, either, do you? Even if it turns out that you made these marks, I won't arrest you again. Trying to trace these prints is going to be a dandy job and I've got to begin somewheres."

"I'll do anything to help," said Emma, smiling but serious. "And I'm very glad for the watchdog. M. LeBotien is a darling but he's not exactly a pillar of strength. And I'm getting so I wouldn't feel safe anywhere but in an armored car. Where, by the way, is my roadster?"

Donovan said that he'd send it around in the morning, unless she needed it that night, and offered to take her home. Emma accepted, resigning herself to dining off what M. LeBotien's supply of groceries could provide. As she straightened up her desk for the night, Donovan recalled the matchbox that had been moved and told her that no fingerprints, other than her own, Jeff's and Hank's, had been found on it. Emma had forgotten the whole thing entirely, which was not remarkable, under the circumstances. "But," she went on, "if I said it had been moved, why it had been. Tim may think that my possessions are in a permanent state of uproar but about keeping things handy, I'm orderly to the point of old-maidishness. The ash tray is there," she said, pointing, "the matches are always back there and the order book and pencil are here. I can always tell if Jeff has been fussing around, though he's pretty good about putting things back."

"I believed you," said Donovan, "I had the things fingerprinted, didn't I?"

"Whoever did it must have worn mittens." Emma got her hat from the top of the filing cabinet (she had been strangely reluctant to hang it in the washroom), bolted and set the lock on the doors and said a pleasant goodnight to McKinnon.

Chapter

14

THE NEXT DAY was a nice enough day as far as weather was concerned but it was a great disappointment to Emma. She got to work early; the roadster, nicely washed, had been waiting for her when she set out but that was the last indication she had that Donovan remembered her existence. Business was dull during the morning. After eleven o'clock, at which time it seemed reasonable to expect that Hank might have recovered from his sleeplessness, Emma kept one ear cocked for the telephone. It rang, several times, but none of the calls were from Hank. Life, Emma felt, was passing her by. She gleaned what crumbs of information she could from the papers but, aside from wild speculation as to the result of the taking into custody of Jeff, the gleanings were meager. Even the reporters neglected her, only one of them feeling that she was of sufficient importance to merit an interview. Emma had half a mind to reward him with the exclusive story of Hank's new theory or her own experiences in jail but something warned her that, if she did, she would never see Hank again.

McKinnon was no help to her, either. He sat solidly in a corner from which he could watch both doors and so abruptly repulsed Emma's hint that he might like to retire to the basement for a smoke that she did not dare offer him the customary drink. Emma laid a side bet with herself that he came from the north of Ireland and was a Presbyterian.

Mrs. Graham created a little diversion by calling up to ask if she could be sent another check, instead of stalking in as usual and demanding one. She did not even berate Emma for withholding the information that Jeff was being held by the police. Emma wondered if words from Donovan were responsible for the unusual meekness and was glad that she did not have to talk to her at closer range. She found herself already thinking of Mrs. Graham as the murderess and felt that it would be difficult to be casual with her. It occurred to her that people might have had the same feeling about her and the realization brought some understanding of Hank's reactions. After all, there was nothing more tangible against Mrs. Graham than there had been against her.

As though to give body to her thoughts, a little woman crept cautiously into the shop, approached Emma as though she wore a scarlet fever sign and released an audible sigh of relief when she caught sight of McKinnon's impassive bulk. She wanted to replace a broken prism on a girandole and had been assured by her son that this was the place to do it. Otherwise, thought Emma, as she rummaged around to find a prism that matched, she wouldn't have come near. The purchase being concluded, the old lady hurried out. Emma didn't know that she blamed her. One murder might be good advertising but two murders came near to being a bad habit. Perhaps they'd better move the shop. Mrs. Arbuthnot was looking for another apartment. She had been out playing bridge on the night that Petty was shot but she said that she was tired of being questioned by the police.

Emma lunched disconsolately on a sandwich and a cup of coffee at the Greek's, conscious of the furtive looks cast in her direction. She realized that up to now she had made her public appearances in the company of Hank or Donovan and, without the bulwark of their casual indifference, she felt naked, and strangely vulnerable.

"This has got to stop," she admonished herself finally and glared ferociously at the next person to glance her way. She practiced glares as she finished her coffee and went back to the shop refreshed in body and spirit.

The afternoon wore on with trying slowness; a thorough dusting, which was badly needed, served only to pass an hour. Emma was finally reduced to sorting a drawer full of escutcheons and bails. Jeff, she thought, would have a heart attack if he could see her. She herself was surprised at her own temerity; the majestic disorder of years openly defied her orderliness.

About five o'clock a telephone call came for Hank. Emma was almost sure that it was from Stephana but whoever it was hung up as soon as Emma gave the information that Hank was not there. Emma held quite a conversation with Stephana, to herself of course, lest McKinnon think she was demented. Stephana needn't, Emma assured her, be afraid to come right out in the open if she wanted Hank. He was a free agent as far as Emma was concerned. If he preferred Stephana, that was O.K. Absolutely O.K., she repeated, for emphasis. Of course that didn't mean (Emma decided that she might as well have the thing out) that she wasn't very, very fond of Hank and that she wouldn't be considerably upset should he decide that he preferred Stephana to her. Yes, Emma conceded honestly, she wouldn't like that at all. And furthermore she, Emma, did not intend to stand meekly by while Hank changed his mind; she was a free agent too, by gum, and she intended to put up quite a fight for Hank. Oh yes, Stephana could have him, if she could get him; but, if she did, it would be over her dead body. Emma was rather surprised at the turn the conversation had taken; she hadn't, she realized, known that she felt quite so strongly on the subject of Hank. Loneliness must be getting her; the silent shop was almost as bad as the jail. She went back to sorting brasses.

At five-thirty Hank and the expressmen with the secretary arrived simultaneously. Emma forgot that she was especially anxious to see Hank and set him and McKinnon to clearing a place on the front aisle for the secretary.

"Everybody," she told them, "has seen its pictures in the papers; so they might as well see it in the flesh. Maybe the advertising will sell it. I can't see why Jeff didn't make a deal with Scott, since he wanted one like it."

"Probably," Hank reminded her, "Mr. Scott didn't want to pay for it twice. He's out what he paid Dunn, unless the police can get his money back."

"Mm-m," said Emma who was running her hands over the secretary, feeling for damages, like a mother cat licking a strayed kitten. She opened the drawers and rolled the tambour doors experimentally. Except for a fresh scratch on one end and a dented leg, the secretary had not suffered in its travels. Emma sighed with relief and regarded it fondly.

Hank slumped down wearily in the wing chair and shut his eyes.

"My sacred aunt," he said, "how tired I am."

"You poor thing," said Emma mechanically. "Now all we have to do is to sell it. You're not going to sue us for that thousand, are you?"

"No," said Hank without opening his eyes, "I'll just take the old desk."

"You'll do no such thing; the secretary is mine and I can prove it."

Hank opened his eyes. "There," he said plaintively, "this just goes to show that, if I could get five minutes rest, I could solve this case. Bring me the receipt you got from the woman in Natick."

As soon as she saw the swooping L's of the signature, Emma knew what Hank meant. The hand that had signed the receipt had written the letters to Emma and Jeff. Hank took one look and waved the paper away.

"Donovan has the letters," he said, "and can check it but that's the baby. See how easy it is for me? I'll have this thing in the bag if I can only keep a chair under me long enough. My minions or, modesty compels me to admit, Donovan's minions, will put the peek on this self-appointed right hand of God tomorrow. Maybe she can't provide an alibi for the night of January sixteenth."

"You're goofy. Success has unbalanced your mind. How could she know that Norwitch was going to buy the secretary and what did she think Petty had to do with it?"

"It's a Messiah complex, see Krafft-Ebing, page 209; she's out to rid the world of antique dealers and maybe that's a good idea; maybe we ought to let her go ahead."

"I'm all for it," said Emma, "up to a point. But the point is me and how do I know when she'll get there?"

"That's right." Hank frowned intently. "To save you, we have to save the rest of the deceivers of old ladies. Forward, Minions! No mercy! And don't spare the horses. Ask me something else."

"All right, smarty pants, who called you up half an hour ago?"

Hank groaned. "That's too, too easy. She called me this morning; she called me right after lunch. Oscar is having a couple of kittens, he's so afraid I've been indiscreet. What," Hank smiled complacently, "do women see in me?"

"It must be your looks," said Emma, dripping irony, "it couldn't be your money."

"Tut, tut, Baby mustn't get jealous. You'd think," Hank went on plaintively, "hell-bent as she was to get me to take her out, that she'd have been ready on time. She kept me waiting in a mangy little front hall, with no place to sit down, for nearly half an hour. I learned the names of all the inhabitants off the buzzers and checked up on their mail—ten minutes more and I'd have been reading it. Mr. Chew Lee lives there and he had three letters, all from Japan. I think he's a spy. Miss Mary Sark and James S. Sunderland co-inhabit. James S. had a letter from a lawyer in Clinton, Iowa. I think his wife is after him. Stephana didn't have any mail. H. H. Henderson had three bills. Miss Adelaide Olsen had a letter from Papa in St. Paul. It felt as though there were a check inside. I bet Adelaide takes all the girls at the school of expression out to Schrafft's. The Quickie Cleaner sent a batch of circulars to all concerned. Mrs. A. S. Matoušek and J. O. Conroy must have moved; letters but no name plates."

"Go on," said Emma. "You're inventing; you couldn't possibly remember all that."

"Don't be silly," said Hank. "I haven't made up a thing. And let me tell you, young woman, if you could do a job of remembering like that you'd be a lot more use to me than you are now."

"How," asked Emma, feeling that a change of subject was indicated, "did Stephana look?"

Hank closed his eyes and blew a kiss dreamily into space. "Divine," he murmured. "Well worth the wait. Shoulders like alabaster—"

"You make me sick," said Emma, stalking into the office.

"I'm a sick man," said Hank. "How about a drink?"

"Sh-h," said Emma, pointing to McKinnon.

"Who, him?" asked Hank. "Don't make me laugh. Hey, Mac," he called, "want a drink?"

McKinnon rose quickly. "Sir," he said, "I'm that thirsty I've had to tie my tongue in knots to keep it in my mouth. But I didn't know how the young lady—"

"There seems," Emma cut in as she went to the washroom for the glasses, "to have been a misunderstanding. It will be corrected."

"I'm not only so tired I'm silly," Hank began, after McKinnon's tongue had been shrunk to its normal size, "I'm in bad. In fact, I'm back in the role of suspect."

"Oh, Hank—you're not," said Emma anxiously.

"Oh yes I am," Hank went on firmly. "You see, last night, as I sat in the theater, thinking, I remembered what Mrs. Graham had said to me. I was kidding her about the boy friend and she shushed me and said she was trying to keep him under cover until she 'got rid of' Jeff. What would that mean to you?"

"That she was going to divorce him," Emma answered promptly.

"Maybe," Hank granted, "but, if she knew about that paper in Petty's room, she'd realize that there were certain difficulties in the way of a divorce."

"Then why didn't she try to get the paper?"

"She did, or at least Donovan thinks she did. She went to Petty's hotel twice the day Petty was killed. The day clerk said that someone answering her description called Petty twice on the house phone."

"Does she admit it?" Emma wanted to know.

"She does not. But, anyhow, Donovan and I decided to pay her a surprise visit and accuse her of it. And what do you think the witch does?"

Emma couldn't imagine.

"She turns on me," Hank's tone was aggrieved, "and says that I tried to call Petty while I was at the Royal Palms. She claims that she went with me because I couldn't find the telephone booth and that she heard me ask for Petty. The operator couldn't get him because he was getting cold by then. She says I told the hotel operator that he'd better start worrying about Petty's bill because he wasn't coming back. Get it? How did I know he wasn't coming back unless I knew he was dead or, more likely, had killed him? And the funny part of it is, I remember going somewhere during the evening but I can't remember where, or what I did. It was a pay phone and I could have called Hobbs, New Mexico, if

I'd had money enough."

"Some people," Emma said profoundly, "have a mania for telephoning when drunk but I never noticed any symptoms in you. What did Donovan say?"

"He said," Hank repeated wearily, "that I needed a guardian. But he also opined that, in my cute way, I had probably meant that Petty had skipped out. You recall that, at the moment, he was our chief suspect."

"What possessed you to call him anyway?"

"Doubtless just a drunken urge to tell him to go to hell for standing me up and, as a reward for my impulsiveness, I have, quite definitely, to find the murderer in order to clear my own fair name. No pun intended." Hank pulled a footstool toward himself with one toe, heaved his legs upon it and closed his eyes again.

"Oh, come now," said Emma, with the callousness of one who had enjoyed a good night's sleep and an uneventful day, "you surely got more than that out of her."

"Not a thing, not even a drink; she wouldn't even admit that she was planning to divorce Jeff or that she ever went to New York with Swartz; but she let us take prints of the heels of her shoes and I'll get her yet."

"Go on," Emma insisted, "that didn't take you all day; haven't you done anything else?"

Hank groaned. "I should have known better than to come here. I'm going home where I can get some sleep." He did not move, however, and, after a wide yawn, he continued: "I've interviewed cobblers and shoe men to see if there was anything unusual about those five nails. All I found out was that it was a standard re-heeling job; new heels like that usually have the little brass screw in the middle. I checked the lab and the dirt is Grade A, number one, Boston mud; you can get the same thing off Tremont Street any day. And I've talked to Jeff. Oh my, have I talked to Jeff! And every time I suggest that we really haven't much on him and that Sullivan can arrange his bail, he goes right back to the point that he was in the shop the night Uncle was killed and that he could perfectly well have killed Petty. I tell you, he wants to stay in that jail. And while I think of it, he sent you a message."

Emma was all attention.

"If I remember correctly, it was: 'Why the hell doesn't she send me some cigarettes and some clean underwear?' You know," Hank continued reminiscently, "it's the little attentions that count when you're in jail."

Emma couldn't think of anything much to reply to that so she went back to Jeff's desire for seclusion.

"Why," she wanted to know, "doesn't he tell you who's after him and get the thing cleaned up? He can't stay in jail forever."

Hank opened both eyes and looked at Emma. "Jeff," he said slowly, "is just the kind of a chump who would confess to both murders rather than tell that his wife was trying to kill him."

"Oh," said Emma aghast. "Oh, I never thought of that."

"Well, think of it, because that's the situation in a nutshell."

"But why," Emma wanted to know, "would she kill Norwitch? Or have you found out that he knew about Petty's evidence?"

"No," Hank said shortly, "I haven't. I don't think he knew anything about it."

"Then why, in heaven's name—"

Hank cut her off. He took his feet off the footstool and addressed her firmly. "Darling, you're a sweet girl, and I'm no end fond of you, but, in your impulsive, helpful, half-cocked way, you do some strange things. For that reason I'm not going to tell you something. Because, if I did, just as sure as God made little apples, you'd think I was wrong and try to prove it in some outlandish way that would probably land you over there," he pointed to the washroom door, "with a bullet in your neat little carcass. Two men have been killed and a third shot at. Why do you think there's a cop here and a cop over at your apartment?"

"Why," Emma answered meekly, "I thought it was because of the key and because Donovan knew I was scared."

"Well, it's not." Hank was almost sitting up straight in his earnestness. "You were seen talking to Petty the night of the first murder. He'd be a lot more likely to tell you about the goings-on in New York than he would Norwitch. When I think how we were running around loose before Petty was killed, I wonder that you're still alive. I'm going home with you and, cop or no cop, I'm going to look under the bed. And get this. Don't you dare go gallivanting off alone, even to buy socks for Jeff. Do your shopping by phone and stick to the shop, or the house, until this thing breaks; if it doesn't break by tomorrow, I'm going to bust it wide open. Now put on your bonnet and let's get going, because I'm going to go home and sleep and sleep and sleep."

Emma drove the roadster because Hank professed to be incapable of so much action and telephoned for a cab to assist him on the return trip. Hank was as good as his word, while Emma was greeting Minnie and again providing herself with dinner from M. LeBotien's supplies, he searched the apartment, looking under the bed and in the closets, and carefully locking the windows that gave on the fire escape. O'Donnell, Emma's watchdog, followed Hank around, questioning him, but Hank was too tired to do more than mumble noncommittal replies. Finally, satisfied that the apartment was reasonably secure, he said goodnight and stumbled into the taxi.

Emma was very grateful for the attention Hank had bestowed on her. She was glad that M. LeBotien was so solicitous of her comfort that he helped her carry her groceries upstairs; O'Donnell was by no means the smallest man on the force but Emma wished that she had been favored with the biggest. She hoped that the Yogi lady upstairs would have company, lots of it; it was too bad that it wasn't M. LeBotien's birthday so that some of his cronies would drop in for a glass of wine. She wanted noises, loud noises, that she could identify as being made by people, not the little noises, the creaks and moans that empty rooms make in the night, though their walls are of brick and their floors are solid.

And speaking of birthdays—Emma put her chop on to cook and went to look at the calendar on her desk—sure enough, she thought, day after tomorrow would be Jeff's birthday. Jail was not much of a place to have a birthday; they usually had such swell parties too. She must remember Jeff's socks. Or was it pajamas that he wanted?

Emma ate her dinner and washed the dishes, not knowing how long her retirement was going to last; then she got into a game of Russian Bank with O'Donnell that cost her forty cents. Further losses were prevented by a series of telephone calls, all of which O'Donnell answered, leaving Emma to explain to all and sundry what strange man was inhabiting her premises. Emma was grateful for the calls; during the last week she had begun to think that Hank and M. LeBotien were the only friends she had left. She visited away cheerfully about the murder with a schoolteacher friend until a violent coughing caused her to look at O'Donnell, who was shaking his head at her.

What, Emma wanted to know, was the big idea?

Her line, O'Donnell told her, was tapped and some officer was listening to the conversations; she shouldn't talk so much. All the fun, for Emma, went out of the calls. She tried saying that there was a cop in her room and another listening in and her callers promptly hung up. She tried being nonchalant and the conversations, if they did not immediately turn to the murder, seemed to deal entirely with new babies and the details of ill-running love affairs. Emma decided that the reason no one had called her was that all of her friends seemed to have been either in hospitals or in Bermuda with their bosses, and that it was unfair to let them pour out their confessions to a third person, who might or might not be venal, but who certainly would be interested. Finally she went to bed, leaving the telephone and the cards to O'Donnell who, having no delicacy, promptly held a long conversation with his girl before settling down to a night of Canfield.

Emma went promptly to sleep, lulled by the murmur of O'Donnell's voice, but sometime during the night she awoke, clammy with perspiration, from a dream in which she stood, helplessly watching, while a figure dressed in Jeff's pajamas bent menacingly over an unconscious Hank. In spite of the pajamas, Emma had known that the figure was that of a woman whose face she could not see but whose raised hand held a blackjack. Emma lay very still in the darkness; the house, which had seemed very quiet at first, began to whisper about her. A rhythmic creaking came from the hall, as though someone were cautiously treading on stairs. There was a rustling just outside the blackness of her window. Emma tried to worry about Hank. He was sleeping the deep sleep of exhaustion in the Norwitch house, with only Oscar, somewhere at the top or the bottom, probably asleep too. What was that? Emma's ears strained to catch and identify a new noise; a deep sigh seemed to well through the room; there were heavy steps and the sound of running water. O'Donnell was not, apparently, doing well at the solitaire; Emma relaxed and went to sleep.

Chapter

15

ON THE NEXT DAY the minions, as Hank termed them, delving in the glacial deposits of Natick, unearthed some very interesting remains. Miss Lydia Latham read the papers and she had not minced words when she told the butcher, the postman and her next-door neighbor what she thought of the little snippet who had bought her secretary and turned out to be no better than an antique dealer. The expression, "ought to be shot," which the butcher quoted her as using, need not, of course, be taken literally; but one of the minions, with unusual perspicacity, inquired at the depot and discovered that Miss Latham had gone to Boston on the days of Norwitch's and Petty's murders and that, further-more, she had gone to Boston that very morning. The information was promptly telephoned to headquarters but failed to excite Hank. He was much more impressed by Connerton's report that the man who had been shadowing Mrs. Graham was the representative of a local de-tective agency and that he had been hired by Mr. Jefferson Graham. Hank persuaded Donovan to say nothing of this to Jeff; it simply strength-ened his conviction that Jeff suspected his wife and he would save the knowledge of that report, along with the paper found in Petty's room, for some dark purpose of his own. Donovan consented, but he was becoming a little grim about Hank's expectations of a break; so Hank left him and went placidly to the shop. He sat limply in Jeff's chair most of the afternoon, refusing all the conversational bait that Emma set out for him. Occasionally he mooned around the aisles. Once he stood for some time quietly opening and closing the corner door. And once Emma found him perched on top of the desk, alternately crouching down, and peering over the partition.

"Are you," she wanted to know, "trying to act out the crime?"

Hank sniffed. "I know exactly," he informed her, "how Uncle's murder was done. But," he added, "I can't seem to prove that she did it. She came in here at about six-thirty the night he was killed and got some money. You and Petty were the proof of that...." Hank paused. "Only, now, Petty is dead, and anything that you say she might have overheard might be misinterpreted by an impartial jury. Then, on the evidence of Swartz and the waiter, she and Swartz had dinner at Lock's and finally, on Swartz's say-so, they went to a movie. I wish," he added bitterly, "that that infant industry had died at birth. Crowds, dark, no tickets, nothing to prove anything."

"But if," Emma put in, "she left the movie, Swartz would know about it."

"And why not? Two people have done a job before. Swartz is undoubtedly Remington and she practically told me that she was going to marry him 'when she got rid of Jeff.'"

"How is she fixed for the time Petty was killed?" Emma wanted to know.

Hank groaned, thinking of that night. "According to her, she was on the subway, coming in to meet Swartz at the Royal Palms."

"But," Emma was all excitement, "if she was at Petty's hotel in the afternoon, she wouldn't go way out to the apartment and come back."

"You forget, my sweet," Hank reminded her, "that the lady denies flatly that she was at Petty's hotel."

"Oh," said Emma, "then all you have to do is to prove that somebody is lying."

"Precisely," replied Hank; "that's all there is to it."

"Well," Emma was very matter-of-fact, "you didn't have much trouble making a monkey out of me."

"You're quite wrong there; you were a lot of trouble because you never lied; things just looked as though you had. And as you so kindly pointed out to me, the appearances would have resolved themselves into the truth without my conference with Roger. But you were constantly on guard and the same is true of a person who has told an original lie; he's always on the watch not to give that lie away. Right now Mrs. Graham says she wasn't at the hotel; the clerk thinks she was. But, even if she were, she didn't see Petty that afternoon; therefore it's hardly worth arguing about unless I can get some stronger evidence to back it up."

"Hmm," said Emma. "Can't you put a dictaphone in her room? Maybe she talks to herself. Did you ask her what her maiden name was?"

"You don't mean a dictaphone and she says her name was Martha Kelley and that she and Jeff were married in West Dudley."

"For heaven's sake, where's that?"

"East of Southbridge, just across the line from Connecticut."

"That fits all right; they'd go out of the state to get married. Can't you check the records?"

"I suppose so but it's such a long way to go."

"Well, of course," Emma put in, "it was only your uncle and you're just working on the case. You could send the sergeant."

"I'm not sure," said Hank, "that he can read. I really couldn't expect Donovan to go; I suppose I'll have to do it myself."

You'll have a breakdown if you're not careful." Emma was not feeling sympathetic. "Did you ask Jeff what that girl's name was?"

"Not yet. If she were Mrs. G. he'd give me a phony name and I couldn't tell whether he were lying or not without checking first."

"By the way," Hank changed the subject. "I got one of those notes from God's secretary this morning."

"Oh, Hank, do be careful. Have they found out anything more about Miss Latham?"

"Nothing much. I think she's touched but harmless. Last time she was in town she went to the movies." Hank seemed to be thinking of other things than Miss Latham. "Say, can I borrow your car?"

"And burn out a bearing or turn over or be arrested for speeding?" Emma was indignant. "I should say not. Those letters may be just the work of a crank but they are awful bad luck. Look at Jeff and then me. I don't think you ought to go to West Dudley at all; something is sure to happen to you."

"Do you," Hank wanted to know, "think of any reason why I shouldn't buy a car?"

"That's the first sensible remark you've made for a week but you can't drive a new car to West Dudley. You'd ruin it."

"Well," Hank was giving the problem his entire consideration, "I could probably get a demonstrator if I told somebody I was going to buy one. What'll I get?"

Emma shook her head. As one to whom the purchase of a car was a serious matter, not to be entered into ill-advisedly, Hank's disregard for anything except his immediate convenience was hardly understandable.

"They say," she opined, with what she thought was obvious sarcasm, "that the Rolls is a nice car."

"Oke," said Hank. "Gimme the phone book."

"Look," said Emma. "You're going to have company."

Stephana was even then in the act of opening the door.

"I don't live here," said Hank. "She's your company." He began to dial a number.

Joe Foster was following close on Stephana's heels. Emma went to meet them.

"Come in, kids," she said. "Hank's buying a car."

"How grand," said Stephana.

"What kind?" Joe wanted to know.

"Any kind," said Emma disgustedly. "He'll be duck-soup for the first salesman that gets to him."

"I know a guy—" began Joe.

"Yes," said Hank into the phone, "a car. Oh, I don't care much. A coupe, I guess, or one of those things that shut up into a roadster."

Emma groaned. "Sit down," she said, "while I get you a drink."

"I came on business," said Joe, "but as long as it's a party I'll stay; so you might as well introduce me."

Emma remedied her omission. Hank, at the phone, had his back to them; Stephana favored Joe with a long, slow lift of her eyelashes. Joe was plainly interested. Emma, defending Hank's interests, demanded Joe's help with the drinks.

"That's it," said Hank. "I'll wait for you here."

He turned to Stephana. "Hello, my dear. It's nice to see you."

Stephana lifted the lashes slowly again. "Hello," she said. "I haven't really told you what a good time I had the other night."

"That's great," said Hank. "We'll do it again sometime."

Emma poked a drink in front of Hank; he glowered at her.

"Pardon the interruption," Emma said haughtily and went over to sit by Joe. Hank needn't be afraid she was going to cramp his style!

"How's Bill? And what's this about business?" she asked.

Just then a long, long sapphire-blue hood slid into view in front of the door. Hank got to his feet hastily, calling good-bys. He motioned Emma aside.

"Good-by, sugar," he said. "I'll try to be back tomorrow night. Keep in touch with Donovan and behave yourself."

Emma picked a piece of lint gently from Hank's coat.

"Please," she said, "don't do anything silly."

"Boo," said Hank and went out the door.

Their relationship, Emma thought, was a very comfortable one.

Stephana, again a dark picture in the pink chair, was purring at Joe and Joe was liking it very much. Emma took her drink into the office and sat down, willing, for the moment, to be an onlooker. She might, she thought, learn some points.

No, Joe was saying, he only knew Mr. Graham very slightly. Did they have to talk about him? Stephana tipped her face and her cigarette toward him for a light. Her lipstick ? It was rust. Did Joe like it? Joe did. Could she get away? She could.

Emma felt that she should join in the conversation. She had been under the impression that Stephana thought she was Hank's girl but apparently she was just after anything in pants that came along.

"What," Emma asked of Joe, "was that business you claimed brought you in here?"

"Huh?" said Joe. "Oh, that. I wanted to know if you would lend us some stuff for a show—antiques, I mean—a couple of chairs and a table and a sofa and some gadgets."

"Lord no." Emma was emphatic, being, perhaps, not in a receptive mood. "You'd smash 'em to bits."

"No, we wouldn't; this is a serious show. I promise to take care of them. Get your name on the program," Joe wheedled. "Your friend Petty got an obit out of Variety," he went on, "because he did the antiques for Sense and Sensibility—of course he backed it too but that's a small matter."

"I'm a sucker for free advertising," Emma weakened. "Bring me a list of what you want."

"I have it right here. That's swell. Gee, you're a good sport. You might, you know, have it in for Bill and me on account of the things we told the cops. What were they stewing about anyway?"

"Just the routine checkup," Emma said shortly. She did not care about revealing her stay at the city's jail to Joe, or to Stephana, either; she didn't want to be a good sport but she supposed she had to. She turned to Stephana.

"You said you knew some of the people who worked on Sense and Sensibility. Wouldn't it be strange if you had seen Petty? Of course, you wouldn't have known him but I bet a nickel you knew someone who did." Emma paused, overcome with the realization that the world really was a small place.

"Where," asked Stephana, "did Hank say he was going?"

"West Dudley," said Emma without thinking and then could have kicked herself for not keeping her mouth shut.

"It's something to do with the estate," she went on mendaciously. "He may be gone for days."

"Go on," said Joe. "I heard him say he'd be back late tomorrow night."

"Did he?" said Emma. "I must have misunderstood."

Just then a belated customer came in, bringing a broken andiron and wanting something for a present. Emma put the andiron under Jeff's desk, promising to attend to it at once and went in search of the something. She was kept busy for some time: paperweights were too expensive; silhouettes were too common. Finally, as a decision was about to be made between a muddler and a bootjack, Joe and Stephana called goodnight. Emma gave them a wave and watched them go. They had the air of being very much together as they went up the street. Did

Stephana, Emma asked herself, have to steal all her gents?

Aloud she said, "Yes, the blackjack would be just the thing." She hastily corrected herself.

Eventually she sold the muddler, said a pessimistic goodnight to McKinnon and went home to bed.

Chapter
16

THE NEXT MORNING it was raining again, and Emma busied herself with visions of Hank skidding on slippery paving, hitting telephone poles and lying in some obscure ditch, unconscious and bleeding. As she drove to the shop, a truck bumped her from behind and its driver laughed at her glowering looks. The morning mail was depressing: the woman from Schenectady again threatened not to take the chandelier; the bill for the month's drayage seemed outrageously large; a woman in Lowell had an empire bureau for which she had been offered one hundred dollars; another person named Milford had some antiques that could be seen at a given address. Emma consigned the Lowell lady to the wastebasket, put the other letters on her desk and played a game of Russian Bank with McKinnon that passed the time until lunch and left her even with the Police Department.

After lunch Emma sent Jeff some cigarettes and a note. She almost told him about her troubles with the chandelier but decided that the tale of her loss of Hank and Joe to Stephana Mathews would amuse him more. McKinnon decided that he was catching a cold and she got him some aspirin. She got a detective story from the lending library, guessed the murderer on page five, confirmed her guess by looking at the last page and then could see no reason for reading the story. No word from Donovan; no customers and, of course, no word from Hank. Mrs. Arbuthnot passed the door but did not stop or even wave a greeting. By four-thirty Emma was having the fidgets. She walked to the door. The rain had almost ceased, the sky was clear in the west and a light wind was blowing. Emma decided that she would shut the shop promptly at five-thirty and take a ride. Only her conscience and the presence of McKinnon kept her from doing it then.

She went back to her desk, lit a cigarette, filed the bill for the haul-ing, heaved a sigh and postponed answering the chandelier lady until another day. Nehoiden Street? Where the dickens was that? Oh, Wakefield, huh. All she had to do was to look at the letter. Out through Maiden and Melrose; quite a long way but she hadn't been out there for some time. She might as well go there as anywhere. Emma read the letter again. Some antiques, it said with delightful vagueness, could be seen at 304 Nehoiden Street on Thursday after six o'clock. Among them was a desk with a round front that the owner had been told was quite rare. A desk with a round front? Emma realized that she had not given the letter sufficient attention at first. It couldn't possibly be that here was another swell-front tambour secretary. Probably just a swellfront desk with a slant top. Still, those were not to be sneezed at and there was always the chance—On Thursday; today was Thursday. What was the rush? Maybe the people were going to move. If she missed something good And if they had a good desk the other things might be good too, though that was almost too much to hope for. If she started now she would get to Wakefield by six-thirty, if the traffic wasn't too bad. Emma put the letter in her purse, knowing that she would forget the address at least by the time she had reached Somerville, told McKinnon she hoped his cold would be better and got into the roadster.

In Melrose it occurred to her that she had not left word where she was going or when she would be back. As she neared Wakefield she remembered that she was not supposed to go roaming off by herself. But that was silly. What trouble could she get into looking at antiques in Wakefield? The thought flashed through her mind that Richard Norwitch, doubtless, hadn't expected to be murdered looking at antiques in Jeff's shop. Emma pulled into a filling station and inquired for Nehoiden Street. The attendant cheered her by knowing, or at least having a sort of an idea, where it was. Four blocks ahead, three to the left, leave the car line and go out into the country to the first crossroad. Emma set off.

It was growing dark. Wakefield, Emma decided, was not too well lighted. A streetcar sang past her, laden with passengers in the semiconscious state of people going home from work to supper. Emma wished that she were meeting Hank and a large steak. The streetcar turned to the left and Emma bumped ahead on a dirt road. The houses were few; the lights ceased altogether. The roadster dropped with an ominous bang into a pothole. Damn, thought Emma, had she broken a spring? Her headlights picked up the fresh grading of a crossroad. Almost disappointed at the cessation of discouragement, Emma swung onto the comparative smoothness of Nehoiden Street, in what appeared to be a new part of town. There were no sidewalks, the lawns were barren of grass, the houses were all of a white likeness and only a few of them seemed to be occupied. The chances of finding a cache of valuable furniture seemed most unlikely; people were moving into these houses, not moving out of them. Emma took cold comfort from the thought that you never could tell and started hunting for number 304. It was the last house on the street and Emma blessed the owner for putting the number on the gatepost. Her headlights showed it plainly. There was a dim light at the rear of 304. The owners, Emma thought with a pang, were probably eating in the kitchen; maybe they'd offer her some nice hamburger and fried potatoes.

She shut off the motor and turned off the lights; then she promptly turned them on again to relieve the utter blackness. Ahead of her Nehoiden Street ended abruptly; a bleak and stony field stretched away into darkness. Emma got out of the car and, having overshot her mark, went back a few steps to the gate. Suddenly she tripped, reached out to steady herself and felt her hand come in contact with something sticky. Rubbing her ankle and wishing that she had not come, she investigated and found that she had made a sorry smear of the numbers on the gatepost. They had been freshly painted. Emma scrubbed at her hand, not wishing to start negotiations under the handicap of an obvious vandalism and looked, with eyes now accustomed to the darkness outside her headlights, at the object which had attacked her. A board, painted white, lay beside her, to it was nailed another, sturdier board which bore the marks of having been partly in the ground. Said the big white board: FOR SALE OR RENT. Well, what of it? The sign was down. Emma looked toward the house. A light flashed on in the front room. Through the uncurtained window Emma caught a glimpse of bare, white-plastered walls. It was only a glimpse, because she made a dive for the car, turned the switch with trembling fingers, and roared backward, down Nehoiden Street. She actually hated to turn onto the short connecting road, because then she could not watch for the horror she was sure had been lurking in number 304. Disregarding the roadster's springs, mindful only of her shaking knees and a sick sensation at the pit of her stomach, she hurtled over the ruts and bumps, fighting down the waves of nausea that threatened to delay her flight. She got as far as the car line, turned down a side street, opened the car door and was very sick for some minutes. Her stomach, she thought, when she could think, was always an awful sissy.

Clammy with perspiration and still shaking, but with her stomach under control, Emma, by a circuitous route, sought out the bright lights of Wakefield's main street. The dime stores and the filling stations and the coal dealers looked so normal and cozy that Emma stopped at a one-arm for a cup of coffee and a recapitulation of the incidents that had sent her fleeing in blind panic from number 304.

Had her guilty conscience, when she realized that she was disobeying Hank's explicit instructions, tricked her into imagining reasons for not completing her errand? Waiting for her coffee to fall to a drinkable temperature, Emma followed the progress of her terror. First there had been the lonely situation of the house; although that had not consciously disturbed her and could be put down, other things omitted, to chance. Her stumble had been largely a matter of chance too, she realized. If she had parked in front of the gate, she would have walked directly in and would not have fallen over the sign or put her hand on the wet paint. After all, if the occupants of number 304 had but recently moved in, their number might well be wet and the FOR SALE sign only just taken down. Emma took a sip of coffee and wondered what she would do first if she had just moved into a house. She'd take down the sign, that was O.K.; but she doubted if she would make a trip to the dime store, buy a can of paint and decorate her gatepost with the house number. Uh, uh. She'd go to the dime store all right, for cup hooks, towel racks, steel wool and shelf paper, but she'd never think of the house number; or, if she did, she'd forget it, along with half the other things she had gone for. Weeks would pass, Emma was sure, before she got her house number up. Somebody had wanted that number up, quick, before six o'clock.

Emma pulled the letter out of her purse. The signature, "W. H. Milford," meant nothing to her; she hadn't even remembered it, there being no reason why she should. "Thursday, after six." The writer might be vague about the antiques but he was very definite about the day and time. And the come-on, the round-front desk; that might be chance or it might be an indication that somebody knew that she got all steamed up about swell-front desks. There were, Emma was aware, a lot of people who possessed that information.

Up to this point Emma could almost explain away the reasons for her panic. But what could she do about the empty, uncurtained room? Maybe the furniture was all in another room; maybe it was down cellar—Emma had a vision of herself, lured to some dark basement and choked on the coffee. That house hadn't had more than four rooms downstairs and if furniture had just been moved in there would be some standing around. Or would there? Emma realized why Hank moaned and groaned at conjecture and pleaded for one little, solid fact to go on. Anything, in this cockeyed world, could happen and frequently did. Who was she to tell movers where to put furniture? Likely enough it was all standing out in the yard. Maybe she ought to go back and take another look? No, Emma didn't think she would do that. Tomorrow, perhaps, with Hank, when the sun was shining. Besides, she was hungry; she was going back to town and eat a lot in some brightly lighted place where there were lots of people. She considered the drive back to town. By now W. H. Milford, whoever he might be, could have passed her and could be lying in wait at some intersection. Emma sighed; she would, she supposed, have to take the risk of running all the stop lights again. But there was one fact that she could present to Hank: she had been badly scared. She was still scared.

Emma paid her check and went out. At three o'clock the night man swept a letter from under a chair but he was too tired even to read it.

Should she, Emma wondered, during the completely uneventful trip back to town, tell McKinnon or perhaps even Donovan of her experience? She decided that she would prefer to reveal her flight from the as yet unknown to Hank's ear. If she had to be laughed at, she would rather that Hank did it.

Chapter

17

THE BRIGHT SUNSHINE of the next day made Emma feel that she had doubtless been a little silly the night before. She went to the shop feeling good and was met by a gloomy McKinnon, whose cold had not yielded to the aspirin and a gloomier Hank, who regarded her glumly from Jeff's chair as she came in.

"Good morning," said Emma brightly. "What is this, half-holiday at the morgue?"

Hank and McKinnon sneezed in unison.

"Catching cold, eh? You two better go home to bed and let the sun come out again."

"Yah," said Hank, hunting for a handkerchief.

"How was the Rolls?" Emma wanted to know as she hung up her hat. "And how was West Dudley, a bit dampish?"

"Burned up," said Hank.

"What?" asked Emma, "the Rolls? That's too bad."

"No, dummy," said Hank. "West Dudley. Five years ago. Whole town, courthouse, records, vital statistics, marriage registry. She could have been Martha Whoosit or an illegitimate child as far as West Dudley is concerned."

"That's a shame." Emma was sincerely, if momentarily, sympathetic. "But while you're thinking up what to do next, you might find out where Mrs. Graham was between six and seven last night."

"Why? What difference does it make? Say," Hank came out of his abstraction and viewed Emma with suspicious interest, "have you been up to something?"

"I don't know." Emma a little sheepish. "I thought it was too good to miss and then I got scared out. I—" She plunged headlong into the tale of the letter and her trip to Wakefield.

McKinnon pricked up his ears and forgot to sneeze.

When Emma had finished, Hank said sternly, "Give me that letter."

Emma opened her purse calmly, pawed through its contents and then emptied it onto her desk. The letter failed to appear.

"Now where?" she began.

"Find that letter!" Hank's voice was harsh.

"I had it," Emma communed with herself, "in the one-arm because I looked at the signature. It's not here; so I must have left it there. Maybe someone picked it up. I'm sorry. Do you think it was important?"

Hank buried his face in his hands.

"It was typewritten," Emma went on, trying to minimize her blunder. "All the writing there was was the signature, W. H. Milford. I don't know anyone by that name. Do you?"

"The paper it was written on," exclaimed Hank, addressing McKinnon, "the machine, the signature and the postmark. And she leaves it all in a joint! I ask you!"

"Get your hat, sweetness and light," he spoke to Emma. "We're going out to Wakefield to see what we can find. I'll tell Donovan."

He swung around to the telephone.

"Ouch and blast," he said, rubbing his ankle. "What have you got under there?"

Emma looked. "Oh, them," she said. "Look, before I forget it again get Hřebec on the phone; Mrs. Riggs will be in here tomorrow for those and my name will be mud if they aren't fixed."

"Who is Hurbick and how do you spell it?"

"He's the Bohemian who mends brass. He's very good. You spell it H-ř-e-b-e-c. There's a whitchet over the 'r.'"

"What, in heaven's name, is a whitchet?" Hank was thumbing through the *H*'s.

Emma, used to his thirst for knowledge, explained patiently, "It's a dingus, like a caret upside down."

"They wouldn't put a mark like that in the phone book," Hank began.

Emma interrupted him. "Well, they ought to. All Bohemian names have them."

"A whitchet, a dingus." Hank looked at Emma wonderingly. "It's impossible; it's a concidence. Please," he said, "this may be important. Think hard. Does the name Matoušek, spelled with a whitchet," he put in, "mean anything to you?"

"Why, no," said Emma blankly. "Should it?"

"I don't know," said Hank wildly. "I don't know but I've got to find out. There was the letter. That name is Bohemian and she was Bohemian and we have to go to Wakefield and I'm going nuts."

"That's right," Emma said kindly. "I haven't the faintest idea what you're talking about. Gimme that phone."

Hank grabbed his hat.

"Stay right here," he said. "Don't," he said to McKinnon, "let her get out. I'm going over to that apartment house before we go to Wakefield."

"What apartment—" began Emma but Hank was in the Rolls before she could finish.

She turned to the phone and called Hurbick. It was queer that a name spelled h-r-e should be pronounced h-u-r.

"Hello," she said. "Send Gus over for some andirons. They have to be ready by tomorrow. That's fine. Look," she went on hesitatingly, "do you know any Bohemians by the name of Matoušek? I don't know how you spell it, probably not the way it sounds if it's anything like yours. Oh, a friend of mine wanted to know. Yes, I guess it would be spelled something like that. Americanized to what? They do? Oh. . .Oh. . . Thank you."

Emma hung up the telephone and shivered. She tried to light a cigarette and broke three matches before she managed it. It was impossible, completely impossible. That was what Hank had said. Emma sat on miserably in the office, waiting for Hank to come back.

Hank had driven around the corner, pulled up in the comparative quiet of Brimmer Street and turned off the ignition. There was no use, he decided, in going off half-cocked, upsetting the applecart, breaking the eggs and scaring the quarry. He needed to sit a while and sort out the facts that had been so suddenly dumped in his lap. He had a hunch that he had finally found something that would spot the murderer, if he could only decide what it was.

The sun was warm. Hank pushed back his hat and shoved his long legs into a corner. He relaxed; his mind stopped chasing its tail and settled down to peaceful contemplation. So; Emma had been induced to go to Wakefield and had almost walked into some kind of a trap. Serve the little mutt right if she had, after being told to stay put! Hank reproved his mind sternly for such a thought and then turned it loose again. Why? The billy bobbed into his mind. The thing would have had to be planted. It began to look as though someone had decided to put Emma permanently, instead of temporarily, out of the way. The planting of the billy had obviously been to clear the shop for Petty's murder and not, primarily, to do harm to Emma. This time had been different. Had Emma been up to something again that she hadn't told about? He had neglected to ask for a play-by-play account of what she had done in his absence. The clue might lie there. But, according to her story, she had been alone with McKinnon until she went to Wakefield.

Hank turned his mind to the letter. The letter had been so worded, if Emma's memory of it could be trusted, that she would be sure to be interested—darn her for losing it—and would be at a certain place after a certain time. What, exactly, did that tell him? The writer had been vague about the antiques, except for the mention of the round-front desk. The desk was the unmistakable come-on. The writer, then, didn't know much about furniture, knew of the excitement caused by the secretary, but didn't know enough to call it by its right name. Was that right? Or was the writer just being smart, concealing his knowledge and counting on the mention of the desk to do the trick? After six o'clock. Any time after, but not before. That was easy; it was dark shortly after six. Anything else? Hank stirred uneasily. By golly, it also meant that the writer was not free himself before six. In other words, he worked. But Mrs. Graham didn't work. But she might think that Emma did. How would Mrs. Graham know about an empty house in Wakefield? Hank sighed; it looked as though the sergeant had a lot of work cut out for him. Matoušek. Why did he bother so about that letter? The sergeant could interview the postman and the janitor and find out where A. S. Matoušek had moved.

Hank told his mind to stop wandering and settle down to business. Suppose he was right, suppose the person he wanted didn't know much about antiques, but knew about the secretary; if he also worked in the daytime and had access to a house in Wakefield, what picture did that make?

"I don't believe it," Hank said aloud, to the surprise of a passerby. But he had to believe it. The picture was finally coming into focus; it had been there all the time, except for the part with the house in Wakefield. What in the dickens had Emma been up to? It was imperative that he be in three places at once. Emma wouldn't believe him; Donovan wouldn't believe him; he'd have to prove it to them. The car shot out of Brimmer Street, onto the parkway, and headed for Wakeheld. Hank got as far as the North Station before he decided that it was not necessary for him to do all the work. Connerton could go to Wakefield and Donovan could go to the apartment. He parked in front of a drugstore and went in to telephone. He told the sergeant what to look for and told Donovan that he would meet him at the apartment. He came out and drove slowly away. It wasn't, he decided, going to be much fun.

It was after the morning mail had been delivered that Jeff wanted to see Donovan. Donovan had, by this time, gone to meet Hank, but he had left word of his errand and was finally reached by phone.

"Well, I'll be a son of a gun," Donovan said in answer to Jeff's incoherences. "That's where we are now. Lemme talk to Ike. He can bring you over and maybe you can help us find what we're looking for."

Donovan went back upstairs laughing. He seemed to think that the joke was on Hank.

Jeff came and joined in the search.

"It's not in the bureau nor the desk nor the closet," said Hank. "Jerry is about to operate on the mattress. You might try the bathroom."

"Honestly," said Jeff, "I don't see how a guy can be so dumb."

"Save the remarks," said Donovan, "and get to work. It's past lunchtime."

Hank knelt down with Donovan to examine the seams on the mattress.

"Would this," asked a pleasant voice, "be what you are looking for?"

Stephana Mathews stood in the doorway holding a little gun, holding it very firmly and pointing it at Hank and Donovan, who were kneeling, open-mouthed, on the far side of the bed.

"Wasn't it lucky," Stephana went on, "that I came home this noon to change my dress? Otherwise, you might have caught me unprepared. I think I shall go out very quietly and lock the door. The telephone, you may remember," she smiled at Hank, "is downstairs. I don't know exactly where I shall go but I'll be back . . . sometime."

Jeff came out of the bathroom; he was still wearing his hat and overcoat.

The change in Stephana's face was instantaneous and horrible. Her lips drew back in a maniacal snarl, her eyes glittered, her body shook, but the hand that held the gun was steady. The three men gazed at her, appalled and fascinated. Stephana spoke quickly.

"First," she said, "you made a tramp of me, and then a criminal. I shan't have to come back."

Her voice rose to a scream; the spell was broken.

Hank thought the shooting would never stop. Stephana must have emptied her gun but Donovan shot only once. The echoes and reechoes were visible, circling about the room. No, that was smoke. Hank could feel the sharp prickle of the smell of gunpowder. The glass in the bathroom door was completely shattered. From behind the door Jeff was crawling slowly; there was blood on his face and one hand left a bloody track on the floor.

Stephana Mathews lay very still. The front of her black dress looked wet; there were pinkish bubbles at her mouth but no more bubbles were coming.

The Italian janitor stood wringing his hands in the doorway.

"Mother of God," said Donovan, "I've killed her. I didn't mean to kill her. I shot at her arm but she kept coming. I didn't mean to kill her; honest, I didn't mean . . ."

Hank took Donovan's gun from him and put it back in its holster.

"That's all right," he found himself repeating. "You couldn't jump over the bed at her and she was trying to kill Jeff."

"The very same place," Jeff was saying, "I swear she got me right in the same place."

Hank turned on him. "If you had any idea she shot at you and didn't tell us, you're to blame for a dandy mess."

Jeff struggled to his feet.

"Don't be a fool," he said sharply. "I thought it was Martha, so help me. I never thought of Anna being mixed up in this until I got Emma's letter this morning."

"This morning," said Hank blankly. "Emma didn't know it this morning. Emma doesn't know it now."

"She wrote me that she wished a Stephana Mathews had never come to the shop because she was after all her boy friends." Jeff's voice was none too steady. "I didn't know Anna was anywhere around. Last I knew she was going to get married. But it didn't take me long to figure that she had been responsible for the hell raising that's been going on."

"Stop jawing," said Donovan. "Somebody telephone for the ambulance."

Donovan's face was still white but he was again in command of himself and the situation.

Hank went down to telephone. When he came back, Donovan had taken the gun from the dead woman's hand and covered her with the cheap pink spread from the bed. They sat down quietly to wait for the ambulance.

"It was six-seven years ago she began to have it in for me." Jeff was holding a wadded-up handkerchief against his shoulder; blood continued to drip rhythmically from the nick in his ear. "I took her to Hartford and stuck around until she got a job with a dressmaker. Then I beat it. I didn't have a dime. I couldn't marry her and, besides, I didn't want to. For a while after I left her she was all right; then the dressmaking got a little dull, I guess; she got a job as a waitress and—you've guessed it—began to take up with the traveling men. To make a long story short, sometimes things were good—some guy took her to New York and set her up there—and sometimes they were bad. When they got too bad she'd write to me and I'd send her money. It was nothin'. I was glad to do it. She'd been a cute kid and I was a young punk that bit off more 'n I could chew when I helped her out of that farmhouse window.

"Well, the crash cut off the sugar money, she was getting a little old and she had to go to work. I guess she got to thinking about that Bohemian farmer and the kids she might of had. Anyhow, she began blaming me for taking her off and ditching her just about the time the people who could afford to spend money for antiques decided that they were broke. They were down to their last yacht but I couldn't pay my rent, let alone send her any cash. She got wilder and wilder. She came up here about three years ago threatening to kill me because I'd ruined her. She called the house a couple of times and Martha got wind of her—without knowing who she was—and that started the trouble between Martha and me. I managed to keep her out of Emma's sight, by the grace of God, borrowed some money of your uncle and got her back to New York. I borrowed from him several times. I wasn't scared of her, exactly, but she wasn't any comfort to have around.

"Then, little over a year ago, I got a letter saying that she was going to marry a Joe that knew all about her and everything was jake. I haven't heard a word about her since, until I got that letter from Emma this morning indicating that she and Anna were buddies, at least to the extent of fighting over the same gents. Right then I decided that it hadn't been Martha who took the potshot at me, but Anna, all wheed up again for some reason."

"You see," Hank said to Donovan, "I was right. He did think Mrs. Graham shot at him."

"Yeh," said Donovan, "and I suppose you're right about her,"—he pointed—"thinking your uncle was Jeff. And she hated Jeff because he got her off to a bum start—"

"It's more complicated than that." Hank was eager to set forth the psychological possibilities. "I've seen enough of her to know that she was preoccupied with men and marriage---"

Donovan ignored him and plodded on, "And Jeff had a wife and money and that'd make her hate him more—"

"—and she got to brooding over the fact that she might have been married if it hadn't been for Jeff—"

"—and that's motive enough for anybody," Donovan finished triumphantly.

"—then this engagement must have been broken off," Hank went on, "and she'd blame Jeff for that too. It's a persecution complex."

"Don't get technical on me." Donovan was satisfied with his own explanation. "She didn't have to be crazy to hate Jeff enough to kill him but, after what I've done, we may never find out why she killed Petty."

"Well, have it your way." Hank abandoned his theorizing. "But don't worry, no one is going to blame you for saving Jeff's life."

"You see," Jeff had been following his own thoughts, "I was having

Petty do a little job for me in New York and I thought maybe Martha had found out about it."

"Following her?" asked Hank.

Jeff nodded.

"We found his report to you. Do you want to see it?"

"Does it have to be made public?"

"No," said Donovan. "It don't."

"Then," said Jeff, "tear the damn thing up. Whatever it is, I guess it's no worse than for me to suspect her of murder."

That, thought Hank, was exactly like Jeff.

The ambulance shrieked to a stop below them. Donovan took Jeff, that the city surgeon might give him some attention, and Hank set off to find out why Stephana Mathews had spent a friendly afternoon with Emma and then tried to murder her.

Chapter

18

EMMA HAD HAD a long time to think before Hank came in. She had tried to dismiss as pure coincidence the fact that the name Mathews was the Americanized version of the name Matoušek which Hank had seen on the letter in Stephana's hall, but the more she tried, the more little things occurred to her to point out Stephana as the murderess. Stephana had always been in the picture; Emma thought wryly of Hank's obsession for the picture. She had been in the background, perhaps, but always there. She had been at the inquest and then had come in and talked to Hank. But—Emma's mind, by devious routes best known to itself, picked its way back— Stephana had been in the shop before that; Hank had referred to her as a customer and Emma had remembered her. That had been just after the first murder, so Stephana must have been in the shop. . . . Emma reached for the bill file. Had she been asking about a footstool? No, Emma found the slip for the footstool; it had been purchased the day after the murder; Stephana hadn't bought it—Emma remembered the woman who had—but Stephana had been there at the same time asking about the murder. Emma turned back to the slips for the day of the murder. She should, she thought, have done that when Hank was pestering her for the incidents of that day. Yes, indeed, she certainly should have.

Because the woman from Schenectady had bought a chandelier—not that there seemed much chance of her ever getting it—yet the slip said quite plainly: "1 tapestry, $200." The woman who had asked to see a tapestry had been Stephana Mathews.

Emma's haste to get away on that night and the subsequent events had driven the incident completely from her mind. Because the chandelier had not been delivered Emma had sent no bill for it and had had no occasion to refer to the slip. Now, holding it in her hand, the scene came back to her. She had been standing at the entrance to the office, making out the slip, when a woman in black, who had been in the shop for some time, had asked about a tapestry. Emma had hastily written tapestry for chandelier and had then tried to sell her the Prodigal Son.

Stephana might, Emma realized, have been in the shop for a long time, she might easily have heard Jeff tell Mr. Norwitch that he would be back at eleven o'clock, for the narrow aisles and piles of furniture offered plenty of places for concealment. Emma was sure that she had seen Stephana leave the shop but she might have waited outside, seen that the door was left unbolted and slipped back in. A chill, as quick as a startled squirrel, ran up Emma's spine. Stephana must have been in the shop when Emma returned. If Stephana had wanted to kill her, why hadn't she done it then? Obviously, because she hadn't wanted to. Emma wondered what she had been up to since to incur Stephana's enmity, but decided that Hank would probably tell her. And what was it that Hank had said about Jeff being afraid that someone would kill him? And the girl Jeff had run off with was Bohemian and she had thought Stephana might be Russian.

"Look," said Emma to McKinnon. "She didn't mean to kill him."

"Eh?" said McKinnon.

"Stephana Mathews—Mr. Norwitch. She meant to kill Jeff. It's the overcoats; they were just alike. The overcoats, I mean. And Jeff and Mr. Norwitch were about the same height and their hats were enough alike so that Jeff mixed them up; but they weren't really alike, Jeff and Mr. Norwitch, I mean, so you never thought about their being the same size; but in the dark they'd look just the same. And I bet Hank Fairbanks thought of that long ago and never told me, the rat."

Emma reached for the phone.

"I'll call Donovan and tell him I've got the murders all solved and it'll serve Hank right. Only maybe"—Emma put the phone down—"that's what he went out of here in such a dither about because it was right after I was telling him about the whitchet."

McKinnon approached Emma cautiously.

"You may have caught it from me," he said, "or Mr. Fairbanks. The flu often makes you lightheaded, kind of."

"Crazy, huh?" Emma wanted to know. "Well, you would be, if you had just decided that one of your pals had been trying to murder you."

"There, there." McKinnon was afraid he was going to have his hands full. "Nobody is trying to hurt you."

"They were too," said Emma. "You heard what I told Hank and now I know who did it. Only I can't imagine why, or why Petty . . ."

Emma's voice trailed off and she fixed McKinnon with her gaze as she wondered about Petty. Petty had been in the shop on the night of the murder of Mr. Norwitch but Emma felt sure that he had come after Stephana had gone. She might have seen him at the inquest, though. They were both from New York; and, while that was reputed to be a large city, they might possibly have known each other. That would be no wilder a coincidence than that Stephana Mathews, a costume designer, should turn out to be a Bohemian girl with whom Jeff Graham had run away. Costume designer. She remembered Joe Foster's remark on the day he had been there.

Emma jumped up and slapped McKinnon on the back. If he had not had to cough, he would doubtless have put handcuffs on her.

"*Sense and Sensibility*," Emma shouted. "I've got it."

"Indeed," said Hank, coming in quietly.

"You know," began McKinnon, "nothing she says makes sense."

Ignoring him, Emma turned to Hank.

"Angel," she said, "Mathews is American for Matoušek and she could be the Bohemian girl Jeff ran off with. She killed your uncle by mistake because they'd look alike in the dark, and she killed Petty because he knew something and she had to kill me too. Only I got away."

Hank threw his hat on the desk and sat down.

Emma stamped her foot.

"I'm not crazy," she said emphatically. "And you knew she didn't mean to kill Mr. Norwitch because you said Jeff was afraid someone was trying to kill him. And you let me think it was poor Mrs. Graham all the time."

"I think," said Hank, "that I shall take up bookbinding; I'm too slow to be a detective."

"Don't be sarcastic."

"I'm not. You're right; absolutely right. You discover the murderer by pure deduction; Jeff spent half the morning trying to find Donovan to tell him who did it, while I come dragging in a poor third. I wonder if Donovan would like to go into the garage business? It's a cinch we're no good as sleuths."

Emma sat down suddenly in the wing chair. Hank's abject agreement had knocked all the argumentative props from under her.

"You don't mean," she said, "that she really did it—them, I mean?"

"Right as rain," said Hank with forced lightness. "I don't suppose you'd consider leaving Jeff and keeping books in a garage, would you? No excitement, no murders; probably no pay."

McKinnon gaped at the two of them.

"Where is she?" Emma asked. "I mean, has Donovan arrested her?"

Hank went to the washroom, poured two drinks and gave each a perfunctory dab of tap water before he spoke.

"Lock the door," he said to McKinnon. "If anyone comes in here wanting to match one of Grandmother Hincklebotham's plates, I shall scream."

Emma, who ordinarily would have chided Hank for such an outburst, took a long swallow of her drink. Hank stood looking down at
her.

"Stephana's dead," he said bluntly. "Donovan shot her."

He watched Emma's eyes grow wide with horror; she shrank away
from him.

"It's not very pretty, is it, to have someone you know shot down by
the police? But it's my business too, you know: snooping and hounding
and trailing and finally catching some poor creature in a trap. And all
too often the death shot is delayed and delayed. . . ."

"Why?" Emma's throat was dry. "Why?"

"Because," Hank went on, "because she found us searching her room
and tried to kill Jeff again. That's not pretty, either, is it? She's had it in
for him for a long time."

He told the story of the growth of Stephana's hatred as Jeff had told
it beside her body.

"The poor, poor thing," said Emma. "What were you looking for?"

"The gun, more letters to identify her, anything." Hank finished
his drink.

"Then it was the letter with the Bohemian name that really put you
on her track?"

"No," Hank was honest. "When I left here I didn't connect Stephana
with that letter. After you pointed out that names with whitchets were
Bohemian I thought of that letter and had the wild idea that Jeff's Bohemian girl might be living in the same house. It wasn't until I got to
thinking about what had happened to you that it occurred to me that it
might be Stephana."

"I don't get it; tell me."

"The real estate office. Stephana worked in one. She was the only
person connected with the case who would know of, and have access to,
an empty house. And since she worked, she couldn't get out to Wakefield
much before six. Once I thought of that I could fit her into the picture,
except for Petty. And by the way, whatever did you do to set her after
you?"

"I know." Life came back into Emma's voice. "I was trying to tell
McKinnon when you came in. You remember that she said that she
knew a man you knew who did the costumes for *Sense and Sensibility*."

Hank nodded, all attention.

"Well, after you left the other day, Joe said something about Petty
having an obituary in *Variety*. Like a dummy," Emma paused but, as no
denial came from Hank, she went on, "I spoke up and said that it was a
small world and that he and Stephana must have had friends in com-

mon. Then Joe was a help, when I said I didn't know when you'd be back, and said you'd be back the next night. . . ."

Hank picked Emma up bodily from the chair, held her close and rubbed his cheek against her hair.

"And to think," he said huskily, "that I went ambling off to West Dudley."

The phone rang. Hank dropped Emma unceremoniously and went to answer it. He was, Emma thought, nice.

"Yes," said Hank, "it's me.

"In her purse? I'll be darned!

"Heel marks, huh?

"They fit?" his voice was jubilant.

"She did?

"At the dime store?

"Connerton surprises me. How'd he happen to think she'd buy paint there?

"Sure, I know he's not as dumb as he looks. I'm the dummy in this outfit. Why, even Emma . . . Look . . ."

He instructed Donovan to send Connerton to interview the cast of *Sense and Sensibility* and asked him to wire Petty's secretary for any connection that Petty might have had with a Stephana Mathews. He turned to Emma.

"The pieces are fitting together," he cried. "They found Jeff's key in her purse; that settles that. And Connerton found some heel marks by the back door of the house in Wakefield and, glory be, they match the marks on the desk blotter. He also went to the dime store in Wakefield and found that someone answering Stephana's description bought some paint last night. The clerk remembered her because she was good-looking and seemed to be in a hurry. A commuters' express gets into Wakefield at 5:25; she just had time to make it to the store."

"But she's dead." Emma was stricken with gloom again. "What possible difference can all this make?"

"Yes," said Hank, "she's dead. And I'm glad. She killed two people, one by mistake, I grant. She tried to kill two more. She would have had to die; but I'm glad she died quickly and was spared the horror of having her poor little life, her dreams and frustrations, haled into court and hawked through the streets. But the rest of us have to go on and finish the thing up; we have to be just as sure of our facts to close the case as though she were coming up for trial."

"Bufferin' snakes, will you look who's here."

Jeff was fumbling with the door latch and with him was a man whom they recognized, from the memory of a previous visit, as a reporter.

"It's Jeff's shop," Emma began reluctantly, "so I suppose we'll have to let them in."

McKinnon opened the door.

Jeff's arm was bandaged; his overcoat hung over his shoulder; a wad of cotton was taped to his ear. A smile of great good-humor was spread across his face and he breathed rather heavily.

"My secretary," he said, "God bless her, and the boy friend, a smart chap. He's the one who can tell you all about it."

"Jeff," asked Emma sternly, "how did you get away from Donovan?"

Jeff managed to look innocent, indignant and hurt, all at the same time.

"He sent me home," he pronounced, "after they had tied me up. I didn't want to go home. I stopped at a bar and had a most interesting conversation with this gentleman. He's a smart chap too."

The reporter bowed gravely.

"Mrs. Graham," said Emma, "will be worried."

"Let her stew."

It was apparent, Emma thought, that Jeff's experiences had not made a changed man of him.

"This is not," Jeff opined, "the reception I had imagined. Drinks are so often offered to utter strangers in this shop, that I thought---"

"—nay, expected," put in the reporter.

"—unless," Jeff divided a baleful glare between Hank and McKinnon, "these squatters have drunk up all the liquor?"

"You nut," said Emma. "You know I'm so glad to see you I could yell but what you don't need any more of is drink."

"Since when," Jeff wanted to know, "have you been the boss around here?"

"Oh, for years and years," said Emma airily, "only you never noticed it. The silken hand, you know."

"The iron hand," corrected the reporter, "in the silken glove."

"You win," said Emma going to the washroom.

"Wonderful woman," said Jeff. And, "That's nice," as Emma came back with the glasses. "And now, if it's not too much trouble, I'd like to know why Mr. Norwitch was killed."

"It was the overcoat," Emma put in. "I thought you knew."

"I don't know anything except about my misspent youth. Where's the bottle? And why the overcoat?"

"Just alike," said Hank as Emma got the bottle, "and you looked alike in the dark and she was hiding here when I came in. I might have found—"

"That's nothing," said Jeff, "to what I found when I came in. The body," he explained to the reporter.

"And when I came in to bolt the door," Emma began.

Jeff looked up, puzzled. "It was unbolted when I got here. I told Donovan that. I bolted it when I came in. I thought of course the fairies had unbolted it."

"Humph," said Emma.

"It works quietly," said Hank. "I tried it. She," unconsciously they were all avoiding the use of Stephana's name, "went out that way while Petty was at the front door. She took the key with her."

"So," said Emma, "that's what you were up to, opening and shutting the door. I thought you were trying to air the place out. Well, I found something too. She was in here that afternoon, asking for something to put on a wall." Emma produced the sales slip, showing how Stephana's request had induced her to write tapestry for chandelier.

Hank took a drink and groaned. "If I asked her once," he addressed the others sorrowfully, "I asked her forty times to tell me all the things that happened that day and never once did she have brains enough to check up with the sales slips."

"You're so smart, why didn't you think of it?" Emma defended herself.

"I," said Hank, "didn't know that sales slips existed."

"You did too; you were smug enough about the one you found on the floor."

They glared at each other.

"Please," said the reporter, "about the overcoat?"

"As I was saying." With dignity Hank took up the tale. "We kept popping in and she had to hide. You can see into the office from the door but you can't see the desk; and from the desk you can keep watch, over the partition, of the door. We know she hid on the desk---" He explained about the finding of the heel prints and the broken spar on the ship model. "She found the paper cutter on the shelf where Emma had left it. Whether she changed weapons because stabbing is quieter than shooting, or because she saw a certain justice in killing Jeff with his own dagger, I don't know. Anyhow, Uncle came in, with a key, mind you, just as though he belonged there, wearing an overcoat just like Jeff's and a hat so like that Jeff later took it for his own, causing Emma much undue concern and landing her eventually in the hoosegow."

"Oh, were you there too?" Jeff asked politely.

"A lot of this wasn't in the papers," said the reporter.

"Shut up," said Jeff. "I am interested in the demise of my deceased client."

"Where was I?" asked Hank.

"On the desk," said Emma.

"Well, I come down off the desk when I see Uncle coming in looking just like Jeff, and strike. She," with the gesture of striking Hank relinquished the role of Stephana, "was in the dark and Uncle probably never knew what hit him. What her feelings were, when she found that she had killed the wrong man, I won't attempt to say. She must have been pretty calm about it because she pulled the body over where it couldn't be seen from the door and started to wash the knife. She heard something—maybe Petty tried the door—and decided that she had better scram. She hung around, though, to see if Jeff would show up. He did, but he bolted the door behind him and turned on the lights, so she waited till he came out to pop him. You," Hank addressed Jeff, "complicated things by crawling off in the bushes—"

"Bushes?" asked the reporter.

"The hospital, he means," Emma explained.

"Oh," said the reporter.

"—so she couldn't tell, along with the rest of us, how badly damaged you were—"

"It wasn't quite in the same place, this time; lower down, just a flesh wound. I thought somebody would ask." Jeff looked aggrieved.

"Why, that's right," said Emma. "Does it hurt?"

"Not much," said Jeff nobly.

"He's had a lot of anesthetic," said the reporter.

Emma giggled.

"In the interests of your public," asked Hank sternly, "do you, or do you not, want the rest of this story?"

"To my public," the reporter drained his glass and refilled it.

They all drank.

"She went to the inquest," Emma put in, "and she came around here with a lot of questions about didn't anyone know where Jeff was."

"As soon as she found out," Hank took the tale back from Emma, "that Jeff was the suspect for Uncle's murder, she could relax. She wasn't involved; and, if Jeff were electrocuted for murder, he was just as dead as though she had killed him herself. She couldn't resist, then, tipping the police off when she found out where he was."

"Who told her that?" asked Jeff with a suspicious look.

"I did not," said Emma indignantly.

"Yes, you did," said Hank. "I found this in her room."

He displayed a crumpled bit of paper of the kind used in the shop for a scratch pad. On it, among Emma's neatly shaded figures, was a telephone number.

"At sometime or other," Hank pointed the paper accusingly at

Emma, "you called this number, the hospital number, and sat making marks on this piece of paper. She was here when you did it or took the paper; and, when she called the number and found what she got, it didn't take her long to figure out where Jeff was; only, by that time, he wasn't."

"I was all alone when I called the hospital," said Emma. "You'd gone off to do something or I wouldn't have done it."

"You were a big help on this case right along," Hank snapped. "Gimme the bottle." The strain of the morning was affecting even Hank's placid disposition.

"Get it yourself," Emma snapped back. "She had the key, didn't she? She could have come in here any time when I was out—"

Hank couldn't resist adding, "And that was often enough."

"So," said Jeff trying to look disapproving, "been neglecting your job, huh?"

"Oh for heaven's sake." Emma glared at both of them. "Who found Jeff's car? Who found Jeff? Who has been working her fingers to the bone supporting doctors and lawyers and boy friends? Who gave you the tip on Petty? Who was most unjustly imprisoned? Who nearly got killed? I ask you, is this gratitude?"

"Somebody," said the reporter lugubriously, "has to keep the home fires burning."

"The trouble with Emma," said Hank, "is that she wants to throw kerosene on the fires. She needn't have gone to jail if she'd had a lick of sense and she wouldn't have got into that jam in Wakefield if she'd done as she was told." He related the tales of Emma's adventures with the dachshund and the house in Wakefield.

"Noblesse oblige," said the reporter, referring, Emma imagined, to the incident of the dachshund.

"Are you sure," Jeff wanted to know, "that there wasn't a swell-front desk in that house?"

Emma looked from Hank to Jeff, shaking her head in selfpity. "My masters," she said, "whom I try to serve. No, you big bully, I'm not sure that there wasn't a gorgeous collection of the earliest Americana at 304 Nehoiden Street. I'll go tomorrow and see. And you," she addressed Hank, "you big dope, if I hadn't gone out there you'd never have known that she wanted to kill Petty."

"Why," asked Jeff, "did she want to kill Petty?"

"We don't know."

"That," said Jeff, "makes everything perfectly clear."

"Unity, emphasis and coherence," said the reporter.

"Extrie, extrie! Cop kills girrul!" The raucous voice of a newsboy came in to them plainly. "Read all about the Norwitch murder."

"Well," said Hank, "there's nothing like reading about it in the papers." He motioned to McKinnon, who went out and returned with two copies.

When the reporter saw the masthead he groaned. "Scooped," he said sadly, "scooped by my own paper."

"Cheer up," said Hank. "Stick around and we'll tell you why Petty was killed."

"What you got," asked Jeff, "foresight or hindsight?"

Ignoring him, Hank took one paper and gave the other to the reporter. COP KILLS GIRL was indeed the headline and there was a two-column picture of Stephana. She looked very lovely; her lids were downcast. Or were they closed? Was it a picture of Stephana taken after . . . ? Repressing his wonder, Hank began to read.

" 'Police Lieutenant Jerome Donovan, veteran of the force, shot and killed one Anna Matoušek, alias Stephana Mathews, as the latter was making a murderous attack on Jefferson Graham, prominent antique dealer—' "

"Paid advertisement?" asked Emma.

Jeff glowered. Hank continued: "'—Miss Matoušek has been identified by means of heel prints as the person who killed Richard Norwitch, wealthy clubman, antiquarian and philanthropist. It is said by the police that she mistook Norwitch for Graham, against whom she had a fancied grudge, and on whose life she had made several attempts.'"

"That's damn white of Donovan," said Jeff. "'Fancied grudge' is more than I deserve."

"That's right," said Emma, who was reading ahead of Hank, further down the column. "Look, it says: 'Henry Fairbanks, nephew, and so forth, who has been working on the case as an amateur detective,' ha, ha, 'was present at the time of the shooting, "Lieutenant Donovan," young Mr. Fairbanks is quoted as saying, "acted with prompt and commendable initative; it was nip and tuck with Mr. Graham---" ' Hank, you couldn't possibly have said anything so original."

"I didn't," said Hank. "That's just some reporter's idea of how the nephew of Richard Norwitch should sound."

"The dummy," said the reporter, "misspelled initiative."

"Looks all right to me." Emma was charitable.

"You wouldn't know," said Jeff.

"Page three, column two," said Emma. "Turn over."

Grumbling that he had not finished page one, Hank complied.

"'The police,'" Emma scooped Hank on the reading, "'are working on the theory that Miss Matoušek was responsible for the shooting of

Richard Petty, though as yet no motive has been found for that slaying. Rumors and gossip about these two killings have been rife'—sic—'and the final success of the police, in the face of false clues and a certain unwillingness on the part of certain persons involved in the case to cooperate—'"

"Yah," Hank interrupted Emma, "I don't suppose you know who that is?"

"It says persons," Emma defended herself.

"Tsk, tsk," said the reporter, "two certains. My, my."

Emma firmly finished the sentence, "'—redounds,' whoopee, 'greatly to their credit.' "

"Must be a misprint," said the reporter. "There's no whoopee here."

"Gimme a paper," said Jeff. "Chap who wrote that must be crazy."

"He is," said the reporter. "Name of Everson."

"He is not," said Hank. "I sat beside him in English 47. But you're right, he couldn't spell."

Emma burst into hoots of laughter. McKinnon, for the second time that day, suspected sudden madness and hastily took a drink.

"What's keeping Connerton?" Hank wondered. "We know all there is in the paper. And a lot more."

The telephone rang.

"Shut up, you," said Emma, answering it. "Oh, hello, M. LeBotien. No, I'm not busy. Yes, I'm fine. Yes, a great relief. Yes, we're just reading the paper. What, you did? She was? Are you sure? Wait, wait just a minute; I want you to talk to Mr. Fairbanks. No, he's right here." She turned to Hank. "Come quick. It's M. LeBotien."

"I guessed as much," said Hank, "from your conversational style. What's the matter? Haven't you paid your rent?" He took the telephone.

"How do you do, sir?" Hank would not be outdone in politeness. "Thank you. Oh no, very little. What? Yes, I saw the picture. You did? She was? Are you sure? Of course it's important. It ties up one of the loose ends. I say it solves one of the problems, answers one of the questions—"

"Don't forget 'fills in the picture,'" Emma helped him.

"I thank you, sir, and good-day to you."

"I can't wait," said Emma feeling very righteous, "for the sergeant to hear that."

"It was before you had the key made, of course—"

"And then coming over here, as though butter wouldn't melt in her mouth—" Emma was more indignant than she had been over the attempt on her life.

Jeff laid his paper carefully to one side and stood up.

"Come on," he said to the reporter. "If they're going to have secrets—"

"Sit down, silly," said Emma. "That was M. LeBotien."

Jeff sank down murmuring, "Yes, so I believe you said."

"He just saw the picture in the paper and he says he saw her coming downstairs from the apartment one day. He'd been busy and didn't see her go up and thought she was one of the Yogi lady's clients. He says he's positive it was she. So that explains how the billy got under my sofa cushions. He's going to put it in writing and I'm going to make the sergeant eat it."

"What 'd she want to do that for?"

"To get Emma in jail where she couldn't possibly gum up the murder of Petty. She had the key to the shop, she planted the billy and then she just sat tight and waited for someone to find it. Connerton obliged her. When Donovan took Emma away from the shop, she knew that the coast was clear for her to get after Petty."

"Assuming, of course, that she killed Petty."

"My assumptions," said Hank with dignity, "are the cornerstones on which this case is built."

"That reminds me," Emma began. "How long ago did you begin to assume that Norwitch was Jeff? That she thought he was, I mean?"

"Oh," said Hank casually, "long ago. The morning I went to meet Jeff. I was a little late, it was a foggy morning and I saw Jeff get off the train from some distance down the platform. Why, thinks I to myself, that could be Uncle just as easy as not, if he weren't dead. Same overcoat, same hat, same general outline. Of course I knew their dispositions were different but that didn't show in the fog. Right then I decided that somebody had made a mistake and that there was more to the attack on Jeff than a card-game quarrel. Toward the identity of Jeff's assailant I had just one clue: Jeff's refusal to identify his assailant and his willingness to go to jail under suspicion of being implicated in Uncle's death." Hank paused, looked at the reporter and chose his words carefully. "There was just one person whom I knew to have a real grievance against Jeff and I knew he was just enough of a sap to protect that person."

"Who was it?" asked the reporter.

"It was the wrong person, so we don't need to go into that."

"I was going to scold you for something," said Emma. "What was it?"

The telephone rang again.

"For you," said Emma to Hank. "Sounds like the sergeant."

Hank listened attentively at the phone; Jeff began to read the racing news; the reporter dozed in his chair; Emma turned on the lights and made a halfhearted attempt to empty the ash trays and pick up the glasses.

"Okay," said Hank triumphantly. "Nice work, old boy. Now here's one for you." He told the sergeant of M. LeBotien's identification of Stephana as the person whom he had seen coming from Emma's apartment. "What? No, he didn't actually see her hide the billy," Hank winked at Emma, "but you'll concede, in view of subsequent events, it's likely she did. Emma," he said grinning, "sends you her love."

"That's that," he said hanging up the phone. "Donovan is on his way over." He lit a cigarette.

"Now," said Emma, "I remember what I was mad about. You don't tell me things. You didn't tell me about Jeff and Mr. Norwitch being alike and now you stand there grinning like a Chessie Cat and don't tell me what Connerton said."

Jeff looked up from the paper. There was a gleam in his eye. "Remind me," he said, "to put fifty on Silver Heels in the third tomorrow."

"Is it hot?" Hank asked. "Put fifty on for me."

Emma stamped her foot.

"Sh-sh," said Jeff. "You'll wake the dead." He pointed to the reporter, who was sleeping quietly, happily unaware of his corpselikeaspect.

They laughed; and suddenly the three of them were happy again together, sensing, from Hank's manner, that their troubles were over. Donovan knocked and was admitted by McKinnon. He was beaming.

"Say, this is great, everybody being here. But I thought," he spoke to Jeff, "that I sent you home?"

"He came here instead," said Emma, "and he brought a friend. He's a reporter."

Donovan looked at Jeff as though wondering if all his trouble had been worth while. "I have," he said, "given a statement to the press. I wanted to talk."

"I think," said Emma, "that he's passed out but just in case some of the others think to come here, maybe we better go to the basement."

"Just like old times," said Donovan.

"Emma misses the sergeant," said Hank and told Donovan the explanation of the billy.

"She thought of everything, didn't she," Donovan said, half-admiringly. "She probably decided to kill Petty as soon as she saw him at the inquest."

"Did she, by any chance," Jeff asked—they were in the cellar now, arranging themselves on the boxes and broken chairs—"did she really kill Petty?"

"Oh yes," said Donovan.

"Well," said Jeff, "it's nice to know. I feel that I should go and tell that chap upstairs."

"And sometime," added Emma, "if we're all very good, maybe we'll hear how and why. Anybody want a drink?"

Donovan took one. Jeff refused. "It's the first time," he explained, "that I ever got sober by drinking more and I'm scared to overdo it."

"It seems," Hank began, "that she was engaged to Petty."

"What?" asked Emma and Jeff.

"Apparently he was the one she wrote Jeff about. The secretary's wire says he was engaged to a Stephana Mathews and several of the cast confirmed it and identified her picture when Connerton showed it to them."

"Then why—" began Jeff. "Her letter to me sounded as though everything was swell."

"The engagement was broken," Donovan explained, "about a month ago."

"Just about the time Uncle had Butterby write to Petty. Apparently Petty decided that she wasn't the wife to go with a quarter of a million and gave her the gate. Didn't you say," Hank turned to Jeff, "that she said the man she was marrying knew all about her?"

"That's right."

"Why, the worm!" said Emma. "I never liked him, anyway."

"And," said Hank to Donovan, "if you'd paid any attention to what I was trying to tell you this morning, you'd understand that she'd blame Jeff for this failure to get married. Only it would be worse this time because she'd almost got Petty to the altar."

"Oh," said Emma, "you mean she was crazy about men, almost any man. Even Joe or Hank?"

"Something like that," said Hank dryly. "I didn't realize it, of course, but as long as I seemed," he glanced at Emma and repeated the word, "seemed to be interested in her, Jeff was comparatively safe."

"You mean," Emma sounded actually reproachful, "if you'd married her she wouldn't have wanted to kill Jeff any more and wouldn't have been killed?"

"If I had only known," said Hank half-wondering if Emma would have sacrificed him on the altar for Jeff's well-being, "I would have been happy to solve our difficulties in that way. Unfortunately, when she found us searching her room, she knew that my intentions were not matrimonial, and when Jeff walked in—" Hank paused, remembering the awfulness of Stephana's face when she glimpsed Jeff. Emma might never fully understand but he was glad that she had not seen that.

"I guess," said Emma, "that I don't want you to marry anybody, at least not right away."

"Thank you, my dear," said Hank.

"As I said," Donovan resumed, "as soon as she saw Petty she knew that she had to get rid of him, because, for the very reason that Jeff told us: Petty knew all about her; so he must have known about her feeling about Jeff. Petty may have thought that she killed Norwitch because, in making Petty his heir, he had been the cause of her broken engagement."

"It's a cinch," Jeff put in, "that Petty would have told what he knew about her if it became necessary to save his own neck. She couldn't afford to run any chances."

"But why," Emma wanted to know, "did she have to kill him in the shop? She could have arranged to meet him most anywhere."

"You forget, my sweet," Hank explained, "that she was the one person with whom Petty would not willingly make an appointment. The fact that she got you out of the way may mean that she pretended to be you and got him here on some pretext, the secretary, maybe. Or perhaps she claimed to have some information about his connection with the murder."

"That is guesswork," said Donovan, "but her gun shot him all right enough, which makes me feel a little better about what I did this morning."

Emma passed him the bottle and he drank without the formality of a glass. In the momentary silence they could hear the telephone.

"Let 'er ring," said Jeff.

"Maybe your friend will wake up and answer it," suggested Emma.

"I'll make the effort." Hank climbed the stairs.

"Incidentally," said Jeff, "it *was* eleven-twenty when I was here and the door *was* unbolted."

"Oh sure," said Donovan. "I never thought you did it anyhow."

Hank was back in a moment. "I told her," he said looking at Jeff, "that she had the wrong number."

"And incidentally," said Donovan to no one in particular, "Remington is a high-class divorce lawyer, with a wife."

"Oh," said Emma, "then she wasn't "

"Who's Remington?" asked Jeff.

"You'll find out," said Hank as the phone began to ring again.

Jeff looked at Emma. "Tell her," he said firmly, "that I won't be home to dinner."

"That's an idea," said Hank. "Let's go over to the house and send Oscar out for some steaks."

They followed Emma upstairs. The sound of the phone had finally aroused the reporter. He blinked at the sight of Donovan, then he caught sight of Jeff and rose, unsteadily, to his feet.

"I've been meaning to ask you," he began. His voice faded out, he swayed, righted himself and began again. "Did they ever find out—" He shook himself, brushed a lock of hair from his eyes, and managed a complete sentence. "Who," he asked, "killed Petty?" But the effort was too much for him. Before anyone could answer, he fell back in the chair, gentle snores coming from his mouth.

"What we ought to do," said Hank, "is to write it all out, pin it on him and send him to the office in a taxi."

"He don't deserve it," said McKinnon.

"I'm hungry," said Donovan.

"Will you answer that phone?" asked Jeff.

"Yes?" said Emma. "Yes, Mrs. Graham."

"Yes, he's here."

Emma held the telephone away from her ear. Violent crackles were audible in the office.

"But he's with Lieutenant Donovan," Emma said soothingly. "No, just a scratch. They're going out to eat and then," Emma turned a wicked eye on Jeff, "he's going to wire a chandelier."

THE END

Other Rue Morgue Press titles

Murder, Chop Chop by James Norman (ISBN 0-915230-16-X, $13). Writes Jane Dickinson in the *Rocky Mountain News*: "The Rue Morgue is bringing back out-of-print books that the publishers feel deserve a second look. *Murder, Chop Chop* certainly qualifies. The book has the butter-wouldn't-melt-in-his-mouth cool of Rick in *Casablanca*, but the setting is China in 1938 during the Sino-Japanese War. The fortunes of war have brought together an unlikely cast under the guidance of Gimiendo Hernandez Quinto, possibly Pancho Villa's cousin, who runs a training school for guerrilla fighters in the resort town of Lingtung. When another foreigner is killed, Quinto is quick to look for answers, but questions pile up like cellophane noodles as denizens of the foreign quarter turn out to be more (or less) than they appear." The *Rocky* reviewer neglects to mention Mountain of Virtue, the beautiful and mysterious Eurasian woman who aids—and often confounds—Quinto. There's also a cipher or two to crack, a train with a mind of its own, and Chiang Kai-shek's false teeth, which have gone mysteriously missing.

The Mirror by Marlys Millhiser (ISBN 0-915230-15-1, $14.95). This magical novel may well be the first time travel novel to feature a woman protagonist. How could you not be intrigued, as one reviewer pointed out, by a novel in which "you find the main character marrying her own grandfather and giving birth to her own mother?" You'll have the time of your life watching as a very modern Boulder, Colorado, girl is transported back in time to 1900 and is forced to spend the rest of her life in her grandmother's body. Nor are things much easier when a very old-fashioned girl is transported forward in time to the sexually liberated Boulder of 1978. After all, it isn't easy being a virgin *and* pregnant. So how does one categorize *The Mirror* (which was a Mystery Guild selection twenty years ago)? Is it science fiction? Fantasy? Supernatural? Mystery? Romance? Historical fiction? You'll find elements of each but in the end it's a book driven by that most magical of all literary devices: imagine if...

"*The Mirror* is completely enjoyable."—*Library Journal*
"A great deal of fun."—*Publisher's Weekly*
"A fascinating tale."—*Atlanta Constitution*
"Settle down for a good read."—*The Denver Post*
"Highly imaginative"—*Pittsburgh Press*
"The homely detail is enthralling."—*Los Angeles Time*
"*The Mirror* is just fun."—*The Tennessean*
"The best reading I've had in a long while."—Phyllis A. Whitney

Cook Up a Crime by Charlotte Murray Russell (ISBN 0-915230-18-6, $13) Meet Jane Amanda Edwards, a self-styled "full-fashioned" spinster who complains she hasn't looked at herself in a full-length mirror since Helen Hokinson started drawing cartoons for *The New Yorker*. But you can always count on Jane to look into other people's affairs, especially when there's a juicy murder case to investigate. This one starts when Jane's friend, Detective Captain George Hammond, puts the idea of publishing a cookbook in her mind. That leads her to visit Jessie Nye, an irritating woman who unfortunately is the safekeeper of her family's famous recipes. Jesse thinks a cookbook a marvelous idea but immediately announces that she is far better suited to put it together than Jane. So when Jessie turns up dead, Jane decides to look for clues—and recipes—among the murdered woman's effects. In the meantime, Jane's hapless brother Arthur—a true lily of the field—gets a valentine from a secret admirer and goes courting, only to find himself accused of the murder. Sister Annie warns Jane to stay put and goes off to watch female wrestling on television. Through it all, Theresa, their long-suffering cook and general housekeeper, keeps one and all well fed with tempting treats from her kitchen (the recipes for these and other dishes are included between chapters). First published in 1951, it's what you might get if Joan Hess or Charlotte MacLeod wrote the culinary mysteries of Diane Mott Davidson.

The Man from Tibet by Clyde B. Clason (ISBN 0-915230-17-8, $14). Locked inside the Tibetan Room of his Chicago luxury apartment, the rich antiquarian was overheard repeating a forbidden occult chant under the watchful eyes of Buddhist gods. When the doors were opened it appeared that he had succumbed to a heart attack. But the elderly Roman historian and sometimes amateur sleuth Theocritus Lucius Westborough is convinced that Adam Merriweather's death was anything but natural and that the weapon was an eighth century Tibetan manuscript. First published in 1938, this is a locked room mystery that compares favorably with the works of John Dickson Carr.

The Black Gloves by Constance and Gwenyth Little (ISBN 0-915230-20-8, $14). The two sisters who put mirth into the malice domestic mystery for nearly a quarter of a century are at their best in this 1939 screwball mystery set in the New Jersey countryside. It features Lissa Vickers Herridge, a spoiled and bored young wealthy divorcee, who hears mysterious sounds in the cellar at night, dips dandelions in blue ink, and engages in a sparkling battle of wits with her father, her ex-husband and a quick-witted policeman.